CS HIGH

WHAT OTHERS ARE SAYING ABOUT CS HIGH

"As a forensic science teacher, I cannot recommend *CS High* enough! It's a page-turner! This mystery is packed with many exciting forensic science terms and techniques for aspiring young Sherlocks. The characters are relatable and the scenes so vivid, one might feel as if they are tagging along behind Simon, Marcus, and Laurel. I cannot wait to use this novel as a supplement to my own curriculum. I know my students will be inspired by the teamwork and skills of this incredible sleuthing trio. I guarantee yours will be too!"

—Mary Fran Park, forensic science teacher

CS HIGH

JULIANNE ZEDALIS

SWEETWATER BOOKS
An imprint of Cedar Fort, Inc.
Springville, Utah

ISBN 13: 978-1-4621-4034-3

Published by Sweetwater Books, an imprint of Cedar Fort, Inc.
2373 W. 700 S., Springville, UT 84663
Distributed by Cedar Fort, Inc., www.cedarfort.com

Library of Congress Control Number: 2021936729TA

Cover art by Tom McGrath, www.spikedmcgrath.com
Cover design by Shawnda T. Craig
Cover design © 2021 Cedar Fort, Inc.

Printed in the United States of America

10 9 8 7 6 5 4 3 2 1

Printed on acid-free paper

For my students, who always inspire me.

AUTHOR'S NOTE

This work is fiction. I am not a forensic scientist nor a professional crime investigator of any kind. I teach a forensic science course called Bugs, Bullets, and Blood at a high school in San Diego, California. Some of the lab techniques described in the book have been modified and simplified for the sake of storytelling. My hope is that this story sparks interest in the STEM disciplines for young students.

livor mortis: *a purplish discoloration of the skin starting twenty minutes to three hours after death*

TUESDAY MORNING, ZERO HOUR

Simon ripped the sheet of notebook paper out of his binder, crumpled it into a tight ball, and flung it across the room. *Ping.* It ricocheted off the whiteboard and landed in a heap of a dozen others around the perimeter of the recycle bin. *So much for a basketball scholarship,* he thought. He bit the eraser off his pencil and spat it out. At this rate, he could kiss off his math scholarship, too.

He glanced at the clock above the teacher's desk. Thirty-eight seconds. Why couldn't he differentiate the function of $f(x) = e^{(3x)}$? This was elementary math. Calculus 101, not multivariable. He had solved more difficult equations in fourth grade.

Simon's hand shook as he plugged another set of numbers into his graphing calculator. *Why can't I solve this? Is there something wrong with my brain's left parietal lobe?* He'd never had such difficulty before. "Brilliant," teachers wrote on his report cards. "A gentleman and scholar." Simon had never earned anything less than an A+ in any course at Pinehurst Academy, even advanced placement. He had always been able to solve Mr. Smithson's math problems.

Until now.

Another peek at the clock. Twenty-three seconds. Sweat pooled under his armpits.

Simon looked to his left. Bobby Tate had just set his pencil down and was leaning back in his desk, his hands folded behind his head and a snotty grin plastered on his face. *Seriously? Impossible.* No way had Bobby solved the problem that he couldn't. Simon doubted if the loser could calculate his GPA. He pushed his glasses higher up his nose. Just beyond Bobby, Marcus was furiously scribbling on his paper—in fact, all five members of the varsity basketball team were. They didn't look stuck at all. What universe was he in? Why was nobody else struggling?

Twelve seconds. He would need a shower before his engineering class.

Simon gnawed on his lower lip and tried to focus on the paper in front of him. If the graph of f was obtained by compression, the graph of $e^{(x)}$ was . . . That was it! All slopes were magnified by a factor of 3. The answer was $f' = 3e^{3x}$.

The chimes rang before his pencil touched the paper.

"Time's up," Mr. Smithson said, peering over Simon's shoulder. "You know the rules, Mr. Musgrave. Pencil down, please."

Simon stabbed his pencil on the desk so hard that its lead tip broke off. "Aaaghhh!"

A shrill buzz followed by the first notes of "Eine Kleine Nachtmusik" silenced his scream.

Simon jerked awake. Unburying his arm from under the covers, he punched the snooze button on the alarm clock. Even Mozart was grating at the crack of dawn.

Pegasus, Simon's Labrador puppy, jumped off the foot of the bed and scampered out of the room. His heart racing, Simon rolled over on his back and, swallowing hard, peeped over the edge of the blanket. *Thank God.* He was in his bedroom, not a classroom. That was the last time he'd eat four scoops of triple mint fudge before going to sleep.

Simon rubbed the crust off his eyes. Without his glasses, the clock's green neon numbers were blurred.

"Oh, no!" he blurted and jumped out of bed. He was late.

It was Tuesday. He couldn't be late on Tuesday.

Luckily, he had ironed and laid out his school uniform the night before.

* * *

It was still dark when Simon and his father exited the interstate and tooled along Ocean Crest Road. "C'mon, Dad, can't you speed it up?" Simon was jamming his own foot into the floorboard, as if by miming he could get his dad to drive faster. "Mr. Smithson's got a problem on infinite sequences for us to work on."

The fog had thickened overnight and reduced visibility to a few meters despite the Tesla's climate control system, forcing his father to drive well below the posted speed limit. Martin Musgrave turned left on Academy Drive and carefully navigated around the curves and up the hill toward the campus. He signaled to turn into the school's front parking lot and glanced over at Simon. "Good luck on your chemistry test. Stoichiometry equations can be tricky. I know you'll do—"

"Dad! Watch out!" The Tesla's collision warning system had activated before Simon's scream.

A dark Mercedes sedan had bolted out of the blanket of fog and was heading directly toward them. The car nearly clipped the Tesla's left front fender as it swerved around the bend and crossed over into their lane. Simon's father jerked the steering wheel to the right and slammed on the brakes. The tires squealed on the wet asphalt.

Simon twisted around and looked out the rear window. The Mercedes' red taillights disappeared down the hill.

His dad shouted several curse words that Simon had never heard him use. "Who the heck was that?"

"Don't know." The car wasn't unique. Three-quarters of the parents at Pinehurst Academy drove top-of-the-line S-Class Benzes. "I only caught the last two digits of the license plate."

"Probably some—" Martin clamped his lips shut, censoring himself this time. "Some *parent* dropping off his kid before the stock market opens. We'll keep an eye out for it. I've got a few things to say to the driver." Martin muttered several choicer words.

Simon's heart was still pounding when his dad pulled alongside the curb in the drop-off zone in the parking lot. The only other car in the lot was Mr. Smithson's older model but freshly detailed Volvo parked against the back fence in the area reserved for the faculty. Simon grabbed his backpack from the back seat and slammed the car door. The chapel bells chimed the half hour as his dad pulled away. If he sprinted, he could reach Hartford Hall in one minute and seven seconds—or exactly one-hundred-and-forty-two paces.

OneTwoThreeFourFiveSix . . . Simon darted in and out of the shadows cast by clusters of pine trees, squishing through the damp grass of the central quadrangle. He took the key Mr. Smithson had given him, but the main door to Hartford Hall was ajar. Strange. The building was usually locked this early in the morning. Maybe the others had arrived ahead of him for zero hour, which would be a first. Zero hour was the time before school reserved for club meetings, and as the youngest member of the Math Club, Simon always was the first to arrive.

Although the front door was unlocked, the hall lights were off except for the chandelier bathing the foyer in a yellowish glow. Simon's wet sneakers squeaked on the tile as he quickly walked down the dim, shadowy corridor. Mr. Smithson's classroom door was closed, and no light spilled into the hallway from underneath it. That was unusual, too. Mr. Smithson always propped open the door . . . waiting.

Simon knocked. "Mr. Smithson?"

No answer. No familiar, "Good morning, Simon. I've got a tricky one for us this morning."

Simon rapped again, a bit louder. "Mr. Smithson? Are you in there?" He placed his ear against the door. Classical music played softly in the background. Chopin. "Mr. Smithson?"

Still no answer.

How could he not be there? Mr. Smithson was never late, always arriving well before zero hour.

Slowly twisting the doorknob, Simon pushed open the door a few inches and fumbled around for the light switch. The fluorescent bulbs flickered several times before illuminating. His eyes strayed along the rows of empty desks, moving toward the front of the room, and then froze.

The teacher was slumped over his desk, motionless.

"Mr. Smithson?" Simon took a small step forward. "Are you okay?"

Even as he spoke, Simon knew it was a stupid question. The man was pitched forward on the desk with his right arm extended forward as if reaching for the pull chain on the small Tiffany lamp. His tie dangled in a pool of liquid near an overturned traveler's mug, and his left hand was knuckle-white around an amber plastic medicine vial. The gray head that Simon was so used to seeing nodding proudly as they worked their math problems was turned to the side, its neatly trimmed beard resting on a pile of papers. Mr. Smithson's eyes behind his wire-rimmed glasses were open but vacant. The melancholic strains of "Etude in A Flat Minor" floated from the pair of stereo speakers on the bookcase.

"Are you asleep?" *Please be asleep.* "Mr. Smithson?" Simon rushed forward but stopped short of the desk, jerking back at the close-up of Mr. Smithson's huge, dark, dilated pupils and mottled purplish skin. Livor mortis had already set in.

Simon stood there a moment, motionless. *Help.* He had to get help. Where were the others? Had the Math Club meeting been canceled? His legs felt like they were made of granite, his feet trapped in sludge, but he willed them to move. Spinning sharply, he dashed out of the classroom and ran full-speed down the hallway, his backpack pounding against his shoulders. Panicked, he didn't even think about rooting for the iPhone buried at the bottom of the bag. "Someone help!" he cried.

Crashing open the door to Hartford Hall, Simon plunged into the fog and raced across the quad toward the administration building. *Please someone be there. Please someone be there.*

The steps were slick, but he bounded up them two at a time anyway, slipping just once. Bashing his knee sharply on the brick barely slowed him. Using the iron railing, he launched himself up the last steps and slammed into Marcus Jackson, who had just come through the security office door.

"Whoa! Slow down, buddy!" Marcus grabbed Simon's elbow to prevent him from falling backwards. A basketball popped out from under his arm and bounced down the steps. "What're you doing, trying out for the track team?"

"Wh-where's the security guard?" Simon struggled to catch his breath. "I need help!"

"He went to unlock the back gates. What's up? Are you okay?"

Simon pulled loose and lunged at the door. "Call 9-1-1! Call 9-1-1!"

"What's wrong?" Marcus turned and peered into the fog. "Is there a fire?" He craned his neck as if looking for smoke.

Simon threw the office door wide open and bolted in. "Mr. Smithson's dead!"

Kastle-Meyer test: *a chemical test to identify blood*

MONDAY MORNING, THE DAY BEFORE

"Oh my gosh! Is that blood?" Laurel nearly broke Marcus's arm as she tried to push past him into the classroom.

"Ow," he squawked as her backpack slipped off her shoulder and fell on his foot. He bit back the words on his tongue, instead grabbing the sleeve of her polo shirt and yanking her back. "Don't! Can't you see the glass?"

"Not with you blocking the door." She tried knocking his hand free, but the six-foot-four basketball player held tight. He made her settle for looking under his armpit.

Not that what she saw would make any sense. Their high school forensic science lab looked like a riot scene. Four student desks were overturned at the front of the room, and broken pieces of glass were scattered across the floor along with several wet, red drops. *Plink . . . plink . . . plink.* Marcus's eyes focused on the teacher's desk where droplets of brownish liquid fell from a venti-sized paper cup tipped over on the desk, collecting in a puddle on the linoleum.

"What happened?" Laurel asked. "Did somebody get hurt?" She twisted and pulled without success. "Move!"

Marcus wasn't about to let her go. By now their other classmates had gathered in front of the door and strained to see inside room 102.

"What's going on?" a boy's nasal voice shouted from the back of the group. "Let us in!"

Marcus assessed the scene. Somebody had been thorough to the point of leaving a roll of crime scene tape and a box of disposable nitrile gloves for them on the epoxy blacktopped lab counter nearest the door. Marcus knew what to do from here. He had watched every episode of every season of CSI—the original Las Vegas series and the half-dozen spin-offs—at least twice. He was grateful to late-night cable TV, Netflix, and Amazon Prime for the reruns. His favorite iconic Vegas character, Grissom, would take charge and make sure a crime scene wasn't contaminated. It didn't matter to Marcus that his idol had been written out of the show at the end of season 9 and was last seen trekking through a rain forest with a butterfly net. Grissom would always be The Man. Better than Cumberbatch's Sherlock. The jury was still out on the newest Nancy Drew and Criminal Brains. There might be hope for NCIS: San Diego, but he doubted if any series would replace the original CSI. He had mourned for a week when the network had canceled the series. He hoped the rumors were true that a sequel was in the works.

Marcus raised his right arm above his head, his fingers spread wide as if taking a shot from the free throw line. "Stay back!" he commanded. "The room's off limits."

"But that's *blood*." Laurel pointed at the drops spattered on the floor. Her polished nail was redder than the drops.

"Can't handle a little blood?" Marcus let go of her sleeve and stared down at her. She was more than a foot shorter than him. He wondered how she could see anything with all that makeup on her eyes. So much black eyeliner outlined her blue eyes that she looked like a raccoon.

Laurel stared at him, as if she could read his mind. He tried to think of shooting a three-pointer in Saturday's game. "Where's Ms. Mason?" she asked.

"Don't know. She told me I could meet her before class to review for the quiz, but when I—" *Bzzz.* Marcus's phone vibrated in his jacket pocket.

"Yo, Marco Polo. C'mon, man, this sucks," Nasal Boy said, this time much louder. "Let us in."

"Okay, folks, keep it down." Dr. Gladson, the biology teacher in the classroom next door, came into the hall, his white lab coat soiled with several rust-colored stains. The pungent odor of something formaldehyde-like permeated the corridor. "In case you haven't noticed, the bell has rung, and I've got a rabbit dissection going on." He held up a scalpel and retreated into his room, shutting the door with a sharp snap. A girl's fake shriek from inside the anatomy lab rose above the buzz of Marcus's classmates.

"Ew," Laurel said, shivering. "Cutting open dead animals. That's so disgusting."

Marcus pointed at the blood spatters on the floor of the classroom. "And this isn't?"

The phone buzzed again. Marcus pulled it out of his pocket, looked at the screen, and frowned. *Great*, he thought. The man doesn't call for weeks, then picks now, eight o'clock on a Monday morning. Priceless.

"You could get a detention for using that," Laurel said, gesturing at the phone. Classes had started.

"I'm sure you'd know." A low-pitched hum signaled a new voice mail.

Laurel smirked as Marcus stuffed the phone back in his pocket. It vibrated yet again. *Jeez*. Didn't his father know that he was supposed to be in class?

Dr. Gladson walked back into the hall and pulled a folded scrap of paper from the pocket of his lab coat. "I almost forgot," he said. "Marcus, this is for you."

Marcus read the familiar scribble on the note and grinned.

You're in charge. You know what to do.
Ms. M

The ball was officially in his court. Now *he* was The Man.

"C'mon, everybody. We've got a crime scene to process," he said with the same authority he used on the basketball court.

Marcus stripped off his varsity athlete's jacket and, crouching, used it to prop open the classroom door. *Crap!* he thought as he stood up. He'd left his fingerprints on the doorknob. He had broken Grissom's rule number one: Never contaminate the crime scene. "C'mon, everybody." He grabbed the roll of crime scene tape and began ushering his classmates to a small alcove at the end of the hall. "Let's go. Hurry it up."

Laurel's heels clicked on the tile as she struggled to keep up with his long strides. "What's this about? Where's Ms. Mason? Do you know where—"

"Listen up!" Marcus waited for his classmates to quiet down. "*This* is our quiz. Ms. Mason has set up a mock crime scene, and she put me in charge. I think she's the victim. We've got about forty minutes to figure out what happened in here and find Ms. Mason."

"Why do you get to be the primary?" Laurel asked.

Marcus showed her the note. "Satisfied?"

"Not really." Her pout made her mouth look like a blowfish's.

He knelt down and, rummaging through his backpack, tossed out a tattered paperback copy of *The Great Gatsby*, a U.S. history textbook, and several crumpled old homework assignments until he found his forensic science notebook and a pencil. He pulled out his tablet, too, just in case. He also extracted a pair of nitrile gloves. "We all can't work in the room at the same time, or we'll contaminate the scene." He pitched the roll of crime scene tape to Manny. "Make sure nobody gets in who doesn't belong."

"Why're you always in charge?" Bobby Tate—Nasal Boy—was slouched against a locker with his arms crossed over his chest. Captain of the basketball team, Bobby wasn't used to taking orders, especially from his center. He spat a wad of bubble gum toward a nearby trash can. It bounced off the rim and landed on the freshly mopped tile. "This is stupid. C'mon, let's go."

"We can't blow it off," Marcus said. "We're gonna get a grade on this."

He wrote down three names and asked the water polo players to search the campus for Ms. Mason. "Be sure to check the faculty lounge. Maybe she's using the copy machine." They sauntered off without their backpacks, but at least they wouldn't be around to mess up the crime scene.

Marcus jotted down another name. "Laurel, can you run over to the admin building and ask the headmaster if Ms. Mason called in sick or had a flat tire or something this morning?"

"Nuh-uh," she said. "Not with these shoes."

He looked down at her black patent platforms. Her navy and green plaid uniform skirt was about twelve inches too short, and it looked like she had borrowed her polo shirt from a sixth grader. He struggled not to stare. A single strip of pink in her chin-length black bob was tucked under a tortoise shell clip, and at least a dozen bracelets adorned her arms despite the school's "no excessive jewelry" policy.

"How do you get away with them?" Marcus asked. "You know, the UVs." Uniform violations normally sent teachers into fits.

Laurel shrugged. "My dad paid for your gym."

"Fine." Marcus erased her name and asked the Wang sisters to go to the headmaster's office. "Ask the receptionist at the front desk if Ms. Mason signed out or grabbed her mail." The twins grabbed their bags and scurried off.

"You can check if Ms. Mason's Prius is in the parking lot," he told Laurel. "I think it's white. License plate is CS HIGH."

"And walk way over there?" she said, glancing down.

Right, Marcus thought. *The shoes.* "Would your highness care to be on the crime reconstruction team?"

"You got the name right." She batted her spidery eyelashes innocently and then frowned. "But not the assignment."

Marcus chewed on the end of his pencil. He was running out of things for her to do. Laurel Carmichael was one of the strangest and most annoying girls he had ever met, but she was also one of the smartest. He really could use her help. "Who do you want to work with?"

"Myself."

Marcus sighed. "You'll work in the classroom. With me."

"Lucky me." She swiveled on her heels and stalked off toward room 102.

"Watch out for the broken glass," Marcus called after her.

Five minutes later, only two students remained without assignments: Bobby Tate and Simon Musgrave. Simon stood behind a large potted fern in the corner of the alcove outside the classroom, counting leaves on a frond. With his slender frame, khaki uniform pants, and green Pinehurst sweatshirt, he was camouflaged behind the plant. His shaggy light brown hair hung past his eyebrows, and his eyeglasses were slightly crooked. Simon was the only thirteen-year-old freshman among the juniors and seniors in the class.

"If you're done hiding, I've got a job for you, too," Marcus said, walking over to Simon. "Can you diagram the crime scene?" Simon nodded. "Start with a hand-drawn sketch, like Ms. Mason wants us to do. Then you can make another using the CRIMESKETCH app."

Simon grabbed his lab notebook and rushed off, appearing glad to have something specific to do.

Marcus found Bobby slumped behind a desk in the classroom, his eyes closed. With his head lolled back, Bobby's Adam's apple protruded like he had swallowed a golf ball. Marcus punched his shoulder. "Wake up."

"Huh? What's up?" Bobby yawned. Drool trickled from the corner of his mouth.

Marcus recoiled at the sour breath mixed with Big League Chew. "You, now. C'mon. You'll help Laurel and me. You can take photos. Use the new digital camera on the equipment cart."

Bobby stretched and tossed his long, straggly blond hair away from his face. He stood and hitched up his pants, which had fallen below his hips, exposing red plaid boxer shorts. "I've got my own." He pulled his phone out of his pocket. "Quit bossing me around, dude."

It would be better if Bobby took photos with a camera real forensic scientists use, but he wasn't going to argue. "Start outside in the hallway," Marcus said.

Bobby tripped over his untied shoelace as he shuffled out of the room.

"Loser," Laurel said. "*Total* loser."

Marcus glanced at his varsity jacket wedged under the door. He and Bobby had played basketball and football together since middle school and now were starters on both varsity teams. "He's not so bad."

"Yeah, right. A real Einstein."

"Speaking of geniuses," Marcus said, "Simon's going to sketch the scene."

"*Now* we stand a chance of passing," Laurel said.

Laurel pulled on a pair of nitrile gloves. "Too bad these don't come in another color. Plum would be nice." She slapped a pile of yellow triangular evidence markers into Marcus's palm. "If it's okay with you, *boss*, let's each search half the room. I'll take the back."

"No problem," he said. Laurel ignored the tinge of red tinting his caramel cheeks.

Room 102 was larger than a standard classroom, but the rectangular space was crowded with student desks, lab counters, equipment, and storage cabinets. Laurel carefully picked a path around the glass fragments and blood drops and yanked open a cabinet. It was crammed with textbooks, lab manuals, DVDs, three-ring binders, and other teacher crap. The next was filled with test tubes, beakers, graduated cylinders, and Ehrlenmeyer flasks. The third cabinet she opened contained microscopes and specimen jars, some with dead stuff floating around in amber liquid—beetles, spiders, a couple of crustaceans, a jellyfish, and a few critters she was glad she couldn't identify. Embryos or something. Laurel shivered. She'd start with the floor.

She placed an evidence marker next to a cigarette butt and jotted information in her iPad:

> Evidence #1: A partially burnt 2-inch cigarette butt found on the floor near the safety shower in the northwest corner of room 102 in Weatherly Hall

"Hey, Mr. Basketball," she called over to Marcus, holding up the cigarette. "You need to start hitting the trash can with your butts."

"Funny," he said. "Get back to work."

The mental image of him coughing and gagging over a nasty cigarette made her smile. *Nobody* smoked anymore. "Hey, brainiac," she said to Simon, "I've got some evidence for your sketch."

Simon hurried over with a spool of measuring tape, but he didn't use it. "Fifteen centimeters to the left of the lipstick and about twenty-one centimeters from the wall." Brushing his hair out of his eyes, he squatted and stretched out the tape. "Bah! Off by forty millimeters. It's 14.6 centimeters from the lipstick tube."

Not bad, Laurel thought. "I need a photo over here," she yelled.

Bobby didn't answer. He wasn't in the room.

Laurel cussed, causing Simon to scribble furiously in his note-book. "I knew we couldn't depend on that jerk," she said. "If *I* was in charge, I would've let him sleep."

Simon kept sketching.

Laurel picked up the cigarette butt with a pair of tweezers, sealed it in a small plastic bag, and labeled it with her initials and the date. With any luck, they could pull DNA from the saliva. She placed evidence markers next to other objects she found: two burnt matches, one pearl earring, a tube of coral lipstick, and a gold fountain pen. No way Ms. Mason smoked—she was a competitive tennis player—but the lipstick and earring could belong to her.

Laurel leaned down and examined the fountain pen. "Mont Blanc. Impressive. Ms. Mason has expensive tastes in pens."

"It's probably not hers. She uses cheap ballpoints—the ones you buy in bulk at Costco," Simon mumbled.

"Really?" Laurel said. She'd have to check if the school bookstore sold Mont Blancs. "Hey, Marcus, over here."

"In a minute." He was sifting through a stack of papers on Ms. Mason's desk. "Don't forget to confirm that the drops on the floor are blood. Check the brown smudges on the door frame, too. I've got some Kastle-Meyer in my bag."

"Please tell me you're not serious." Who carried blood-testing chemicals around in a backpack? She dug into Marcus's bag and found a small gray box labeled *Kastle-Meyer Reagent*. "Unbelievable," Laurel muttered under her breath. "Sherlock Holmes in a varsity jacket."

She removed two glass vials containing clear liquid from the protective Styrofoam mold inside the box, poured a sample of each into the kit's plastic spray bottle, and gently mixed the chemicals. "Where did you get phenolphthalein?"

"Amazon," Marcus said without looking up.

Laurel took aim and squirted a stream of Kastle-Meyer reagent onto the smudges.

"Stop! Don't do that!" Simon dropped his notebook and sprinted across the lab, skidding to a stop in front of the door.

She whirled around. "Why not?"

"Look!" Streaks of bright magenta dripped down the cream-colored door frame and formed a pink pool on the linoleum.

"So?" Laurel asked. "What's wrong?"

"If you did a Kastle-Meyer test, that's a positive reaction, but—"

"But what? It's blood."

Simon pushed his glasses higher up his nose. "I . . . um . . . I couldn't help but notice that there appeared to be a fingerprint in one of the smudges. It says in chapter 13 in our textbook, page 247, second paragraph, third sentence that you're supposed to lift the print first and *then* test for the presence of blood." He pointed at the door frame.

Laurel's shoulders sagged as she stared at the magenta splotches. The fingerprint had disappeared. *Lovely, Laurel. Freakin' lovely.*

"Crap!" Marcus said, stepping away from the drippy pink mess. "Why didn't you just swab a small sample instead of spraying the whole door with K-M?"

"It's not *my* fault. *You* said to check for blood. You didn't say anything about a fingerprint." Laurel's cheeks were flushed, her voice an octave higher than usual. "You're the primary, remember?"

Laurel was right. Grissom's rule number two: The supervisor was responsible for the actions of his team. He should have watched her more closely, but there was nothing he could do about it now. "Let's just finish up." This CSI stuff was definitely harder than it looked on TV. "Here, I want to show you something."

He led her over to Ms. Mason's desk and pointed to the stack of homework papers saturated with brown liquid. Luckily, her laptop had been spared. He sniffed the puddle. "Coffee." He picked up the paper cup. "*Cold* coffee." He pointed at the distinctive blue-circle logo on the cup. "From the Coffee Mug." He sealed it in an evidence bag he pulled from his pants pocket. "I also found this in her laptop case."

Laurel grabbed the plastic sandwich bag half-filled with white powder out of his hand. "*Now* this is getting interesting," she said.

"Maybe . . . " Marcus's voice trailed off. "Simon, what've you got?"

"I found the source of the broken glass. A 500-milliliter Ehrlenmeyer flask." A sharp jagged piece rested in his gloved palm, one of its edges smeared with a reddish stain. "It's positive for blood."

He held up a Q-tip stained magenta with Kastle-Meyer reagent. "Hydrogen peroxide combines with hemoglobin in erythrocytes, producing a—"

"Bag and tag it," Marcus said. He turned back to Laurel. "Here's what I'm thinking. Ms. Mason was typing up a lesson plan or something when somebody came in and tried to grab her. She struggled, and the flask fell off the counter and broke. Somebody got cut. Just hope it wasn't her."

"Nice hypothesis," Laurel said, "but how do you explain the cigarette butt, fountain pen, and other stuff I found at the *back* of the room?"

"Good question," Marcus said. "Ms. Mason set up this fake crime scene. Everything means something. We need an evidence trail."

"You got here first, didn't you?" Laurel asked. "What time? Was the door open or closed? Lights on or off?" She looked around the room. "And where's Bobby? Aren't you supposed to be supervising him? Do you think he could've *planted* some of the evidence? You know, to mess with us?"

"Whoa," Marcus said, holding up his hand like a traffic cop. "Enough with the questions. I'm doing my best here." He ran his hands across the closely shaved sides of his short, curly black hair. "Ms. Mason told me to meet her at 7:45. Zero hour. The door was open, lights on, but she wasn't here."

"See anybody else?"

"Just Mr.—" A scrap of paper on the floor, partially hidden behind a large bromeliad plant, caught Marcus's eye. He stooped over, picked it up, and read it twice.

Before he could show the note to Laurel and Simon, a woman's voice from behind him said, "Well, what happened to me?"

Ms. Mason pulled her dark brown shoulder-length hair into a ponytail with a scrunchie and fiddled with her left gold hoop earring. After buttoning her lab coat, she circled the room and examined each piece of evidence they had collected, comparing each item to a list she had pulled up on her iPad.

"Nice work," she said, nodding. "You bagged and tagged everything I planted. Even the gross cigarette butt." She fake-shivered. "Don't even ask where I got that nasty thing." She picked up the Mont Blanc fountain pen. "Hmm. A student must have dropped this. It isn't mine." She put it back with the other evidence.

"So we passed?" Marcus asked.

"This is 'A' work. With one exception." She smiled and pointed at the magenta stains on the door frame. "Learn from your mistakes."

Marcus's cheeks grew warm. "Sorry. I screwed that up," he said, glancing at Laurel.

Laurel caught his gaze but said nothing.

Ms. Mason avoided the puddle of coffee on the desk and opened her laptop. "Tomorrow you can process the evidence and reconstruct what happened in here—after I finish my lecture on DNA." She typed in her password. "Please read the Simpson case in your textbook for homework. You'll realize the consequences of poor evidence collection."

Marcus zipped the box with Kastle-Meyer reagent in his backpack and slipped on his varsity jacket. "Hey, Simon," he said, "before you disappear again. You did a good job."

With the slightest nod, Simon stuffed his notebook, tablet, and measuring tape in his bag and dashed into the hallway, blending into the crowd of students shuffling to second period.

Laurel was almost out the door herself.

"Hey, Nancy Drew. Wait up," Marcus said.

"Can't be late to French," she called over her shoulder. "I'm not going to spend another Wednesday afternoon in detention. And . . . " She paused. "*Never, ever* call me Nancy Drew."

"I thought you'd be flattered," Marcus said. "She's back on a new TV show." Her glare convinced him never to make that mistake again. Veronica Mars, maybe? At least he had her attention. "What do you think of this?" He showed her the words scrawled in elegant script on the torn scrap of paper he had picked up off the floor.

Meet me in 102. Bring the money.

"Weird," Laurel said. "Ms. Mason said we found all the evidence."

"Either she's wrong," Marcus said, "or our 'A' just slipped to a 'B.'"

calculus: *a branch of mathematics focusing on the study of change*

LATER MONDAY MORNING

Marcus slid into his seat seconds before the final chimes rang.

Mr. Smithson stared at him with raised eyebrows. "Nice of you to join us, Mr. Jackson," he said, checking off Marcus's name from the attendance sheet in his grade book. Preferring to keep track of his own calculations, Mr. Smithson was old-school and disliked online grading and attendance recording, much to the annoyance of the school's deans.

"Sorry, sir." Marcus draped his jacket over the back of the desk and rummaged through his backpack. Mr. Smithson wasn't a fan of online textbooks either. Marcus scooped up the nitrile glove that fell out of the bag along with his math book and stuffed it in his pocket. "It won't happen again." He was barely winded from sprinting across the campus from the forensic science lab to Hartford Hall.

"Hurry it along," Mr. Smithson said. Marcus settled into his seat, but not before glancing out the window.

Pinehurst Academy was nestled on several acres of prime California real estate with postcard views of the Pacific. Even in February, thick green stems of ivy mixed with red and pink bougainvillea streamed down the cream-colored stucco buildings with curved archways and terracotta-tiled roofs that enclosed a central quadrangle. Clusters of eucalyptus trees and an occasional Torrey pine erupted out of the lush lawn of the quad. A small chapel, complete with bell tower, made the school look like it belonged in a tourist guide along with photos of the missions of Santa Barbara and San Juan Capistrano. Marcus could think of worse places to go to school.

Mr. Smithson crept up and down the aisles between the rows of desks, looking right and then left at each student. He stopped at the first seat in Marcus's row and removed an exam from the stack resting on his forearm. His large gold ring with a crimson stone sparkled under the fluorescent lights.

"Good morning, Mr. Santana," he said. "And how do you think we did today?" Without waiting for an answer, he thrust the exam at Manny, who looked at the grade and gagged.

Feeling his friend's pain, Marcus prayed for a C for himself. Mr. Smithson's calculus tests were killers. Not only were the equations nearly impossible to solve, but the man penalized the smallest mistakes. Once he'd taken five points off a quiz because Marcus had written the date on the upper left corner of the page instead of the right. "Just giving you your parents' money's worth," was his standard reply when students complained.

Still, despite Mr. Smithson's reputation as Pinehurst's toughest teacher, the waiting lists for his courses were long. His students excelled on their SATs, his Quiz Bowl team was undefeated, and there was a waiting list for students to join the Math Club. A recommendation from him almost guaranteed acceptance to a top college. Marcus hoped that Mr. Smithson would help him get into the Ivy League, assuming that he didn't bomb this course.

Mr. Smithson inched closer. He paused at the desk in front of Marcus's and tugged the sweatshirt hood off Bobby's head. "*Another* outstanding mathematical performance, Mr. Tate," he said.

Even from his seat, Marcus caught a whiff of the man's peppermint breath. Tall and trim, Mr. Smithson leaned forward at a forty-five degree angle to make eye contact with Bobby. A lemony scent of cologne clung to his freshly starched white dress shirt. His black wing-tipped shoes were polished to a mirror-like shine, and the creases in his navy dress slacks were razor-sharp. With his wire-rimmed glasses

and neatly trimmed gray beard, he looked like a Hogwarts professor—minus the robe. He slowly extended his hand clutching Bobby's
exam like a viper preparing to strike its prey. "At least you spelled your
name correctly." He slapped the test on Bobby's desk.

Mr. Smithson rose to his full height and stared at his next victim:
Marcus.

Not only did Marcus feel queasy, but the inside of his mouth felt
like it was stuffed with cotton, making it impossible to swallow. A
surge of adrenaline doubled his heart rate. Mr. Smithson handed him
his exam upside down, and Marcus hesitated before slowly turning it
over. A large B+ was scrawled at the top of the page. He nearly leaped
right up onto his desk.

"Nice job, Mr. Jackson," Mr. Smithson said before slithering
down the row.

Marcus couldn't help but grin. It had taken several high test scores
to show Mr. Smithson, and some of his classmates, that he wasn't just
another kid recruited to play ball at a prep school. He was here to
learn. He wasn't the smartest student at Pinehurst—that distinction
belonged to Simon Musgrave—but he could hold his own in the classroom if he studied hard. He had made the honor roll every semester.

Bobby twisted around. "Bummer. I got a D," he said. "If my GPA
falls below 2.0, I can't play varsity."

Marcus gave an obligatory groan of solidarity to his teammate, which
was about all he could muster. Bobby wasn't dumb, just lazy, something
Marcus didn't get. They were lucky to attend a school like Pinehurst. But,
then, Bobby's performance in math wasn't Marcus's problem. The guy
could shoot the three-pointers, and that's all that mattered to the gods of
Pinehurst. It was enough for Marcus to take care of himself.

Rubbing his hands together, Mr. Smithson strode to the front
of the classroom. "We have derivatives to solve." He sounded glee-
ful. "Who can work the first problem from last night's assignment?"
Without waiting for a reply, he handed a piece of chalk to Simon, who
quickly covered the board—Mr. Smithson had rejected the school's
offer to replace it with the newest interactive whiteboard—with equations and then hurried back to his seat.

"Brilliant as usual, Mr. Musgrave," Mr. Smithson said. "Who's
next?" He surveyed the room. Not one hand was raised.

Marcus hunkered down in his desk and buried his head in his textbook. With his height, hiding behind Bobby was difficult, if not impossible. He wasn't sure if he had correctly solved the second problem, although he had checked his answer three times. He glanced up. Mr. Smithson was staring in his direction. Marcus lowered his eyes.

"Mr. Tate," Mr. Smithson said, "I'm sure you would relish an opportunity to redeem yourself, especially if you want to play in the game on Saturday."

Relieved, Marcus exhaled again. It was his lucky day. First being in charge of the mock crime scene, then an A- on the test, and now spared possible public humiliation.

Mr. Smithson tossed a piece of chalk toward Bobby, who reached to grab it but missed. Marcus's arm instinctively shot up, and he snagged the chalk in mid-air. *Crap!* he thought. Now he'd have to work the problem.

The chapel chimes signaled the end of the period.

"Ah. Saved by the proverbial bell," Mr. Smithson said. "For homework please solve the problems at the end of chapter 11. All of them. You will have another test on Friday."

A dozen simultaneous groans reverberated off the classroom walls.

"That sucks," Bobby said under his breath.

Flipping to chapter 11, Marcus had to agree with him. He didn't even understand the title: *Vectors and Matrices.* How was he going to get all his homework done? Coach Decker had scheduled extra practices to get the team ready for the St. Francis game on Saturday night, and Marcus had a Spanish quiz the next day and a test in AP macroeconomics on Wednesday. He also hadn't started his paper on *The Great Gatsby*, and English was his second weakest subject. Spanish was his first. Now fifteen math problems. And he couldn't forget to write up the reconstruction of the mock crime scene. Mercifully, his Spanish class had been canceled for the afternoon because the whole school was invited to a special ceremony to dedicate the new football stadium. Marcus stuffed his book and test in his backpack, grabbed his jacket, and followed Bobby toward the door.

"Not so fast, gentleman," Mr. Smithson said.

Ugh. "I'm sorry for being late, sir," Marcus said, turning around, "but I had to finish processing a crime scene, and then I had to—"

Mr. Smithson held up his hand. "That's not what this is about." He selected a tea bag from a wooden box he kept on top of his desk, twisted the top off his traveler's mug, and, dunking the tea bag, stared with narrowed eyes at Bobby. "You are close to failing this course, Mr. Tate. You deserve an academic warning, but maybe I'll speak with your father in person—or, better yet, with your basketball coach. Perhaps *he* can help you study."

"N-no, no, no. You can't talk to Coach Decker." Bobby sounded panicked. "He'll kick me off the team. I, uh, told him I'm passing everything."

"You did, did you? Then I suggest you study hard between now and Friday. Very. Hard." Mr. Smithson stopped dunking his tea bag. "Or find a tutor."

Bobby pulled the hood of his sweatshirt over his head, whirled around, and shoved a student desk so hard that it nearly toppled over as he ran out into the hall.

Marcus remained standing in front of the teacher's desk and shifted from one foot to another in the uncomfortable silence. Mr. Smithson took an amber medicine vial from his desk drawer, popped a small white pill into his mouth, and washed it down with a sip of tea. "Basketball is important to you, right? I still play pick-up hoops in the gym on occasion," he said, taking another sip. "I have a suggestion. Perhaps *you* can study with Bobby."

Great, Marcus thought. He could squeeze tutoring in during the passing period between English and econ *if* he didn't stop to use the bathroom. "I'll see what I can do." Teaching Bobby math would be harder than training a sea anemone not to squirt.

Mr. Smithson loaded a disc into the CD player on the bookshelf behind his desk. Some screechy classical music exploded out of the speakers. Mercifully, he lowered the volume. Marcus doubted if Mr. Smithson was familiar with voice-activated smart speakers, or even Pandora. He couldn't picture him talking to Alexa or Siri.

"I'm sure you'll do whatever you can to help the team, especially with the game on Saturday. District semi-finals, right?" Mr. Smithson flicked his wrist as if shooing a fly. "You're dismissed."

Marcus dashed down the hallway and caught up with Bobby, who was roughly elbowing his way through the crowd.

"Hey, man, chill." Marcus wrapped his arm around Bobby's shoulders. "I'll help you study." He'd skip the bathroom break.

Bobby shook him off. "What if Smithson calls Coach?" He kicked over a large trash can, and crumpled papers, discarded water bottles, milk cartons, and candy bar wrappers spilled across the floor. "I hate that guy! He's ruining my life!"

No way Coach D. will bench him, Marcus thought, watching Bobby storm down the hallway kicking and screaming. He was the team's golden boy. The rules were different for him. Still, Marcus contemplated the worst case scenario. Could they beat St. Fran without Bobby?

"Hey, Sherlock," Laurel said, stepping up behind him and jabbing the back of his shoulder with her fingernail. "Tell me you're not still thinking about the bloody fingerprint. This is Pinehurst Academy, not CS High."

"Huh?" Marcus jerked and whipped around.

"What's Bobby flipping out about?" she asked. "Let me guess. Mr. Smithson?"

Marcus shrugged. "Nothing. Just the usual." He had stopped to pick up the trash that littered the hallway.

"So much for the 'spirit of the community' the headmaster's always preaching about."

She was going in his direction, so he walked with her. Even with his long legs, though, he had to hurry to keep up with her short, brisk steps as they made their way out of Hartford Hall.

"Now that I know your backpack's a crime scene kit, is it true that you're doing some weird experiment with a squirrel in your backyard?" Laurel asked.

"A chipmunk. I'm trying to find out changes in body temperature when the ambient temp—"

She put up her hand, the stack of bracelets on her wrist jingling. "I've heard enough."

"Have you started the essay on *Gatsby*?" Marcus asked.

"You're joking, right? It's not due until Friday." She stopped to pull up the black fishnet stocking that had slipped to her ankle. "I bet you have, though."

Marcus shook his head. "I can't even get a good thesis going."

No way would he be able to get that paper done, especially with the extra basketball practices and now tutoring Bobby in math. And he bet his father was going to be at the game. Jeremiah Jackson never missed an opportunity to be in the spotlight. The media was playing up the rivalry between Pinehurst and St. Francis, and Marcus imagined the headline—something like *Son of NBA Star Takes Dad's Place Behind Free Throw Line*. His father was probably calling to give him some last-minute pointers before tip-off, but Marcus had something else he wanted to talk to him about. And he already knew how that conversation would go. Bad.

He and Laurel walked toward the terrace where students and faculty gathered for the morning's fifteen-minute break between classes, fondly called Milk Break. "Are you going to the dedication ceremony for the new football stadium?" Marcus asked. At least today he wouldn't have to endure his Spanish teacher's torture chamber.

Laurel answered by rolling her eyes. "Ugh. No."

Marcus gazed over the quad as he and Laurel climbed the half-dozen flat concrete steps leading up to the terrace. A breeze was blowing in from the ocean and blanketed the campus with a fishy smell. Kelp, probably. A pair of squawking seagulls wrestled in the center of the lawn, pecking apart a bagel.

"Can I get you a cinnamon roll or something?" Marcus said.

"Do I look like I eat junk like that?" Laurel replied. "Besides, shouldn't you be eating with the jocks?"

Was the word tattooed on his forehead? Despite earning letters in three varsity sports—football, basketball, and track—he hated being called a jock. People rarely meant it as a compliment. "We're not joined at the hip."

"You could've fooled me." She turned on her heels and disappeared into the crowd scrambling for snacks.

Man, what was up with her? No wonder she didn't have many friends. Looking like a fashionista with a touch of Goth, he thought that she of all people would be out to destroy stereotypes, not sling them.

Turning, Marcus saw his teammates at the table behind him, waving him over. He sighed. Bobby had folded a napkin into a hat and was standing on the table, miming out some silly march. He hated to admit it, but Laurel was right. Bobby was a loser. Spinning away, Marcus strode over to the snack bar, grabbed a banana, two cartons of chocolate milk, and three cinnamon rolls, and then walked off toward the library. *The Great Gatsby* beckoned.

forensic science: *the application of scientific techniques to collect and analyze evidence found at a crime scene*

TUESDAY MORNING, THE NEXT DAY

"Crap!" Laurel said. "Crap, crap, crap!"

She had driven twice around the block before squeezing into a parking space on South Coast. The car shuddered to a stop. She was going to be late and should've known better than to start working on yesterday's mock crime scene reconstruction before school. She still had to check her look, especially because her hair would be a horror after trudging up the hill in the fog. She must remember to ask her dad to bid on a parking spot on campus at the spring auction.

Laurel cut through the back gate and dashed into the nearest girls' bathroom. Strange. At this time of the morning, she usually had to elbow her way through a crowd of girls checking *their* looks. Today the only girl in the bathroom was Sarah Morgan-Something who was scrubbing her hands like Lady MacBeth.

A glance in the mirror confirmed her prediction. She looked like a hot mess. Laurel fastened her hair's damp limp strings behind her ears with crystal clips, careful to hide the single strip of pink. Then she unrolled her skirt from the waist until it skimmed the top of her knees; the change made her shiver, but yesterday her French teacher—who apparently was unaware of who Laurel's father was—had given her a UV for her very short skirt. Next she wrapped the tattered shoelaces around the soles of her well-scuffed saddle shoes until they resembled Egyptian mummies. The blisters on her feet from the platforms she had worn the day before were raw. A slash of magenta across her lips and another layer of kohl eyeliner added the finishing touches.

Laurel popped in her earbuds and strutted out into the hallway. She reached her locker just as the chimes signaled the passing period to homeroom. Laurel had dialed the first number of the lock's combination and was halfway to the second when someone grabbed her shoulder. Whirling around, she stomped on an enormous Nike-covered foot.

"Ow!" Marcus yelled, backing away. "Jeez! What's up with that?"

"Are you psycho or something?" Laurel glared up at him. "You should know better than to sneak up on people." Luckily for him her can of pepper spray was buried in her bag.

He tugged the earbuds out of her ears. "No wonder you didn't answer. I even sent you three texts."

Now Laurel noticed the buzz. The chatter between the few students who were around was louder than usual, especially early in the morning when they usually shuffled zombie-like to homeroom.

"Did you hear?" Marcus said.

"Hear what? I just got here."

"Mr. Smithson's dead."

"Really?" Laurel wasn't surprised. With his uptight personality, the man was a stroke waiting to happen. She reached into her locker again.

"Simon found him this morning. In his classroom."

Laurel spun to face him. "He died *here*? At *school*?"

Marcus nodded.

"Wow. What happened?"

Marcus shrugged. "Don't know. Heart attack or something. The paramedics left about thirty minutes ago."

"Wow," Laurel said again. Boy, had she picked the wrong morning to be late.

The final chimes rang. Marcus hustled off to homeroom, leaving Laurel standing in front of her locker, her eyes still wide. Turning slowly, she closed her locker. No need to hurry. She doubted if anybody was tracking tardies or UVs now.

* * *

Marcus found an empty seat at the back of the lab. Laurel crept in several minutes later, her skirt rolled back up to mid-thigh. Their classmates were sitting behind their desks, quietly focused on the molecule of DNA swirling on the SMART board's projection screen. *This is weird,* Marcus thought, glancing around. He assumed everybody would've heard about Mr. Smithson by now. With everyone plugged in, news usually traveled fast through the student body. Why was everybody so quiet? And what about Ms. Mason? She calmly clicked to the next slide. Surely, the headmaster would've at least told the faculty.

Marcus scribbled on a scrap of notebook paper and passed it across the aisle.

Think Ms. M knows about S?

Laurel glanced at it and shrugged.

Ms. Mason pulled up the next slide. As hard as Marcus tried to concentrate, the hydrogen bonds connecting the double helix blurred together. He was usually so into this stuff, but he couldn't stop thinking about Mr. Smithson's class the day before, about how good he had felt when he saw the B+ scrawled on the front of his exam. Now he wouldn't be able to ask him for a letter of recommendation. Marcus shuddered, disgusted by his selfishness. The man was *dead*, for crying out loud, and he was thinking about college.

"Analyzing DNA requires high-tech equipment," Ms. Mason said. "Television makes it look easy. Tomorrow we're going to extract DNA from our cheek cells. Does anybody know how to do that?"

"Use a Q-tip?" Manny said.

Ms. Mason nodded. "That's right. But it's called a swab, not a Q-tip." She pulled one out of its sterile package, careful not to touch the cotton tip. "Kelly, come here. Open your mouth."

Kelly slowly walked to the front of the room. "Will it hurt?"

Ms. Mason waved the swab. "Say 'ah'."

Kelly stuck out her tongue as Ms. Mason demonstrated the technique on her.

"Gently—no blood, please—scrape the inside of the cheek to collect a sample of epithelial cells." Ms. Mason took the swab out of Kelly's mouth. "See? Nothing to it. I'm sure some of you have done this to trace your family's ancestry."

Kelly pretended to gag as she strolled back to her desk.

Marcus couldn't stand it anymore. "Psst," he whispered, leaning toward Laurel. "When do you think they'll give us the official word abut Mr. Smithson?"

"How am I supposed to know?" Laurel snapped, a little too loud.

"Excuse me," Ms. Mason said. "In the back. Quiet."

"Sorry." Marcus jotted down a few notes. *DNA, epi cells, no blood.*

"Next you'll add a little SDS to your sample." Ms. Mason held up a small plastic bottle. "Too bad Simon's absent. He could tell us how sodium dodecyl sulfate digests cell membranes."

Absent? Marcus thought. It wasn't like Simon was ditching or something. The poor kid was probably sitting in the headmaster's office talking to the police. Maybe they'd sent him home. He'd seemed pretty shaken on the steps outside the security office.

"Marcus, do you know?" Ms. Mason said.

He jerked. "Huh? What? Sorry. Can you, uh, please repeat the question?"

"I asked, how can we amplify a small amount of DNA? I'll give you a hint. The scientist who invented the procedure is from San Diego."

"You can run a PCR," Marcus said. "Polymerase chain reaction. Kary Mullis invented it."

Ms. Mason smiled. "You have been paying attention." What looked like a bar code on a grocery product popped up on the next PowerPoint slide. "Here's how DNA fingerprinting works. To run a gel electrophoresis, you must first—"

The classroom door squeaked open, and Mrs. Hudson, the headmaster's assistant, barreled in without knocking. Sixteen heads swiveled around. Dressed in a drab tan pantsuit and her silver hair neatly knotted in a bun at the back of her head, she strode to the front of the classroom on short, stocky legs. With her typical no-nonsense efficiency, she handed Ms. Mason a yellow Post-it. She turned on her chunky brown heels and left without a word.

Ms. Mason read the note and gasped.

"I bet we know what this is about," Marcus whispered to Laurel.

"A Post-it? Seriously," Laurel said. "What century is this? Why didn't they just text everybody?

CSI: *crime scene investigator or investigation*

LATE TUESDAY AFTERNOON

"Wrap it with a bag of ice and come back in the morning." The trainer handed Marcus a note. "Give this to Coach D. No practice today, but we've got to make sure you can play Saturday. On second thought, I'll talk to Coach myself."

Marcus limped out of the gym but then pitched the note into the nearest trash can. His ankle had never felt better. He hated lying, but Coach Decker rarely accepted excuses for missing practice, except from Bobby. Faking a bum ankle might land Marcus on the bench, but so what? He had something more important to do than practice jump shots.

Hartford Hall appeared deserted. It should be, since last period had ended an hour ago. Marcus sprinted down the hallway just in case.

Mr. Smithson's classroom door was closed. But, then, what had he expected? Crime scene tape? Checking the hallway again, he twisted the doorknob. The door was unlocked. He slowly pushed it open, and halfway through the door, he froze. Somebody else was in Mr. Smithson's room.

"What're *you* doing in here?" he said.

Laurel sprang out of her seat and whirled around so quickly that drops of mocha sloshed out of the paper cup she held in her hand.

"Jeez, Marcus." She pulled a Kleenex from her bag and dabbed the spots spattering her uniform. "I'm running out of clean skirts."

"Don't you usually hang out at the Coffee Mug after school?" Marcus asked.

"Shouldn't you be in the gym?" she snapped back.

Marcus stuck his head back into the hallway. It was still empty. He stepped all the way into the room and quietly closed the door. He took his usual seat, and, rapping his fingers on the desktop, glanced around.

Laurel shot him a dirty look. "Hey, Little Drummer Boy."

He stopped rapping. "The headmaster said that Mr. Smithson had a heart attack, but I'm not so sure. He was always shooting hoops after school with the younger faculty. He was good!"

"But he was old, at least fifty," Laurel said.

"I know, but . . . "

"Let me guess. You think somebody *murdered* him." Laurel settled back into her seat and took a long sip of her drink. "You're here to look for clues." Another sip. "Your imagination never ceases to amaze."

"Something like that." Marcus looked at her intensely.

"You're taking this *CSI* stuff way too seriously," she said, glancing around. "Do you see any crime scene tape around here?"

Marcus shrugged. "What's your excuse for being in here?"

She held up her copy of *The Great Gatsby*. "I needed a place to read, and the Coffee Mug's getting too crowded. Who would've thought anybody would visit *this* room?"

Neither spoke for several long seconds. "It's weird that somebody died in here," Marcus said, glancing around. "Everything looks so . . . normal." The desks were neatly arranged in rows, the chalkboard completely erased, the textbooks precisely lined up on the bookshelves according to math level and author's last name. Even the slightly worn carpet looked as if it had been recently vacuumed.

"Do you think they'll assign this room to another teacher?" Marcus asked.

Laurel shrugged. "Where did Simon find the body?"

"Behind Mr. Smithson's desk. He had fallen over on top of it. According to Simon, he was in full livor." He shuddered at the vision of the teacher's stiffened body.

"Ironic, huh? A teacher dying in his classroom. Probably while grading Bobby's test." Laurel took another sip. "Sorry. Too soon, right?"

"Yeah," Marcus said. Laurel wasn't known for her tact.

He thought about the day before when Mr. Smithson asked him to work the homework problem on the board. That would've been his last chance to impress the teacher, and yet he had tried to hide. *Coward.*

The classroom door opened, its hinges creaking. They whipped around.

"What the h—" Marcus leaped out of his seat, grabbed Simon's sleeve, and dragged him into the classroom. "Did anybody see you?" He peered out into the hall.

"I don't think so." Simon cringed into himself. His eyes were red-rimmed, the eyelids slightly swollen.

He looks like he's seen a zombie or something, Marcus thought. *In fact, Simon* looks *like a zombie.* "What're you doing here?" He figured for sure Simon would've gone home by now. It's not every day that somebody discovers a body.

"I—I sometimes study with Mr. Smithson after school. We were working on the Poincare conjecture, although Perelman apparently solved it." Simon stared down at his shoes. "I didn't want to go any-where else."

"It's okay," Marcus said, looking at Laurel. "We get it."

She picked up her backpack and tossed her empty cup toward the the recycle bin. It missed the target by several inches. "C'mon. Let's go. This room's starting to freak me out."

"Hold on," Marcus said. He picked up her cup by the rim, careful not to touch the smudged lipstick stain. "If this is a crime scene, we don't want to contaminate it."

Simon's pupils dilated behind his glasses. "Crime scene? You think so, too? Yesterday after school while I was waiting for my dad—"

"What's that?" Marcus pointed at a gray metal filing cabinet next to Mr. Smithson's desk. "Over there."

"A *filing cabinet,*" Laurel said slowly, as if speaking to a baby.

"Real funny. I meant, what's that shiny thing?" A small, round object caught in the space between the filing cabinet and the wall sparkled in a beam of sunlight streaming in through the window blinds. Marcus crouched down, reached for it, and froze his arm in mid-air. He had almost made another mistake. Grissom would've fired him by now. He bounded off his knees, unzipped his backpack, and pulled out a pair of tweezers.

He picked up the shiny object: a gold cuff link.

"Mr. Smithson won't be needing that anymore," Laurel said. "Let's go."

Marcus examined the cuff link. "Check out the insignia." Simon brushed his mop of hair out of his eyes and saw ΣΩΕ.

"They're letters of the Greek alphabet. Sigma Omega Epsilon."

"Shh!" Marcus said. "Did you hear that?"

Crkk crkk came a soft but high-pitched squeaking noise from the hallway.

"What is it?" Laurel asked.

Marcus stood up quickly.

Crkk crkk crkk CRKK CRKK. The squeaking grew louder.

"I can't get a detention for being caught in here." Laurel was whispering now. "I'm maxed out for the week, and it's only Tuesday!"

"We need to get out of here." Marcus gently positioned the cuff link on the corner of Mr. Smithson's desk by the Tiffany lamp. "But obviously not through the door." He tried the latch of a window and then another. The windows were sealed shut. That ruled out escaping through the courtyard behind the building.

The squeaking was much louder now—and much closer.

"Hide!" Laurel glanced around the room and then opened the coat closet. It was neatly filled with textbooks, prehistoric AV equipment, a small collection of Mr. Smithson's jackets and shirts, and two athletic duffle bags. "We can cram in here."

"The closet's too small," Simon protested, "unless we can somehow reduce our mass to—"

"No math!" Laurel hissed. "Marcus, you take the closet. Brainiac and I will squeeze under Smithson's desk."

CRKK. The squeaking stopped—right outside the classroom door.

Laurel tossed her book and bag under the desk, grabbed Simon's arm, and pulled him beside her in the cubby hole. It was big enough for two curled in the fetal position, heads nearly touching.

Marcus stuffed himself into the closet. He could barely breathe in the tight space. And what was that nasty smell? *Probably Mr. Smithson's sweaty athletic gear,* he thought. If they got caught, how would they explain to the dean why they were snooping around in a classroom after hours? Especially *this* classroom. Marcus's parents would ground him for life if he got suspended, and Coach Decker would probably kill him—if he didn't suffocate first. He plugged his nose and breathed through his mouth.

Click!

Marcus nearly choked. That sound he recognized. Somebody had locked them in!

The squeaking started again—and then faded away.

After several long seconds, Marcus slowly opened the closet door and peered out. "C'mon. It's clear." He grabbed Laurel's arm and helped her out of the cubby hole. It took her a couple of seconds to stand up straight, shaking out a cramp in her left calf. Simon crawled out on his own.

"What's that funky smell?" Laurel asked, sniffing. "It's almost as bad as Simon's shampoo."

"You don't want to know," Marcus said, shutting the closet door.

"Moth balls," Simon muttered.

Laurel stuffed her copy of *Gatsby* in her bag. "I'm out of here."

"How?" Marcus said. "The windows are sealed, and somebody just locked us in. Weird, but there's no latch on the inside, just a keyhole. Do you happen to have a key?"

Laurel glared at him through her thick clumps of mascara. "You'd better think of something, Sherlock. I'm not the auto club, and I'm not spending the night locked in here."

"Hey, guys," Simon said, opening his hand. "I found this under Mr. Smithson's desk." A tiny, oval-shaped pill rested in his gloved palm.

Laurel shrugged. "Probably one of Mr. Smithson's breath mints. Or an aspirin."

"Or maybe not," Marcus said, examining the pill. He remembered Mr. Smithson taking one yesterday when he'd asked him to tutor Bobby.

"As if Mr. Smithson would abuse prescription drugs," Laurel said.

Using the tweezers, Marcus placed the pill on the desk next to the cuff link.

"Seriously, how are we going to get out of here?" she said. "This is like a cheesy movie. *Death Kill Six.*"

"It's not really a problem." Simon pulled a ring with a single brass key out of his pocket. "Mr. Smithson said I could come in here anytime to work on math."

Laurel reached for the key, but Marcus snatched it out of her fingers.

"Simon, you really are a genius," he said, unlocking the door. "Quick! You guys go first. I'll catch up with you."

Laurel and Simon fled down the dim, shadowy hallway.

Marcus slipped the key into his jacket pocket and crossed back to Mr. Smithson's desk. He picked up the pill Simon had found, sealed it in a small plastic evidence bag he pulled out of his backpack, and labeled the bag with a Sharpie. He left the cuff link on top of the desk. *That* belonged with Mr. Smithson's other personal property.

Marcus took several steps toward the door and stopped. Turning, he stared at the grade book resting on the corner of the teacher's desk. Marcus glanced over his shoulder despite doubting if Laurel and Simon would come back looking for him. He probably wouldn't have another opportunity to see what he had earned for the mid-quarter. Surely, Mr. Smithson wouldn't mind if he peeked. After all, it was *his* grade.

He cautiously opened the book, fortunate that Mr. Smithson likely was the only teacher at Pinehurst to use an old-fashioned grade ledger to record his students' marks. Marcus thumbed through the pages until he located the section Mr. Smithson had labeled *Calculus*. He scrolled his index finger down the alphabetical list of names until he came to his own: *Jackson, Marcus, 92%, A–*. Marcus smiled. The extra studying had paid off. He glimpsed at the names below his. *Lopez, Mariana, 85%, B. Musgrave, Simon, 115%, A+.* One-hundred-fifteen percent? Of course. Extra credit. *Santana, Manny, 78%, C+. Morgenstern, Sarah, 96%, A. Tate, Bobby, 85%, B. Van Berkel, Victoria, 98%.*

Marcus re-read the last two names. Impossible. Mr. Smithson had said Bobby was close to failing the class, yet he had earned a B. He must've miscalculated Bobby's average.

But when was the last time Mr. Smithson had made a mistake?

Confused, Marcus closed the grade book, picked up his backpack, and, using Simon's key, locked the classroom door behind him. As he sprinted down the hallway and rounded the corner, he nearly collided with one of the housekeeping staff who was slowly pushing a cleaning cart—a cart with a squeaky wheel. *Crrkk.*

Ah, Marcus thought, nodding. At least one mystery was solved.

eyewitness: *a person who sees something happen and can give a first-hand description*

TUESDAY AFTER SCHOOL

Simon's dad was waiting at the curb in the front parking lot. Simon plopped in the passenger seat of the Tesla and pulled the door shut.

"Mr. Smithson's dead," he blurted.

The car's interior reeked of citrus, either from his father's aftershave or a fragrance pad from the car wash hidden under one of the seats, causing Simon's already queasy stomach to somersault. This morning he had thrown up in the headmaster's office—twice. He opened his window just in case.

"The headmaster called. You could've come home, son," his father said, starting the car. "The school also sent a community email."

Simon nodded.

"I would've rescheduled a few meetings, and your mom could've canceled her classes."

How could Simon tell his dad that he had *wanted* to stay? At school he could pretend that Mr. Smithson was still in his classroom, grading exams or finding obscure and complex math problems for them to solve.

"I'm sorry, Simon. I know you were fond of Mr. Smithson."

"He . . . he asked me yesterday if I wanted to be c-captain of the Quiz Bowl team," Simon said, wiping his eyes with the sleeve of his sweatshirt. That was the last question Mr. Smithson would ever ask him.

"That's quite an honor, son. I'm sure one of the other teachers will coach the squad. Ms. Goldman, perhaps." Martin Musgrave slowly pulled away from the curb.

A late afternoon marine layer had moved in, and the low, gray clouds matched Simon's gloomy mood. "The headmaster said Mr. Smithson had a heart attack, but I don't believe him." His tone was sharp.

"What? Why not?"

"Don't you remember? Yesterday after school? In the parking lot? The fight?"

"Simon, please," his dad said. "I know you feel terrible, but we discussed this several times. We have no idea what was going on. That corner of the lot was really dark."

"But I know what I saw!"

"You've had a traumatic day. Why don't you recline your seat and rest? I'll get us home as quickly as I can." He tuned in to his favorite nineties rock station. "Is Aerosmith too much for you? How about classical? Chopin, maybe?"

"No!" Simon punched the mute button. The etude that was playing when he found Mr. Smithson echoed in his head. He doubted if he'd ever listen to Chopin again.

Unfortunately, traffic on Ocean Crest Road was bumper-to-bumper despite the city's road construction efforts to improve traffic flow. *SevenEightNineTen* . . . Staring out the window, Simon tried calming the roller coaster in his stomach by counting the eucalyptus trees on the side of the road as they drove up the curvy hill toward the university. The trees' camphor-like odor drifted in through the open window, making the inside of the car smell like a cough drop. That was better than the lemony smell, though. He lost count by the time they reached Surf Side Lane. Not even math could help wipe away the horrible image of Mr. Smithson sprawled over his desk. Where was his mind's "delete" key?

Taking his dad's advice, he reclined his seat and closed his eyes, determined not to vomit in the car when he remembered for the hundredth time the fist headed directly toward Mr. Smithson's right eye yesterday after the dedication ceremony for the new football stadium.

Although Simon was allergic to anything athletic, the dedication ceremony had been impressive, even by Pinehurst standards. A faint odor of sulfur and chlorate from the fireworks display lingered over the campus. He stood on the sidewalk in front of Weatherly Hall and gazed at the clusters of students lazing on the grass in the afternoon sunshine. Some were flopped on their stomachs, barefoot, with their textbooks, laptops, or tablets propped open in front of them, their eyes protected by Gucci or Maui Jim sunglasses. Others stared at their phones, thumbs tapping the screens. Nathan Tsu, a senior boy on Simon's Quiz Bowl team, was reclining against the trunk of a palm tree, strumming Ed Sheeran's latest ballad on his guitar. A quartet of girls giggled as they jogged past, dribbling soccer balls on the way to the fields on the other side of campus. Not one of them so much as looked his way.

Simon had fifty-two minutes to kill before his dad picked him up.

He had already studied for tomorrow's chemistry test and Wednesday's quiz in history. The Paleontology Club meeting had been canceled because Dr. Jay, the club's faculty sponsor, had twisted her knee after stumbling over a mouse that escaped from its cage during fifth period. And, with the chairs of the academic departments meeting every Monday after school, he couldn't work math problems with Mr. Smithson. What else was there to do? He could always look over the problem set for tomorrow morning's Math Club meeting.

Simon pulled a wadded-up dollar bill from his pants pocket. By the time he had made his way through the mob grabbing refreshments on the terrace after the dedication ceremony, there wasn't a crumb left. Eating would kill a few minutes, and he had enough to buy a Twix bar from one of the vending machines near the athletic center. Unfortunately, Bobby was heading in the same direction with a basketball tucked under his arm. So much for the vending machine. Simon ignored the grumbling in his stomach and found a vacant bench in the shade under a California sycamore near the front parking lot. He opened his forensic science textbook to the pages

Ms. Mason had assigned for homework, and was soon so engrossed in the reading that he didn't notice the shadow looming over him.

"Good afternoon, Mr. Musgrave," Mr. Smithson said, leaning over his shoulder. "Ah. The O.J. Simpson case. A particularly sensational crime. Ninteeen-ninety-four, right?" His breath had a faint odor of tuna along with peppermint.

"Mr. Smithson! You startled me!" Simon stood up so abruptly that the book slipped out of his hands, missing the teacher's shoe by a centimeter as it fell.

"I'm the one who should apologize." Mr. Smithson picked up Simon's book and brushed off a few particles of dirt before handing it back. "I didn't mean to frighten you. I thought you heard me calling." He leaned in and lowered his voice. "I intended to talk to you after class this morning, but I had other business to attend to."

"Am I in trouble?"

Mr. Smithson chuckled. "You? Quite the opposite." He pulled a tin of mints from his coat pocket and popped one into his mouth. "I'm so impressed with your Quiz Bowl performance that I'm asking you to be the captain of the squad Pinehurst sends to the city competition."

"M-me? But I'm only a freshman." He was youngest member of the team. The seniors would hate him when they heard about this. They already resented him for being in their advanced placement and honors courses.

Mr. Smithson read his thoughts. "Don't worry about the upperclassmen. Protecting fragile egos is not a priority. They won't question my decision." He put his hand on Simon's shoulder and squeezed. Hard. "What's important is that we win the tournament, right?" He stood so close that Simon could almost see molecules of peppermint floating out of his mouth. "I can always count on you. My little protégé."

"Yeah, I guess . . . I mean, yes, sir."

"Good boy." Mr. Smithson peeked at his watch, a vintage Rolex. "Shall I see you tomorrow morning before school? I found an especially challenging derivative for us." Without waiting for an answer, he picked up his old-fashioned brown leather briefcase and strode off across the parking lot.

"Wow." Simon sank back down on the bench. The Math Club and now captain of the Quiz Bowl team. *I'll have to brush up on medieval literature and geography of the Southern Hemisphere,* he thought. *And they always ask about ancient civilizations and . . .* Simon was totally in his head when a horn beeped twice. Dad's Tesla. Simon sighed and lugged his backpack over. Burying his head in the car's trunk, he shoved and pushed at the boxes, duffle bags, golf clubs, and tools to make room for his bag.

From inside the trunk, he heard a man's voice roar, "Stop messing with my son!"

Simon stood and whirled around in the direction of the voice. A large man in a black athletic warm-up suit shoved Mr. Smithson against the teacher's Volvo and raised his right fist. His swing just missed Mr. Smithson's eye.

Simon slammed shut the trunk, rushed around to the passenger door, and yanked it open. "Dad, get out of the car! Mr. Smithson needs help!"

"What?" Martin cupped his right ear and leaned across the seat.

"Turn down the music!" Van Halen's "Jump" blared from the car's audio system. Simon gestured frantically toward the faculty section of the lot. "Get out of the car! Somebody's assaulting Mr. Smithson!"

But before his father could unbuckle his seat belt, the man in the athletic suit had bolted across the parking lot. The hood of the jacket covered his head, but as he turned to cut through the dense hedge of juniper shrubs separating the lot from the quad, Simon caught a glimpse of the man's face. The genetics were unmistakable. Same stringy bleached-blond hair, same hawk-like nose, same nasal voice. Father and son were clones.

"Th-that was Bobby's father," Simon stammered as he climbed into the passenger seat. "He was fighting with Mr. Smithson!"

"What? Are you sure? It's pretty dark in that shaded section of the lot."

"Yes, I'm sure! He threw a punch at him but missed!" Simon twisted around to peer out the back window of the car. Mr. Smithson's car was gone. He had probably driven out the back exit.

"Should we call security?"

"Never mind, Dad. It's over." He faced forward again and reached for the seat belt over his shoulder. "He'll live."

7

fraternity: *a college or university social club, typically for male students*

TUESDAY EVENING

"I'll have the usual—an extra hot, nonfat, no whip, double shot mocha." Laurel handed her debit card to the pimple-faced teenager behind the counter. She didn't recognize him from Pinehurst Academy. Pacific High, probably.

"Anything else?" he mumbled.

"If I wanted anything else, I would have asked for it, don't you think?"

"A bit grouchy today, huh?" the barista muttered, swiping her card.

Laurel's head was throbbing. Maybe she needed to cut down on caffeine—but not until she recovered from the experience in Mr. Smithson's creepy old classroom.

The Coffee Mug was empty except for a thirty-something guy in a faded gray T-shirt tapping away on his laptop in the back corner. Laurel settled into her favorite overstuffed armchair by the café's front windows. She kicked off her shoes and stripped off her fishnet knee-highs, replacing them with a pair of flip-flops. Then, tugging at the clip in her hair, she released the single strip of pink and sank back into the nest of cushions. "Home, sweet home," she said. She tucked her legs under her and sniffed. The blend of chocolate and coffee in the room was like aromatherapy. She should at least attempt her homework, she knew. But "should" was for people who cared. Instead, Laurel rested her head against the back of the chair and, wrapping her hands around the warm mug, closed her eyes.

Her ringtone jolted her awake. It stopped, then began again. She glanced around, a bit embarrassed because she had forgotten to silence the thing.

She found the phone buried under the seat cushion.

"Mom?" She yawned. "Sorry. I must've dozed off. I'm at the Coffee Mug." She checked the time on her phone. It was almost five o'clock. "Where are you?" She sipped her mocha and frowned. It was now lukewarm. "Where? I can't hear you."

Every seat was now occupied, and the line of customers waiting to be served snaked almost to the door. "What?" She could barely hear her mother's voice over the noise of the espresso machine. "New York? I thought you and dad were flying directly back to San Diego. We're supposed to go to Surfrider for dinner, remember?" So much for parent-daughter time.

Laurel tucked her phone between her ear and shoulder and carried the mocha over to the microwave by the pastry counter. She set the timer for forty-five seconds and listened patiently as her mother described the Paris fashion shows. "Oh. Thanks." Another Vuitton bag. Obviously, her mom hadn't noticed the four others that sat on the top shelf of Laurel's closet, unused.

Laurel tested the mocha's temperature with the tip of her left pinkie and licked off the drop. "No, Marta doesn't need to stay over." She had been taking care of herself since she was seven, and at sixteen she didn't need to be chaperoned by the housekeeper. Laurel stirred the mocha as her mother rambled more instructions. *Jeez, Mom.* Of course she would remember to set the security alarm. She snapped the wooden stick stir stick in half. "Bye, Mom."

She disconnected and, careful not to scald her tongue, took a sip of mocha. *Business? Yeah, right,* she thought, settling back into her chair. They were probably hobnobbing in the Hamptons with New York's elite. And she was missing all the fun. As if she was the least bit interested.

Laurel rooted through her backpack for the sheet of problems her econ teacher had assigned for homework. Anything to take her mind off her parents and Mr. Smithson's corpse. She put the crumpled paper on the coffee table and smoothed out the deep creases. The first problem was a breeze, the second barely a challenge. Fifteen minutes later, she had solved all ten of them. She smirked and erased three of her answers. She had a rep to uphold; all she needed was credit for the assignment to pass the course, no fireworks necessary.

She stuffed the assignment back in her bag and took out a book. She had borrowed a first edition of *The Great Gatsby* from her father's personal library. Marcus, aka Mr. Responsible, had probably finished his essay three days ago but would never admit it. Who was he trying to fool? Certainly not her. She knew who his father was. Jeremiah Jackson, Super Jock. Played for the Lakers. Or was it the Dodgers? She knew virtually nothing about sports and didn't care to know anything. Everybody thought Marcus was at Pinehurst because he could dribble a ball, but Laurel knew differently: Marcus was smart, really smart. And he worked his butt off.

The chatter in the café and the whirring of the espresso machine made it impossible to concentrate. She snapped her book shut and, picking up her phone, tapped the number for Sushi Rocks. "I need a take-out order," she said. "A California roll, seaweed salad, and edamame dumplings. For one."

* * *

"Hi, honey, are you okay? Dr. Welton called me at work." Simon's mother, with a dish towel in one hand and barbecue tongs in another, wrapped her arms around him and, pulling him close, kissed the top of his head. "I'm so sorry. It must've been awful."

It had been. The worst thing that had happened to him since his pet anole lizard had fallen in the toilet. Simon had warned his dad to look before flushing. But right now he couldn't talk about Mr. Smithson's death, not even with his mom.

She read his thoughts. "If you want to talk—Aw, shoot! The steaks." His mom ran toward the back patio. "Dinner will be ready in five. Why don't you take Pegasus upstairs with you while you change out of your uniform?" The white Labrador puppy nipped at his ankles.

Simon's bedroom was neat and organized, just the way he liked it. The walls were painted pale blue, set off by a darker cobalt carpet. A *Star Wars: The Rise of Skywalker* comforter covered a double bed, and Sony's latest 49-inch LCD was perched on top of the oak dresser. His

Xbox was plugged into the unit, but Simon didn't feel like playing a video game—not even *Vikings from Venus*. *Fortnite* was so over-rated. A chess board rested on a side table, the black and white onyx pieces arranged for a game that had been started but not finished. Neatly organized books—mostly math and science—and stacks of scientific magazines crammed the shelves of the bank of bookcases. Stephen Hawking's landmark *A Brief History in Time,* given to him on his eleventh birthday by Mr. Smithson, was open on the nightstand next to a Rubik's cube and two tickets to next summer's Comic-Con.

Simon tossed his backpack on the floor and flopped on top of his bed. His eyes began to tear again, and he wiped them with the corner of the comforter. He hadn't eaten all day, and after hurling in the car, his stomach felt hollow, like a surgeon had reached inside and ripped out his pancreas. And spleen. How was he going to survive at Pinehurst without Mr. Smithson? Would the new faculty sponsor of the Quiz Bowl team have as much faith in his ability?

Simon gazed at the mural of the Milky Way covering the bedroom ceiling. The distance between Dubhe and Merak in Ursa Major was off. The stars were too far apart.

He rarely felt this confused. It *had* been dark in the parking lot, but he didn't need a telescope to identify Bobby's father. He'd recognize the black athletic suit with the iconic three white stripes if he saw it again. And he'd never forget the swinging fist. Was it mere coincidence that Bobby's father had been fighting with Mr. Smithson the day before Mr. Smithson died? Simon had already done the calculations: The laws of random chance suggested it was almost impossible.

Just as disturbing, when had his dad stopped listening to him?

Simon stared at the movie poster of *The Martian* tacked on the wall next to *Guardians of the Galaxy 2* and *Black Panther.* So much for *his* superhero: Dad.

"Simon? Dinner's ready," his mom called up the stairs.

She would be disappointed if he didn't eat. He'd eat a little and then say he had a lot of homework. On his way out, he moved the white rook to h5. He'd worry about the black knight later.

Simon sank into his desk chair as Pegasus curled up on the end of his bed. He moved the framed autographed photo of Apple's Tim Cook to make room for the plate of key lime pie that his mom had forced him to take up with him. He'd barely choked down his steak. What would he do with the pie? He checked his Gmail and found twenty unread messages from cyber-friends he had met in chat rooms. Simon played chess online with Rook II in Albuquerque, and somebody with the username Polaris knew more about astronomy than he did. He wished that just once he would receive an email, text, or IM from somebody at school. Somebody he actually knew. Snapchat was useless. His snap would disappear before anyone could read it. Not that anyone would care what he snapped.

His brain jumped to another question: How could he impress Mr. Smithson one last time? After pondering for a few seconds, the answer popped into his head. He would find a topic for his independent study research paper that would make Mr. Smithson proud—a topic so unique that his mentor could claim it as his own.

Simon Googled "calculus" and waited for the list of references to pop up. He skimmed the first hit and shook his head. A paper on *The Birth of Exponential and Inverse Trigonometric Functions* was too ordinary. The next listing, *Derivatives and Integers,* wouldn't work, either. Too elementary. Simon opened the third posting. This would unquestionably impress Mr. Smithson. He would compare the theories of Isaac Newton and von Liebniz defining infinitesimal calculus *and* incorporate a little from the newly discovered Archimedes document.

Try as he might, though, Simon couldn't concentrate on Newton or von Liebniz despite the controversy about which one of them had invented the study of change known as calculus. Nobody cared anymore; the quarrel had been resolved in the eighteenth century. What had he been thinking? The topic he'd selected would bore Mr. Smithson, not excite him. Simon absently scrolled back to his search. The twenty-sixth listing caught his eye: *Renaissance Mathematics and the Return of Greek Philosophy*. He had forgotten about the three Greek letters on the cuff link Marcus had found in Mr. Smithson's classroom. ΣΩΕ. Sigma Omega Epsilon.

Simon knew where he had seen the letters before.

He bounded out of his chair and peeked into the hallway outside his bedroom. His parents were downstairs watching *Jeopardy!* He could hear the host reading a clue. *Benjamin Franklin,* Simon mentally answered. Must be the kindergarten tournament. Franklin, the inventor of the lightning rod, had also created the first pair of bifocal eyeglasses. Simon crept down the hallway to his father's study.

The wall next to the fireplace was a gallery of photographs, diplomas, and awards his parents had received over the years, including a trophy Simon's dad had earned at the 2006 San Diego Rock 'n' Roll Marathon. Mr. Musgrave was a partner at a prominent Del Mar law firm, and Simon's mom taught biotechnology at the university. The first place trophy Simon had won at last year's science fair stood on the fireplace mantel along with dozens he had earned for chess. Simon found what he was looking for on the wall next to his parents' wedding photograph: his father's fraternity certificate from Yale. The three Greek letters in the gold emblem above the chapter president's signature matched the ones on the cuff link. ΣΩΕ. Mr. Smithson and his dad had belonged to the same fraternity. But this coincidence was impossible. Mr. Smithson hadn't gone to Yale.

Simon dragged the ottoman over, and, cautiously balancing himself, lifted the frame off the wall. The host was announcing the category for *Final Jeopardy*—Sitcom Science—while Simon crept back to his bedroom. Pegasus was still asleep on the bed, snoring lightly.

To his surprise, he had a text message from Marcus.

RU okay?

Simon's heart raced as began tapping away on his screen.

Before school. Hartford. My dad

A sharp rap on the door stopped him cold before he could finish the text.

"Simon? Is everything okay?" his father said, rattling the doorknob. "Unlock the door, son. I need to talk to you."

Simon took a deep breath and pressed the "send" key.

charcoal powder: *fine grains of charcoal used to make latent finger-prints more visible*

WEDNESDAY MORNING, ZERO HOUR

Through the small rectangular window in the door, Marcus spotted Simon waiting in Mr. Smithson's classroom. *Hasn't he had enough of this place?* he thought. The kid looked better, though. His cheeks had a hint of color, and his eyes were less bloodshot. But his shaggy hair still looked like it had been styled with a weed wacker.

"Sorry," Marcus said, shrugging off his backpack. "My alarm didn't go off. I almost missed the bus. What's up?"

Simon opened his mouth, but before he could get a word out, Laurel stomped in with flushed cheeks and strings of damp hair hanging around her face. "Nobody gave me a wake-up call, thank you very much," she grouched. "I barely had time to do my eyes." She looked more pale than usual under the florescent lights despite the bright magenta gloss on her lips.

Marcus turned to Simon. "How did you talk your dad into dropping you off this early?"

"I told him that I had to do some research for my history paper. That got him started on ancient Egypt. Did you know that Tutankhamen was only twelve when—"

"Please tell me that you didn't drag us in here to talk about Egyptian mummies," Laurel said, digging around in her bag. She pulled out a compact of face powder.

"Sorry. I'm off on a tangent again," Simon replied.

"How did you get in here?" Marcus asked. "I have your key." He handed it back, certain that Mr. Smithson would want Simon to keep it.

Simon blushed. "I-I told the security guard I forgot my math book and had to study for the cumulative assessment." He slid the key into his pocket.

"Not bad. I'll have to remember that excuse," Laurel said, outlining her eyes with what looked like a charcoal pencil she'd borrowed from the art studio. "But seriously, 'cumulative assessment'? I guess 'midterm exam' doesn't sound elitist enough." She applied another layer of mascara.

"Sorry you had to lie," Marcus said. This was probably the first time in his life Simon hadn't told the truth.

Simon reached under his sweatshirt and pulled out a rolled up 8.5 x 11 inch sheet of ivory parchment paper. It was slightly crinkled like a piece of dried fetal pig skin from the anatomy lab. He peeled off the rubber band and smoothed out the document on top of a student desk.

Laurel glanced at it and yawned. "I'm impressed that Martin Musgrave, whom I assume is your father, belongs to a frat, but you didn't need to drag us in here at zero hour to brag about it." She plopped down behind a desk at the back of the room and, closing her eyes, rested her head on her arms. The strip of pink hair dangled over her face. "Let me sleep."

Marcus studied the fraternity certificate, brushing his fingers across the three embossed gold letters in the center of the seal. ΣΩE. What the heck? Where had he . . .

The cuff link! It still rested where he had left it on top of Mr. Smithson's desk next to the Tiffany lamp. He held the cuff link next to the certificate. The insignias matched. "Your dad and Mr. Smithson belonged to the same Greek," Marcus said. "Quite a coincidence."

"Impossible," Simon said, shaking his head. "Sigma Omega Epsilon is a *local* fraternity, for Yale students only, not a national one like Sigma Alpha Epsilon or Sigma Chi."

"You mean one of those secret frats, like Skull and Bones?" Marcus had watched a movie on Netflix and had been freaked out by a weird initiation ceremony in a brick-walled basement, complete with burning candles, costumes, and chanting in a strange language.

Simon shook his head. "My dad wouldn't belong to anything that strange. I couldn't investigate the fraternity further because my parents insisted that I get some sleep. They took away my laptop and iPad," he explained. "And my phone. My mom made me drink some warm milk."

"Get to the point, King Tut," Laurel mumbled. "What's the big deal?"

"It isn't Mr. Smithson's cuff link, that's the big deal!" Simon answered, raising his voice. "He went to Harvard, not Yale."

Marcus shrugged. "Maybe one of his students gave him the links as a gift. You know, for writing a letter of rec or something." He'd heard a rumor that an English teacher had received a car a few years back.

"Impossible. *Everyone* knows that Mr. Smithson went to Harvard." Simon pointed at the crimson triangular pennant with the large H tacked on the wall next to the chalkboard.

"Yeah, that's kind of hard to miss," Marcus said.

"Mr. Smithson would never have anything related to Yale in this room!" Simon explained.

Marcus nodded. The Ivy League. He remembered reading that the Harvard–Yale rivalry started generations ago and had culminated every year since with a football game. Simon was right: Mr. Smithson's Harvard college ring with the crimson stone seemed glued to his finger. But if the cuff link wasn't Mr. Smithson's, whose was it?

Simon read his mind. "This morning I checked the faculty biographies posted on the school's website," he said. "Ms. Goldman and Coach Decker are Yale graduates. The cuff link could belong to one of them."

"No way." Laurel's voice was muffled by her arm partially covering her mouth. "Ms. Goldman, okay, I can believe that," she said, sitting up straight. "She's smart. But Decker? Since when do they offer Dribbling 101 at Yale?" She put her head back down on the desk.

Marcus rifled through his backpack, pulled out a magnifying glass, and examined the cuff link more closely. "There's a partial fingerprint on top of the letters, but it's really smudged." He doubted if he'd be able to make out ridge details, but he'd take the cuff link back to the lab. He lowered the magnifying glass and looked around. "We need something to compare it to. What else are we sure has Mr. Smithson's prints on it?"

"What about his Harvard mug?" Simon pointed at the bookcase behind the teacher's desk. "One of his professors gave it to him when he graduated. He never let anybody else use it. Sometimes he drank tea out of it instead of his traveler's mug."

Marcus removed a pair of nitrile gloves and a large evidence bag from his backpack. "Grissom's rule number three: Be prepared." He sealed the graphite gray ceramic mug with Harvard's distinctive crimson *VERITUS* shield in the evidence bag, careful not to smear any fingerprints.

"What if somebody finds out we took these things?" Simon asked. "I-I don't want to get expelled."

"You won't get expelled," Marcus said. "I'll take full responsibility."

The chimes signaled the passing period to homeroom. Zero hour was over.

"C'mon, Sleeping Beauty," Marcus said to Laurel, shaking her shoulder. "Time to go."

Laurel stretched and brushed her hair out of her face. Magenta gloss was smeared above her upper lip.

Simon rolled up his father's fraternity certificate, secured it with the rubber band, and tucked it back under his sweatshirt. "I don't want to be tardy. It takes one minute and twenty-three seconds to get from Hartford to Weatherly unless you cut across the quad, and if the sidewalk's crowded with students, especially early in the morning, the time increases to two minutes and—"

Laurel groaned. "Stop. It's way too early for math."

"Don't worry," Marcus said. "We've got plenty of time." After labeling the two evidence bags with the appropriate information to maintain the chain of custody, he zipped the cuff link and Harvard mug into his backpack.

Simon slowly opened the door and peered into the hallway. "Hurry! Students are coming." He sprinted out of the room.

Laurel tried to get out of her seat, but her sleeve was caught on a metal screw on the back of the desk. Yanking her arm, she ripped her sweater. "Ah, crap!" She poked the tip of her pinkie through the small hole.

"I'll buy you a new one from the bookstore." Marcus flicked off the lights. "We're out of here," he said. "And, uh, you might want to check in the mirror before class." He rubbed the space between his upper lip and nose.

* * *

Marcus settled into his seat and opened his notebook.

"We need to finish our lecture about DNA," Ms. Mason announced to the class, "but it's been a rough couple of days." Her voice was hoarse. Dark circles rimmed her eyes, and the two vertical creases between her eyebrows looked like they had been carved into her skin. "I'm giving you a free period."

"Yes!" Bobby pumped his fist in the air and jumped out of his seat, toppling it over. The crack of metal against the linoleum sounded like a gunshot.

"Not so fast," Ms. Mason said. "Midterm exams are coming up, and your reconstruction of the mock crime scene is due on Monday. Please use this time wisely."

Laurel groaned, but not as loud as Bobby.

Marcus leaned across the aisle and lowered his voice. "Forget the mock crime scene. Let's start with this." He removed the small plastic bag with the cuff link from his backpack.

"I don't know . . . "

"C'mon. You know you're curious."

"What if Ms. Mason asks us what we're doing?" Laurel said, digging a lab manual out of her bag. "On the other hand, who am I to follow the rules?"

"That's the attitude," Marcus said, grinning. "Besides, she'll think we're reviewing for the test or something."

They found a place to work in the back of the lab, away from the other students. Their classmates had pulled their desks together in study circles with their textbooks propped open. Several students asked Ms. Mason if they could go to the library to study. Not surprisingly, Bobby had grabbed his stuff and left without a word.

"Do you need help with anything?" Simon asked, walking over to them. "I've already studied for the cumulative assessments. Twice."

"Get a life," Laurel muttered under her breath. "And please stop saying 'cumulative.' I hate that word! They're just big tests."

Marcus glanced toward the front of the room. Ms. Mason was sitting at her desk, staring at her laptop screen as if hypnotized by the pod of dolphins floating across the screensaver. "Find out anything you can about Sigma Omega Epsilon," he said, lowering his voice. "It can't be *that* secret."

"I'll go over to the IT lab," Simon replied, thankful for something to do.

Marcus covered the epoxy black lab counter with a square yard of white mural paper. He snapped on a pair of nitrile gloves over his wrists and grabbed two clean beakers and a flask from a cabinet. He also picked up one of Ms. Mason's coffee mugs from the drying rack by the sink.

"I'll dust the cuff link," he said, then handed Laurel the plastic bag containing the Harvard mug. "This should have Mr. Smithson's prints on it. They're latent, though." Invisible.

"What's with the other stuff?" Laurel asked, indicating the glassware.

"If we dust this stuff, too, Ms. Mason'll think we're definitely studying for the midterm." Maybe she wouldn't notice what they were *really* up to.

Marcus found other necessary tools—jars of different fingerprinting powders, two camel's-hair brushes, a roll of clear gel tape, microscope slides, and two magnifying glasses—on the supply cart. They'd have to fingerprint the old-fashioned way. Iodine fuming was out of the question. *That* Ms. Mason would notice, especially if they set off the fire alarm. Same with super glue fuming. Besides, he had read that powders worked better on ceramic.

"I'll use charcoal on the cuff link," Marcus said. "You should use a lighter color on the gray mug. You know, for contrast."

Laurel held up a brush she had already dipped into a jar of white fingerprint powder. "I'm one step ahead of you, Sherlock." She already had gloves on, too.

"Sorry." He needed to trust her ability more.

Twirling a brush between his thumb and index finger, Marcus applied a thin film of charcoal to the top of the cuff link. As if by magic, the distinct ridges of a fingerprint appeared on the cuff link. He tore off a small piece of gel tape, placed it on the print, and, careful not to smudge it, gently lifted it. He put the tape on a clean microscope slide.

"We might as well review for the test while we're doing this," he said. "Ask me a question."

Laurel gently swiped her brush over the surface of Mr. Smithson's mug. "How are fingerprints formed?"

Marcus smiled. That was an easy one. "Fingerprints are friction skin ridges that help us get a better grip on things—literally," he explained. "We have two layers of skin—the epidermis, or outer layer that we shed, and a deeper layer called the dermis. A middle layer of cells pushes up and forms the ridges and grooves of fingerprints. Sort of like hills and valleys. Or tire treads."

"Impressive. Did you memorize the paragraph in the book?"

"Just about," he said. "Your turn. What actually makes the print?"

"Oil and sweat," Laurel said. "They leave the pattern on a surface."

"Not bad." *She knows her stuff*, Marcus thought. The cliché about looks being deceiving definitely applied to her.

Using a magnifying glass, he went back to work examining the print from the cuff link. Someday when he worked for the FBI, he could run a print through the Automated Fingerprint Identification System or AFIS and get an ID by digital imaging. In this case, however, the ridge pattern was obvious. "It's only a partial, but it's from a right thumb. And it's got a central tented arch."

"Arches are rare," Laurel said.

"I know. Only five percent of us have them. A central tented arch is even more unique, especially on a thumb."

"The cuff link probably has some skin cells on it. Too bad we haven't learned how to use the new miniPCR equipment. It would be nice to pull some DNA off the link."

Marcus sighed. "Yeah. PCR would be very useful right about now." He bet the forensic scientists at the FBI did polymerase chain reactions all day to replicate small samples of DNA. The local bio-tech companies often donated used equipment to Pinehurst, and Ms. Mason had promised she would get the machines running before the end of the semester.

Laurel picked up Mr. Smithson's mug. It was streaked with white powder. "No central tents. Just loops and whorls."

"Most people have those," Marcus said.

"So if it's not Mr. Smithson's print on the cuff link, then—"

"Whose is it?" *VERITUS*. Harvard's motto was Latin for "truth." Marcus was more determined than ever to discover the truth about what had happened to Mr. Smithson.

Sherlock Holmes: *fictional detective of the late 1800s known for his powers of deduction and reasoning*

LATER WEDNESDAY MORNING

At the end of the period, Marcus and Laurel put away the fingerprinting supplies and wiped off the counters with a dilute solution of bleach until not a molecule of white powder, aluminum dust, or charcoal remained. The room was empty except for Ms. Mason clicking away on her laptop. Intensely focused on whatever she was doing—probably writing the midterm exam—she hadn't noticed that everyone else had left. They deposited their used gloves in a biohazard bag, hung up their lab coats, and grabbed their backpacks.

As they neared the main exit of Weatherly Hall, Laurel stopped in midstride. "Shoot! I left my bracelets on the sink when I washed my hands."

"I'll catch up with you later," Marcus said. "I need a snack."

Jeez, Laurel thought. *The guy's an eating machine.*

The door to room 102 was propped open. Ms. Mason still sat at her desk, her back to the door, but now had her phone pressed against her ear. "How can you say that?" She no longer sounded tired. "That's heartless. Surely, you can't feel that way."

Laurel froze in the doorway. Although hesitant to interrupt, her wrists felt naked without the bracelets. If they weren't from Gems by James, she would leave them.

"I know he wasn't your favorite person," Ms. Mason said, her voice softer, "but you must feel a little sympathetic. The poor man's dead."

Ms. Mason had to be talking about Mr. Smithson, but to whom? It didn't sound like a casual conversation. Laurel backed away from the door, careful not to be seen, but close enough to hear.

"Why weren't you at school yesterday, Audrey?" Ms. Mason said.

Audrey. Why was that name familiar? Laurel's heart quickened. Ms. Goldman's first name was Audrey. The headmaster had used her full name when he presented her with an award award last spring. Math Teacher of the Year or something.

"We'll talk later," Ms. Mason said. "Let's grab a coffee after school. By then you'll feel differently."

Laurel quickly backed away and ducked into Dr. Gladson's anatomy lab next door. She hoped Ms. Mason would put her bracelets in the lost-and-found box.

* * *

"Are you sure she was talking to Ms. Goldman?" Marcus bit off a chunk of cinnamon bun and washed it down with a long swig of chocolate milk.

"No," Laurel said, popping a purple grape into her mouth, "but Ms. Goldman's first name is Audrey."

They had found two unoccupied patio chairs near the locker bay at the far end of the terrace. A group of sixth graders attempted to play four-square with a tennis ball near them, but Laurel shooed them away with one look. The jet stream had shifted, and hot, dry Santa Ana winds had blown in from the desert, trading places with the early morning's damp marine layer. California was suffering from one of the worst droughts in the state's history, and the county would likely issue a wildfire watch alert until the winds settled down. Students clustered around every table, munching on snacks and working on their tans, while the school nurse handed out small packets of sunscreen.

"Ms. Goldman, huh?" Marcus said. "Interesting."

He had seen Ms. Goldman Monday afternoon in room 102 when he went back to the lab after the dedication ceremony for the new football field. Her behavior would've earned a student at least two detentions.

* * *

Monday's dedication ceremony for Hart Stadium had ended early, and if Marcus skipped the refreshments, he'd have time before b'ball practice to analyze the white powder he'd found in Ms. Mason's laptop case at the mock crime scene. If he identified the powder, he'd earn an A on the crime scene reconstruction, no sweat.

The door to room 102 was propped open. The yellow crime scene tape had been taken down and the broken glass fragments and blood spatter cleaned up. A faint but familiar chlorinous odor of bleach tickled his nose. Somebody—Ms. Mason probably—had scrubbed the magenta Kastle-Meyer stains off the door frame, and the plastic bags containing the "evidence" they had collected were neatly lined up on the lab counter at the back of the room.

Marcus fingered the note he had found at the crime scene. It was safely tucked away in the pocket of his varsity jacket, but if Ms. Mason had planted it as evidence—and found out that he hadn't properly bagged and tagged it—he'd get an F on the assignment, guaranteed. He'd read the note a half-dozen times and had come up with a half-dozen different hypotheses fitting blackmail into Ms. Mason's faked abduction—but rejected all of them. He couldn't shake the feeling that there was something oddly familiar about the note. Marcus shoved it deeper into his pocket, hung up his jacket, and grabbed a lab coat and pair of safety goggles.

From his lab drawer he removed five quart-sized plastic bags filled with other white powders and opened his lab manual to "Exercise 18: Drug Bust at Pacific High." Last week Ms. Mason had set up a crime scene in which Pacific High's principal—Ms. Mason always poked fun at Pinehurst's rival school—asked CSIs to identify mysterious substances confiscated from student lockers. Pretending that the powders were illegal drugs, Ms. Mason had really used common household products, including sugar, baking soda, and salt, and had creatively renamed them. Marcus would compare the white powder he had found in the laptop case to the *Drug Bust* samples. He was stretching a large-sized nitrile glove over his huge hand when Ms. Mason walked in.

"Ah, Marcus. My number-one student. Always in here," she said, heading toward one of the lab sinks. "I need to leave by four o'clock, and so do you. There's a faculty dinner at Beach Inn, and I need to go home and change into something dressier than slacks. I hope the babysitter shows up on time."

"I'll be fast." Marcus unzipped one of the *Drug Bust* bags and, using a small spatula, scooped a small sample. "Hey, Ms. Mason, ever notice how much fake *Zocaine* looks like real sugar?" He peeked at her slyly. "You'd probably kill me if I tasted it."

"Tasting it would probably kill you before I did," Ms. Mason said, smiling. Her healthy sense of humor tempered the course's often grisly subject matter. She squirted a stream of liquid detergent into the sink, picked up a bottle brush, and began scrubbing a 500-milliliter graduated cylinder.

Marcus laughed and reached for a test tube. Judging from its physical appearance, the powder from the laptop case wasn't crystalline like sugar but powdery. Maybe it was baking soda. He scooped a gram of powder labeled *Devil Dust* and was about to transfer it into the test tube when Ms. Goldman, the school's young and popular math teacher, burst into the classroom.

"He's insane!" she shrieked. "I hate him!" Streaks of black mascara streamed down her flushed, tear-stained cheeks.

Startled, Marcus dropped the test tube. It hit the linoleum with a shrap ping and shattered into several small pieces. A puff of *Devil Dust* drifted upward. Marcus instinctively held his breath but then relaxed. Ms. Mason wouldn't use a nasty biotoxin in class; it had to be baby powder or something.

"I'm not going to let that lunatic destroy my career. I'll quit first!" Sinking behind a student desk, Ms. Goldman covered her face with her hands and began sobbing. Her usually neat shoulder-length blonde hair tumbled forward in a tangled mass.

"Marcus, can you give us a minute?" Ms. Mason turned off the faucet and stripped off her dishwashing gloves. "You can finish up tomorrow."

He stooped to pick up the broken glass. "I'll just—"

"No. Leave it. I don't want you to cut yourself."

"Yes, ma'am." Marcus stripped off his lab coat and gloves, grabbed his backpack, and rushed out of the classroom. First Bobby kicking trash cans and now Ms. Goldman flipping out. Laurel was right: So much for the "spirit of the community."

* * *

Milk Break was nearly over, but luckily Marcus had a free study period.

He scanned the crowd. "What's taking Simon so long? He owns the IT department." He fired his empty milk carton toward a trash can several yards away. A clean shot. Grabbing Laurel's arm, he pulled her to her feet. "C'mon. Let's take a walk."

"Why? Let go!" she said, wrestling to wriggle free. "Break's not over. I'm not going to class early."

"Shh. I'll explain in a second. This won't take long."

Holding her elbow, he dragged her across the terrace to the garden behind the chapel where students found refuge from their hectic schedules or couples found a bit of privacy amid colorful blooms and ivy-covered trellises. Sixth graders had planted an organic vegetable garden as part of their life sciences curriculum. This morning, however, the only visitors seeking comfort were birds, bugs, and Princess, the chapel cat. The chaplain's most recent addition to the garden was a small stone fountain, complete with water spouting from the mouth of a chubby naked cherub.

Marcus let go of Laurel's arm and pointed at a small bench under a palm. She refused to sit. "You're acting psycho again," she said.

"We've got to go back to Mr. Smithson's room," Marcus said.

"What? Are you crazy?" The administration had made it very clear that the classroom was off limits to curious students. The dean of students had hinted at suspension for rule breakers.

"Quiet!" He glanced around the garden. Reverend Allworth might be around walking Dallas or Diego, the chapel dogs. The chaplain's menagerie of rescue critters was larger than many animal shelters. "Just hear me out."

Laurel sat down on the bench and crossed her arms over her chest. "This had better be good."

"Ms. Mason told us the first day of class about intuition," Marcus said. "She told us to listen to the little voice in our heads. *Follow your instincts* were her exact words." He paused. "We need to go back."

"We can't keep snooping around in there," she said. "You heard the dean."

"Yes, we can. There's no crime scene tape to keep us out." Soon Mr. Smithson's classroom would be occupied by his substitute. Life went on at Pinehurst. "This is the last time, I promise."

"You're not Grissom. Or an NCIS guy. We're not anybody on TV," she said. "What about the big game on Saturday? If we get caught, we'll get a detention—or worse. You won't be able to play."

Marcus sat down next to her. She scooted over to make room for him. "The game doesn't seem so important anymore," he said quietly.

"What's going on with you?" she asked. "You always follow the rules. *I'm* the one who breaks them, remember?" She swatted a fly away from her face. "I don't know. Maybe Mr. Smithson did have a heart attack, like the headmaster said. Everything we're doing . . . or thinking . . . we're probably the world's biggest idiots."

"I haven't done my homework for two days, and we have cumulatives—er, midterm—exams, coming up," Marcus said. Coach was threatening to bench him if he didn't get his head in the game. Nor had he called his father back, and Jeremiah had left three new voice mails and two texts. "Something . . . something just doesn't feel right."

"What else besides fingerprints not matching? And the cuff link could belong to anybody."

"Yeah. Anybody who went to Yale *and* belonged to Sigma Omega Epsilon. What a coincidence that would be," Marcus said sarcastically. "Simon can calculate the odds."

"What else?" Laurel asked.

Marcus stood and, surveying the garden to make sure they were still alone, started pacing in front of the bench. "The security guard said that the paramedics took Mr. Smithson away in an ambulance."

"What else would they use? A school bus? Uber, maybe?"

"Shouldn't they have sent a crime scene unit, too? You know, because a teacher was found dead in his classroom under mysterious circumstances?"

"Are we reading too much into this?" Laurel asked. "Surely the first responders would've noticed if something seemed off. You know, 'mysterious circumstances'."

"What about the pill Simon found under his desk?" he asked. "I don't think it's Advil—or a breath mint."

"Sometimes a breath mint is just a breath mint, Sherlock."

"Maybe Mr. Smithson was the man Ms. Goldman was flipping out about when I was in the lab. And what about the conversation *you* overheard?" Marcus said. "You're pretty sure Ms. Mason was talking to Ms. Goldman on the phone."

"This sounds like *American Crime Story*," Laurel said. "Or *Forensic Files.*"

"What about Bobby?" Marcus asked. "Everybody heard his threat, and he was *smiling* when he heard Mr. Smithson was dead." Despite interrupting classes with Post-its to teachers, the headmaster had summoned the students and faculty to the gym and announced formally what had happened, offering counseling services. Okay, so Bobby's problems were solved. But a big smile? That wasn't right.

"Bobby's a loser," Laurel said. "But harmless. You said so yourself."

Marcus intentionally didn't tell her what he'd discovered in Mr. Smithson's grade book. With no hint of white-out or erasure marks, he had no proof that somebody had changed Bobby's grade. False accusations about grade tampering had just about shut down a school across town last year, and without solid evidence, he couldn't risk Pinehurst's reputation. Who knows? Maybe Bobby had done some extra credit.

Marcus sat back down on the bench and picked at his thumbnail. "I just want to check things out while I still can."

Laurel stared at him. "Why do you even care? It's not like Mr. Smithson can write you a letter of rec from the grave or something."

"It's . . . it's the right thing to do," Marcus said, looking down at his shoes. *And,* he thought, *if I want to be a real CSI, now's the time to start.*

"Don't you get sick of always being Mr. Responsible?" she asked.

"I'm lucky to be at a school like this," he said.

"Lucky? We *pay* to go to school here!"

"No," Marcus said, shaking his head. "Pinehurst just isn't about the money. We're getting a good education, and we'll get into good colleges."

"You sound like a testimonial in the admissions brochure," Laurel said. "What if we get caught?"

"Then I'll accept the consequences," Marcus replied without hesitation.

The garden was silent except for the buzzing of insects and the trickling of water from the fountain. Princess appeared from under a shrub and brushed against Laurel's legs. After several long seconds stroking the cat's head, Laurel finally said, "I'll help you under one condition. If we don't find anything this time, you'll let this go. Deal?"

Marcus nodded. "Deal." He resisted the urge to fist-bump.

"And if we get caught, maybe public school won't be so bad."

Not for her, Marcus thought. She'd go to Pacific High. He didn't even want to think about where he'd go. His father would disown him if he quit the team *and* was kicked out of Pinehurst. Having a son at a prestigious prep school was a more important status symbol to Jeremiah Jackson than his Ferrari.

He gave her a weak smile. "Look on the bright side. They make a big deal about what we learn inside the classroom being meaningful outside it."

"Yeah, well, we're going to test the school's mission statement," Laurel said.

But Marcus knew it was no test. Intuition told him that they had stepped into a *real* crime scene.

Laurel glanced at her phone. "Now I'm late for class. Really late." She picked up her bag and gave the cat one last rub. "But what's more important: learning about the Treaty of Versailles or solving a murder?"

On his way out of the garden, Marcus plucked a ripe cherry tomato off a vine and popped it into his mouth.

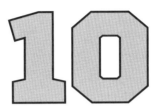

arrhythmia: a medical condition in which the contraction of the heart is irregular

WEDNESDAY LUNCH HOUR

"I feel like I'm in church," Marcus said.

"Or a toy store." Laurel picked up a brown teddy bear from the front of the door and squeezed it. It was the firm, unhuggable kind. She tossed it back on the floor. "I didn't know Mr. Smithson was *this* popular."

Despite the dean's warning to stay away, students and faculty had assembled a makeshift shrine in front of Mr. Smithson's classroom door. Bouquets of roses, sunflowers, tulips, and flowers Marcus couldn't identify despite a semester of botany were heaped in a colorful pile along with an assortment of stuffed animals. A droopy-eyed panda held in its paw a black balloon with *Good-Bye* printed on it in blue and silver, the school's colors. Dozens of sympathy cards, some handwritten, were taped on the door along with photographs of Mr. Smithson and his students.

"There weren't this many flowers earlier," a voice whispered behind them.

Laurel whipped around and clutched her chest. "Simon! You almost gave *me* a heart attack!"

"What're you doing here?" Marcus said. He glanced up and down the hallway. "The building's off limits during lunch. And you know what the dean said about this room in particular."

"When I didn't see you in the dining hall, I deduced that you were coming back here. Lunch was the logical time since the teachers are eating." Simon nudged the brown bear upright with his toe. When it teetered back onto its side, he bent down and propped it up next to a bouquet of daisies. He rearranged the daisies before standing back up again. "*Gerber jamesonii* was Mr. Smithson's favorite. Everything else made him sneeze."

"Are you sure you feel okay about being here?" Marcus could use the kid's help, but the last thing Simon needed was trouble with the dean of students.

Simon nodded and brushed his finger over a photo tacked on the door. "That's Mr. Smithson and me at last year's Quiz Bowl competition." Simon was holding a large trophy. "He chose me for the team even though I was in middle school."

"It's a nice picture," Marcus said. "First place, right?"

"Enough with the trip down memory lane," Laurel said. "Let's get this done. I've changed my mind about going to Pacific High."

Mr. Smithson's classroom was dim but not dark. The shades covering the windows let in just enough light to work by, but not enough for them to be seen if someone was in the courtyard outside.

"Treat this room like a crime scene," Marcus said, tossing them each a pair of nitrile gloves he pulled from his backpack. He also took out a handful of evidence markers and bags. "We're looking for anything that doesn't seem to belong. I've got a penlight if you need it. Or use the flashlight on your phone."

"I get that we don't want anybody to know we're in here, but why do CSIs on TV always use flashlights?" Laurel asked. "Why don't they just turn on the lights?"

Marcus looked at Simon, who shrugged. Finally, a question even a genius couldn't answer. "Who wants to take photos?" Marcus asked. "We don't have time for a sketch."

"I'm on it." Laurel dug through her bag like she was looking for lost treasure, extracted her phone, and turned on its flashlight.

"Laurel, you start in the back and work your way to the front," Marcus instructed. "Simon, you search Mr. Smithson's filing cabinet and bookcase. I'll take his desk. Tag and bag anything unusual."

* * *

On the desktops Laurel discovered hundreds of smudged and overlapping fingerprints that would be impossible to identify. How many students had studied in here over the years? Thousands, probably. She mentally divided the carpet into small grids and deliberately examined every square inch. Like the door and walls, the only evidence the floor revealed was reminders of student occupation—ink stains, shredded pieces of notebook paper, broken bits of pencil lead, and slivers of pink eraser.

"What did I expect?" she mumbled. Bloody fingerprints on the light switch? Muddy shoe prints on the carpet? Blood spatter on the walls? This wasn't Hollywood.

"Did you say something?" Marcus asked.

"There's nothing except—"

"Be sure to check *under* the desks."

"On it, *boss*," she snapped. She crawled under the nearest one. "I can't believe I'm doing this . . . Hey, Simon, did you know that Sarah Morgen-something loves you?" Someone had scribbled their names inside a heart drawn with a red Sharpie.

"What?" Simon turned in her direction, peering around but not seeing her. "What'd you say?"

"Never mind." A big wad of chewed bubble gum was stuck to the bottom of the next desk. *Gross.* It was still a bit slimy. *Must be Bobby's seat.* She placed a yellow evidence marker on the floor under the desk, snapped a photo, peeled off the sticky blob with a pair of tweezers, and sealed it in an evidence bag. The gum would be loaded with DNA. Laurel glanced over at Marcus. Even if they couldn't do DNA analysis without PCR, she didn't want Sherlock Holmes accusing her of not being thorough. Maybe she could get a few tooth impressions off the gum. Bobby had impressive canines.

Laurel continued down the row of desks. More graffiti. *Yikes.* She thought *her* language was bad. Somebody who had sat here *really* didn't like Mr. Smithson. Seriously. His horns weren't *that* big. She thought everybody idolized him but apparently not. She came to the desk she had sat in during zero hour. Threads from her sweater were twisted around a metal screw on the back of the chair, and she began plucking them free with the tweezers.

She had collected a half-dozen navy fibers when another small knot caught her attention. "What the heck?" she said aloud.

"Find something?" Marcus said.

"Yeah. Some black-and-white fibers tangled up with the navy ones from my sweater," Laurel said. "Kind of strange, huh?" With the strict uniform code, Pinehurst students were allowed to wear only blue sweaters over their polo shirts. One uniform violation equaled one detention, not that Laurel kept count.

"Bag and tag 'em," Marcus said, hovering over her shoulder. "I lifted several prints from Mr. Smithson's desk drawers to compare to the ones on his mug. And check this out." He showed her an evidence bag, already expertly labeled with his name, date, time, and location to maintain chain of custody. Grissom had taught him well. The bag contained a plastic amber medicine vial. "I think it's Mr. Smithson's."

"Duh," she said, squinting at the label on the vial. "It says *Douglas Smithson.*" She kept plucking at the threads twisted in the screw.

He crouched next to her. "If Mr. Smithson had a prescription bottle in his hand when Simon found him, wouldn't the paramedics have taken it?"

"I'd assume so."

"Then what's this one?

She shrugged. "A spare, maybe?"

"The date on the bottle says he filled this prescription three days ago." Marcus stood. "Hey, Simon. Do you know what Cardiotalis is?"

"Digitalis." With his head buried in the top drawer of Mr. Smithson's filing cabinet, Simon's voice was slightly muffled. "Cardiotalis is the brand name, not generic, for digitalis. It's a glycoside synthesized from the foxglove plant. It effects the myocardium by—"

"In English," Laurel said. "*S'il vous plait.*" She sealed the knot of mixed fibers in an evidence bag and moved on to the next desk.

"It causes the heart to contract more forcefully." Simon removed a yellow folder from the drawer and tucked it under his armpit. "For certain arrhythmias it—"

"How the heck do you know this?" Laurel asked. The kid's knowledge of just about everything blew her away.

"So he *did* have a heart problem," Marcus said. Medicine. That's what Mr. Smithson had taken after class when he asked him to tutor Bobby.

"No." Simon shook his head as he walked over to them. "Mr. Smithson would've told me if he was sick. Can I see the vial?" He studied the label. "I . . . I can't believe he needed digitalis."

Marcus wouldn't have suspected that Mr. Smithson had a heart problem either. Not the way the man played hoops. Using tweezers, he fished a pill from the vial. "Does this look like the one you found under his desk?"

"It's similar, but not identical. The one I found was cream-colored, not white. This one's also less ovoid." Simon glanced over at Mr. Smithson's desk. "Where's the pill that I found?"

"It's in my . . . it's in a safe place," Marcus said. He wasn't ready for them to know what he kept in his locker, especially after Laurel had given him flak that his backpack was a crime scene kit.

"Can I see the back of the pill? Pharmaceutical tablets typically have a sequence of letters and numbers etched on them that are specific for the type of medicine, the dosage, and the manufacturer."

"Like lot numbers on stuff at the grocery store," Marcus said.

"Not exactly analogous, but sufficient." Simon examined the tablet and shook his head. "This sequence doesn't match the one on the tablet I found."

"You noticed something like that?"

Simon shrugged. "It's math."

"We'll compare these tablets to the pill you found under the desk and try to ID them," Marcus said. "Maybe run a chromatography."

"It won't be as accurate as using a mass spectrometer, which as you know we don't have, but it will give us some qualitative information."

"It's better than nothing," Marcus said. Working in a high school lab—even a well-equipped one like Pinehurst's—had its limitations. A mass spec was way above the department's budget.

"May I get back to my area?" Simon asked.

"What've you got there?" Marcus indicated the file folders under Simon's arm.

"Mostly irrelevant. Copies of Mr. Smithson's old exams, homework assignments, and lesson plans. All labeled and organized. However," he said, pulling several sheets of paper from a blue folder, "these were mixed in with old course syllabi. They're faculty evaluations Mr. Smithson wrote. He rated Dr. Gardner's teaching skills as superior, and commented that Miss Scarletti needs to challenge her algebra students more. Look what he said about Ms. Goldman."

Marcus scanned the report and whistled. "Wow. Mr. Smithson recommended that she be fired." Luckily for them, Mr. Smithson was as old school about his filing as he was about recording grades. Marcus couldn't remember ever seeing him use the laptop on his desk, but surely he kept some sort of electronic records, too.

"Ow!" Laurel yelled in unison with a loud bang. She backed out from under a desk, rubbing her head. Crossing the room, she snatched the sheet out of Marcus's hand. "He says, and I quote, 'Her teaching fails to measure up to the standards of Pinehurst Academy.' Sounds like one of my report cards."

Simon held up yellow file folder. "I also found this buried in the bottom drawer of the filing cabinet. It contains Mr. Smithson's old pay stubs. Years' worth of them."

Laurel shuffled through the papers and then glanced around the room. "Something's off."

"That's exactly what I thought," Simon said.

Marcus raised his eyebrows. "Meaning?"

"Mr. Smithson has some nice things in here," Laurel said. "His desk's antique mahogany and a bit scratched, but not like the crappy veneer one Ms. Mason has. And the lamp on his desk? Tiffany. The stained glass pattern's unmistakable. It's old and some of the tiles are cracked, but it's definitely worth a few bucks."

She'd know, Marcus thought. "So? He was a department chair at a prep school. Probably had a nice salary."

"Not that nice," Laurel said, still fumbling through the pay stubs. "What kind of car did Mr. Smithson drive?"

"He drives—I mean, *drove*—a 2010 Volvo," Simon answered.

"It probably cost a nice chunk of change back then," Marcus said.

"We can rule out a second job," Laurel said. "The teachers practically live at school. Maybe he inherited some money."

Simon shook his head. "He never mentioned anything like that."

Laurel peered at Simon intensely. "How do you know so much about him? It's kinda weird."

"We spent a lot of time studying math," he said matter-of-factly. "Here's something else." He handed Marcus what looked like an old-fashioned accounting ledger out of a Dickens novel. Its black leather cover was stiff and etched with scratches, and the pages inside were crisp and yellowed with age. The ink had faded to gray and was barely legible.

Marcus read the carefully written notes on the first page.

1000E8	91000
1000F8	92000
1000G8	93000
1000H8	94000
1000I8	95000

"It's a record of some kind," he said, "but it's written in some kind of code. Do you understand it?"

"Not off hand. It meant something to Mr. Smithson, though," Simon said.

Marcus checked his watch. Lunch was almost over. "You can decipher it later. We need to get out of here." He sealed the ledger, file folders, and medicine vial in separate evidence bags and jammed them in his backpack. "I hope nobody notices this stuff's missing."

"Horrors," Laurel said, widening her eyes and putting her hands on her cheeks. "We might get a detention." She handed him the evidence bags containing the fibers and the wad of bubble gum. "Cram these in there, too."

Marcus picked up the traveler's mug from the corner of Mr. Smithson's desk, twisted off the lid, and sniffed. "Tea. With lemon." Mr. Smithson often sipped tea while lecturing. Marcus put the mug in a large evidence bag and hoped it wouldn't leak as he took it back to the lab. *That* evidence trail he didn't want. "C'mon," he said. "Let's go."

"What about Mr. Smithson's grade book?" Laurel said, reaching for it. "It might be interesting."

"Leave it!" Marcus said, brushing her hand away. "The, uh, sub might need it."

Laurel shrugged. "Whatever."

"C'mon. Let's go," he said again, this time more firmly. They had less than ten minutes before the bell rang signaling the end of lunch hour.

"I haven't had a chance to process the bookcase," Simon said. "I was thorough about the filing cabinet, however."

Marcus glanced at Laurel. "We'll help you."

She started to protest, but he walked over to the bank of bookcases that covered the wall behind Mr. Smithson's desk. Dozens of math textbooks were lined up according to size, topic, and grade level on the top shelves, and student papers were neatly stacked on the bottom ones. Several photographs were displayed on the middle shelf along with a well-organized collection of paperweights, calculators, boxes of pencils, staplers, packages of graph paper, chalk, erasers for the chalkboard, and enough other office supplies to compete with the school bookstore's inventory.

"Check out the photos," Marcus said. "I think they're pictures of Mr. Smithson's advisory groups." Each teacher was assigned a dozen homeroom students—an advisory group—for four years, from ninth grade to senior year. Pinehurst's middle school had a slightly different system. Advisors took attendance, read the daily bulletin, received copies of report cards, chaperoned class retreats and dances, and wrote letters of recommendation for college. Ms. Mason had once remarked that being an advisor was labor intensive and more time consuming than teaching a class, but Pinehurst parents appreciated—if not expected—the individualized attention their children received.

"Simon, help me do the math," Marcus said. "The headmaster said that Mr. Smithson started teaching here in 1981. How many advisory groups should he have had?"

"Ten, including this year's," Simon answered without hesitation.

"There are nine photos," Marcus said. "One's missing."

"How do you know one's missing?" Laurel asked. "Maybe he doesn't have a photo of that group."

Marcus picked up one of the picture frames. A film of dust outlined a clean area underneath it. He picked up another frame. It was also clean underneath. "This shelf hasn't been dusted in a while."

"The housekeeper was sloppy," Laurel said. "Like ours at home."

Using the flashlight on his phone, Marcus shined a beam at another place on the bookshelf. A strip about six inches long and a half-inch wide was dust-free—a clean outline of a picture frame, but without the frame. A photo had been removed recently.

Marcus gathered the nine remaining frames and filled the gaps with Mr. Smithson's trinkets. "Maybe we can figure out which one's missing."

Marcus stuffed the photos in his backpack and struggled to zip it shut. "We get out early today, and the faculty meeting should keep Ms. Mason occupied for hours. Let's meet in the lab after school." He hoisted the heavy, bulging bag over his shoulders. "Simon, what've you got next?"

"A free period. I'm going to work on my research paper for history."

"That can wait," Marcus said. "Find out everything you can about Cardiotalis. Stuff that you don't know." *If anything,* he almost added. He turned to Laurel. "You go on ahead, too. You don't want to be late to class. I need you in the lab, not the detention hall."

"You got that right." She grabbed her bag and followed Simon out the door.

Marcus had one more piece of evidence to collect—for his eyes only. If caught, he'd be expelled for sure, but something just wasn't right. No way Bobby could've earned a B. Marcus bagged and tagged Mr. Smithson's grade book.

Pausing in front of the makeshift shrine outside the door, he unfastened the small gold basketball pin tacked on his varsity jacket and jabbed it into the belly of the panda holding the Pinehurst Academy balloon.

"Good-bye, Mr. Smithson," he said. "I'm going to find out what *really* happened to you."

aqueous sodium citrate isopropanol: *a chemical solvent used in chromatography to analyze compounds*

WEDNESDAY, AFTER SCHOOL

"Wait up, Ms. Mason," Marcus said, bounding down the hallway. "You can't go yet."

"Why not?" Ms. Mason locked the door to room 102 and dropped the key ring into her purse.

"I . . . um . . . I want to work on the mock crime scene," he said, not making eye contact, surprised at how easily the lie flew off his tongue. "I didn't get much done after, you know, the thing with Ms. Goldman." At least that part was true.

"I'm sorry, but you can't be in the lab without supervision." Ms. Mason adjusted the laptop case over her shoulder and started walking down the hall. "And please forget about what Ms. Goldman said. She was having a bad day."

Marcus kept pace with her quick strides. "Can I come back later?"

"Sorry, but no. I've got a faculty meeting and then a class at the U. I won't be back until morning. It's been an exhausting few days," she said.

They passed the anatomy lab. "What about Dr. Gladson?" Marcus asked. "Can he supervise?" Nursing a sprained knee, he'd probably skip the faculty meeting. With luck, the teacher wouldn't feel like hobbling around to check on them often.

"I'd like to help you out, Marcus, but I can't ignore the safety rules."

"I really want an A in the course," he said. Definitely not a lie.

Ms. Mason sighed. "I'd expect nothing less." She did an about-face. "Let me see if Dr. Gladson can keep an eye on you. He asked me to take notes for him at the meeting while he's grading tests."

"Thanks, Ms. Mason. I won't use any dangerous chemicals or anything."

"Ms. Mason's letting us work in here by ourselves?" Laurel asked, taking her purple lab coat off the hook. "What did you do, wave a magic wand or something?"

"Dr. Gladson is supposed to check in with us. Maybe even grade some tests in here," Marcus said. "He'll think we're working on the mock crime scene, not the real one."

Marcus had scribbled a list of "evidence" they had collected from Mr. Smithson's classroom on the whiteboard.

> Cuff link w/fingerprint
> Harvard mug w/print
> Pill Simon found underneath desk
> Prescription bottle w/Cardiotalis
> Black-and-white fibers from screw
> Old ledger with weird numbers
> 9 photos of advisory groups (one missing)
> Fingerprints from teacher's desk drawer
> Wad of bubble gum, freshly chewed

He intentionally left Mr. Smithson's grade book off the list. That was for his eyes only.

"You forgot my dad's fraternity certificate," Simon said.

Marcus hesitated—reluctant to get a parent involved in their investigation—but added the certificate to the list. "Who wants to do what?"

"I'll work on the threads since I found them," Laurel said. She grabbed a box labeled *Fiber Analysis Kit* out of one of the supply cabinets.

"Simon, you take the pills," Marcus said. "Run a TLC." Genius would be able to whip out a thin-layer chromatography in no time. He would ask him to analyze the tea in Mr. Smithson's traveler's mug later.

"What're you going to do?" Laurel took several small bottles of chemicals out of the kit. "Not that I'm in charge or anything."

"I'll work on the prints I lifted from Mr. Smithson's desk drawer to see if they match the ones on the cuff link or his Harvard mug," he said. "And if you want to be in charge, be my guest."

"Perfect," she said. "And after you're done with the cuff link and mug, you can deal with the missing photo."

"No problem," Marcus said, biting his tongue. Does it really matter who's in charge as long as they got this stuff done?

Simon pulled out his iPad. "Google confirmed what I thought. Cardiotalis is a trade name for digitalis. It causes the myocardium, or heart muscle, to contract more forcefully."

"Could Mr. Smithson play basketball if he had a heart problem?" Marcus asked. Manny Santana had asthma, and all he needed was a few puffs from an inhaler before each game.

"I'd assume so, especially if he was taking digitalis. Millions of people take medicines for preventive measures. Insulin, for example, regulates blood glucose levels, while warfarin—"

"We're talking about a heart drug," Laurel said, "not something given for a virus."

"Actually, warfarin helps prevent blood clots. It works by—" Laurel flashed Simon one of her looks. "According to *The Patient's Drug Reference* website," Simon continued, reading from his iPad, "both Cardiotalis pills we found are manufactured by the same company. The cream-colored one with the sequence CAZ125—the one from his prescription bottle—should contain 125 micrograms of digitalis. The white pill I found under Mr. Smithson's desk with the sequence JWZ250 should have twice as much. I can confirm the approximate amounts by running a TLC on both pills."

"Why would he have pills with different amounts of digitalis?" Marcus asked.

"It's unlikely that Mr. Smithson would have two different prescriptions," Simon said. "My mom, who knows a lot about pharmacology, said patients should take the same amount of medicine at the same time every day. An overdose of digitalis can cause bradycardia."

Marcus raised his eyebrows. "What's bradycardia?" He wasn't taking Dr. Gladson's anatomy class until next year. Nor had he taken Latin at Pinehurst.

"Too much digitalis can slow the heartbeat," Simon translated, "or even cause cardiac arrest."

"Stop it completely," Marcus said. That he remembered from an episode of *Albuquerque Med* or *The Bad Doctor*.

"Maybe Mr. Smithson accidentally took an overdose," Laurel said, rifling through her lab drawer. She tossed out several crumpled pieces of paper and a half-eaten protein bar. "Have either of you seen my safety glasses?"

"No," Simon said, shaking his head. "Mr. Smithson would never have taken too many pills."

"Sure he could've. Don't you read the tabloids?" Laurel opened the cabinet above the sink and pushed aside beakers and flasks. "Remember that celebutante last week? She accidentally overdosed on Tums or something."

"I agree with Simon. We all had Mr. Smithson for math. You know how precise he was," Marcus said. "He caught the smallest mistake."

"Your point?" Laurel asked.

"Did you ever see a messy stack of papers on his desk? A book out of order on the shelf? He even kept the same number of pencils in the container on his desk."

"Eleven," Simon said. "Always eleven."

"Not ten, not twelve. Eleven yellow number-two pencils, always sharpened, with tips pointing upward." Marcus had counted them when he was bored. "Ever see a wrinkle on his shirt or a stain on his tie?"

"No, but—" Laurel said.

"A scuff on his shoe?"

"Never, now that you mention it."

"Exactly!" Marcus shouted. "Mr. Smithson was a neat freak. He literally lived by the numbers."

"Fine. I hear you. Mr. Smithson would never take too many pills." Digging through her bag, she pulled out a handful of pens and pencils, several small bottles of hand sanitizer, a large makeup bag, two pairs of sunglasses, and her phone—but no safety goggles.

"That's why you need to run that TLC, Simon," Marcus said. "We need to confirm if both pills contain digitalis and how much." Although only a screening test, thin-layer chromatography would tell them if the tablets had the same chemicals and a guesstimate of amounts.

"I'm not sure which solvent to use." Simon adjusted safety goggles over his eyes. "I'll try aqueous sodium citrate isopropanol first. If that doesn't give good resolution, I'll experiment with ethyl acetate."

"Is there anything you don't know?" Laurel asked.

"I'm not too proficient at—"

"Just run the TLC," Marcus said, smiling. *And where was Dr. Gladson?* Not that they needed supervision.

* * *

Simon broke off half the pill he had found underneath Mr. Smithson's desk and saved the other half in case they needed to turn it over to the police or something. He shook off the thought of reporting Mr. Smithson to the Drug Enforcement Agency. He ground the pill fragment into a fine power and put it in a clean test tube and did the same with a tablet from the prescription bottle. Simon added 150 milliliters of deionized water to each sample and mixed them by gently flicking the bottom of the tubes with his index finger, careful not to spill any. The powdery granules slowly dissolved. Next he applied one microliter of each sample side-by-side on a ten-by-three centimeter TLC plate; the droplets stuck to the cellulose that was bonded to the glass plate. After the spots dried, Simon carefully lowered the bottom edge of the plate into a jar with a small amount of sodium citrate isopropanol and quickly screwed on the top to prevent the toxic fumes from escaping. Almost immediately, the solvent began creeping up the plate, like soda moving up a straw. The compounds in the tablets should begin separating from each other.

Eight minutes later, Simon had results.

"The pill from the floor is chemically similar to the one from Mr. Smithson's prescription bottle, but not identical," he said, showing the TLC plate to Marcus. "The one I found has almost twice as much main ingredient, which I assume is digitalis. I calculated the Rf values which show that—"

"Man, I wish we had a mass spec," Marcus said. "Then we could specifically identify the substance. And accurately quantify it." Only in his dreams would a biotech company donate something that expensive, even to a school with a strong science program. They would make do with they had, which was impressive enough.

Simon placed the TLC plate back under the fume hood. "We can't *prove* that both pills contain digitalis, but the results show that the pill I found on the floor *didn't* come from Mr. Smithson's prescription bottle of Cardiotalis."

"Now we just gotta find out where it came from," Marcus said.

He was glad that the evidence confirmed that it was unlikely Mr. Smithson had died from an accidental overdose. Simon would've been devastated if his mentor had made such a terrible and fatal mathematical mistake.

* * *

Sheep or goat? Wool or cashmere? Laurel hadn't a clue. The black-and-white fibers she had found twisted around the screw in Mr. Smithson's classroom definitely came from an animal. Hairs, really. Under the microscope, their round, scale-like pattern resembled shingles on a roof. By comparing them to photos in her lab manual, she ruled out dog, cat, rat, cow, horse, and rabbit. Nor did the fibers match the threads from her sweater. Those were cotton, from a plant; their twisted, ribbon-like shape was unmistakable.

Laurel hadn't found her safety glasses, so she was forced to wear a pair of ugly scuba-like green goggles, praying the tightened elastic straps didn't give her a headache. She lit a small votive candle, and, using tweezers, plucked a few blue threads from her sweater and cautiously moved them toward the flame. She said a silent prayer that she wouldn't set off the smoke detectors in the lab. *That* somebody would notice. The fibers ignited instantly and kept burning when she took them out of the flame, leaving a small amount of ash. By comparison, the black-and-white fibers curled away from the flame and smelled like burning hair. They also self-extinguished, leaving a brittle, black residue. She blew out the candle flame and then moved to the fume hood that Simon had vacated.

Next Laurel performed several simple chemical tests, even though they were mainly used to identify synthetic fibers, such as polyester. She labeled six small test tubes—A1, A2; B1, B2; C1, C2—and added two milliliters each of acetone to the A tubes, hydrochloric acid to the B tubes, and sodium hypochlorite to the C tubes. She dropped navy threads from her sweater into the #1 tubes, and a few black-and-white fibers into the #2 tubes. Popping in her earbuds, she hoisted herself onto a lab stool and waited for results.

Laurel was nodding off when Marcus tapped her shoulder. "Any luck?"

Startled, she jerked, and her elbow bobbled the test tube rack. A few drops of solvent splashed onto the counter. Luckily she was working under the fume hood. "Seriously? You never learn," she said.

Marcus grabbed a paper towel and mopped up the drops. "Simon's done with the chromatography, and I finished the fingerprints. What've you got?"

"The fibers from my sweater are definitely cotton," she said, "but the other ones are animal in origin, sheep or goat."

"Wool or cashmere."

"Because they're so soft, I'm betting on goat. Cashmere."

"Okay . . ." Marcus massaged his temples. "Now all we need is to find out who had a heart problem, took digitalis for it, chewed bubble gum, sat in a student desk in Mr. Smithson's classroom wearing a black-and-white sweater and a shirt with a cuff link, went to Yale, *and* belonged to Sigma Omega Epsilon," he said without taking a breath. "Easy."

"As if we'll get that lucky," Laurel said.

"Most of the prints on the desk drawer belong to Mr. Smithson, but there's another set."

"Who would look in Mr. Smithson's desk drawer besides Mr. Smithson? We can't print everyone on campus."

"Here's what I'm thinking," Marcus said. "Remember the faculty evaluation Simon found? I'm sure Ms. Goldman wouldn't want anyone to see what Mr. Smithson wrote about her." He was convinced Ms. Goldman's outburst wasn't just her having a bad day, despite what Ms. Mason had said.

"If I was Ms. Goldman, I would've found it and torn it up," she said. "Her classroom is right down the hall from his, so she had opportunity."

"Then we should start with her. I'll find something with her prints on it. You know, for comparison."

"Leave it to me. I have an idea." Laurel *knew* she'd been right about the conversation she had overheard. If Ms. Goldman had been angry enough at Mr. Smithson for writing a poor evaluation—a possible career ender—could that be motive for murder?

"Check it out," Marcus said, pointing at the test tubes. "Look which ones dissolved."

The black-and-white fibers were cashmere, just as Laurel had thought.

Marcus glanced at the clock. "It's time to work on the missing photograph." He lowered his voice. "Here's my plan."

Her eyes widened and for once she was speechless.

"Do you want tell Simon about what we're going to do, or do you want me to?" Marcus whispered.

Laurel jumped off the lab stool, nearly toppling it over. "Hey, Simon," she called across the room, "enough with the TLC. We need to talk."

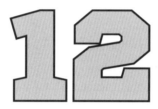

honor code: *a set of rules that define appropriate behavior within a community*

TWENTY MINUTES LATER

"Wake up!" Laurel said, jabbing Marcus's upper arm with the tip of her nail.

"Ow!" he yelled, jerking upright. "Watch the claws." He'd been reclining in a chair in the hallway in the administration building with his eyes half-closed, day-dreaming about where he'd go to school if he got expelled from Pinehurst. Explaining the dismissal to his father would be the real nightmare.

"The headmaster's in the theater watching the rehearsal for the musical."

Laurel's breath smelled like chocolate.

"You were supposed to meet me in front of the dean's office in ten minutes, not twenty," Marcus scolded.

She held up two paper cups from the Coffee Mug, one in each hand. "Sorry. I should've asked if you wanted one, but I couldn't carry three. My bad."

He should've guessed. Caffeine Queen couldn't miss her afternoon dose. "Let's do it," Marcus said.

Laurel strutted down the hall to an office several doors down with her two mochas and several sheets of paper tucked under her arm. A few minutes later, she emerged from the office, now at the heels of Mrs. Hudson, the headmaster's no-nonsense assistant. Marcus had ducked around the corner, careful enough not to be seen, but not so hidden that he couldn't eavesdrop.

"This is really an imposition, Miss Carmichael," Mrs. Hudson said. "It's almost time to go home. I appreciate the mocha, however."

"I know. But the machine in the library is, like, *so* jammed, and I need to make a copy of my *Gatsby* essay." Laurel's voice was syrupy sweet, making her sound like a very polite sixth-grade girl. Marcus imagined that she was probably rolling her eyes, too. "Ms. Mullins won't accept a Google doc. Hard copy only. She'll kill me if I'm not prepared for the read-and-critique."

"We certainly don't want that to happen," Mrs. Hudson said. "Oh, those shoes, Miss Carmichael! How do you get away with the uniform violations? In my day, shoes like that would have . . . " She led the way to the faculty work room with Laurel flashing Marcus a behind-the-back thumb's-up before they disappeared inside.

When he could no longer hear their chatter, Marcus slung his backpack over his shoulder and sprinted to the headmaster's office door. He knocked softly. "Dr. Welton?" His armpits were damp, and his mouth was as dry as Phoenix. He knocked a bit louder. "Dr. Welton? Are you in there?" No answer. He hoped the headmaster would enjoy the rehearsal for several more minutes.

Marcus took a deep breath and exhaled slowly. Breaking and entering was definitely a violation of the school's honor code. But so was everything else they had done. *Do or die*, he thought. With a final glance over his shoulder, he slowly turned the doorknob. Fortunately, the door was unlocked. Had it been locked, he would've resorted to Laurel's plan B—which definitely would've landed him in jail, not just the detention hall. He peered into the headmaster's office. As expected, it was empty. He gently closed the door behind him and quickly navigated around the well-worn brown leather couch and two stuffed accent chairs to the wall of bookcases flanking the fireplace at the far end of the room. The headmaster had a gazillion books, most of them dusty and thick, haphazardly stacked on the shelves, a striking contrast to Mr.

Smithson's well-organized library. Marcus scanned the top two shelves. "C'mon, c'mon. Where are they?" he said under his breath. "I know I saw them when—"

Bzzz. The vibrating of his cell nearly gave him a heart attack—a *real* one. He grabbed the phone out of his pocket. A text from Simon.

Rehearsal over.

Shoot! Marcus glanced at the books on the third shelf. *C'mon, c'mon . . . Faulkner, Fitzgerald, Austen, Hemingway, Shakespeare, Conan Doyle, John Grisham, Douglas Preston and Lincoln Child—yes!* He knew he'd seen them last fall when he'd been in here with the football team for the headmaster's pre-season pep talk. Lined up in chronological order between *The Mysterious Mind of the Adolescent* and *America's Most Wanted Prep Schools* were copies of *Knight Time,* the Pinehurst Academy yearbook. He trusted Simon's calculations that the missing advisory group photograph was taken in late 1980s. He shrugged off his backpack, grabbed several yearbooks from that era off the shelf, and, kneeling down, began stuffing them inside his bag. No time to look through them now, but he doubted if Dr. Welton would notice if they were missing.

As he reached to remove the 1989 edition of *Knight Time* from the shelf, a shrill but slightly muffled female voice from behind him said, "In the future, Miss Carmichael, I suggest you plan your time so you don't wait until the last minute."

Marcus froze, his fingers grazing the spine of the yearbook. *No way!* Mrs. Hudson was just outside the door. She'd call the police if she found him in here. Laurel's job was to keep her occupied. Frantically looking for a place to hide, he sprang up, rushed to Dr. Welton's desk, and dove under it, curling up like a fetus until he felt his knees would snap. Luckily, this cubby was slightly bigger than the one under Mr. Smithson's desk. *Crap!* He'd left his backpack sitting on the floor in front of the bookcase. If Eagle Eyes noticed it, he'd be toast. But Mrs. Hudson didn't come in. Instead, he heard a faint rattling that he recognized instantly: keys. She was going to lock him in!

Great, he thought, *just great.* He'd be locked in here all night, and when the headmaster found him in the morning, not only would he be expelled, but he'd also be arrested. *Dang Laurel!* So much for keeping Mrs. Hudson occupied. Couldn't she have jammed the copy machine or something?

"I apologize," Laurel said in the girly voice, but louder this time. "It won't happen again, Mrs. Hudson. I really appreciate your help."

"I should've gone home five minutes ago," the assistant said, rattling her keys again. "I don't know where the headmaster is, but I need to grab some papers off his desk and then lock up."

"Don't!" Laurel cried. "I mean, I need one more favor."

"What now?" The rattling stopped.

"The . . . um . . . the battery on my phone's dead, and I need to call my dad. He gets worried if I'm late. May I use the land line in your office?"

Yes! Marcus thought. Mrs. Hudson's office was two doors down from the headmaster's, and Laurel was giving him the opportunity to get the heck out of there. He'd have a clear shot from Dr. Welton's door to the opposite end of the hallway.

"I'm surprised that you don't have a phone charger in that big bag of yours. It's certainly big enough," Mrs. Hudson said. "Has anyone ever told you that you can be really annoying, Miss Carmichael?"

Marcus smiled despite the jackhammering in his chest. *Mrs. Hudson's got that right*, he thought.

"Please?" Laurel asked. "I'll be quick."

"I certainly don't want your father to worry," Mrs. Hudson said. "I'll have to dial for you. School rules."

"I owe you a favor, Mrs. Hudson," Laurel said. "Not just a mocha."

"Hmm. Maybe you can ask your father if he can get me a good deal on a condo by the marina."

"With beach access and . . . " Laurel's voice faded as she followed Mrs. Hudson to her office.

Marcus unfolded himself from underneath the desk and, shaking out the cramp in his left calf, hobbled across the room. With his ear pressed against the door, he heard Laurel slowly recite a phone number. The cramp gone, he dashed back to the bookcase, grabbed the 1988 and 1989 editions of the yearbook, zipped them inside his backpack along with the others, and hoisted the heavy bag over his shoulders. He scrambled to rearrange the remaining books to fill in the gaps on the shelf. Opening the door a few inches, Marcus stuck his head out and peered up and down the hallway. *Crap!* He ducked back inside the office, praying that he hadn't been spotted by the dean of students who was waddling toward the faculty bathroom.

He waited several seconds and then peeked outside again. Laurel was talking to someone on the phone, and the dean had disappeared. If he was fast enough, he'd make a clean getaway. If he wasn't . . .

Marcus crept out of the headmaster's office, silently closed the door behind him, and sprinted down the hallway, away from Mrs. Hudson's office, the thick carpet silencing his strides. His backpack slammed against his shoulders. Only a few more yards and he'd be in the clear. As he neared the end of the hallway, he pulled his phone out of his pocket and began punching in a text. Skidding around the corner at the end of the corridor, he glanced up just before he collided with the headmaster. The phone flew out of his hand and bounced off Dr. Welton's shoe before landing.

"I'm-I'm so sorry, Dr. Welton," Marcus said, grabbing the headmaster's arms to steady him. "Are you okay, sir?"

The headmaster adjusted his thick-framed glasses and straightened his tie. "You knocked the wind out of me." He gave Marcus a stern look. "Mr. Jackson, I'm shocked. What are you thinking?"

Images of his future exploded in Marcus's head as he readjusted his backpack over his shoulders. *City High. No college.*

Dr. Welton picked up Marcus's phone and held it between them. "Cell phones on campus during the day? I don't care how smart they are." He chuckled at his pun. "I'm disappointed in you. You know students can only use their phones in designated areas, and this isn't one of them." He looked at his watch. "You're lucky it's after school. Otherwise, you'd be serving detention tomorrow."

Walking in the direction of his office, he looked back at Marcus and winked. "Kick St. Fran's—" His voice dropped off as he disappeared around the corner.

"Yes, sir. Kick butt, sir. I will, sir!" Marcus darted out of the administration building and sprinted toward Weatherly Hall as if the entire St. Francis team were on his heels. What *had* he been thinking? He had just escaped not only expulsion but a jail sentence.

But it was worth it. Seven yearbooks were safely zipped in his backpack. Still, he had violated the school's honor code.

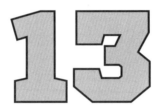

Locard's Principle: *every contact leaves a trace*

A FEW MINUTES LATER

Staying twenty yards behind, Simon tracked the headmaster out of the theater. Disguised by his khaki uniform pants and green sweatshirt, he hid behind a eucalyptus tree—he was getting good at camouflaging behind plants—and, peeking around the trunk, watched Dr. Welton cross the nearly empty quad in the direction of his office. He punched in a text.

He's coming

Marcus didn't reply. *Dang it, Marcus. Where are you?* He waited a few seconds and then sent another message.

911

Still no response from Marcus. Creeping out from behind the tree, Simon hugged the wall of the dance studio and peered around the corner of the building. The headmaster had vanished, but a movement out of the corner of his eye caught his attention. He snapped his head around. The man he had seen fighting with Mr. Smithson in the parking lot was heading in his direction. Simon ducked behind a large juniper shrub and crouched down. As the man passed, Simon clearly saw his face: Bobby's father.

Mr. Tate's black athletic jacket had three iconic white stripes on each sleeve. *Locard's Principle at work*, Simon thought. A suspect always leaves something behind at a crime scene. If Bobby's father had been in Mr. Smithson's classroom, the threads Laurel had found twisted in the screw under the desk could be from his jacket. She'd said that the fibers were cashmere, but Mr. Tate's athletic suit looked like a polyester blend. It was hard to tell from this distance. What if Laurel had been wrong?

Bobby's father cut around the side of the English building in the direction of the athletic complex. Spying through the juniper shrub's branches, Simon looked across the quad and glanced at his phone. Where was Marcus? Had the headmaster caught him in his office? That was the only logical reason he wasn't texting back. Maybe Marcus was already sitting in jail, but he hadn't heard any sirens. Simon's heart rate quadrupled when he realized what he had to do. Even though he would rather walk through a pit of rattlesnakes than go where he *really* felt like a clumsy geek, he had to follow every clue.

Even if the evidence trail led to the gym.

Simon ditched his backpack under a manzanita bush and sprinted toward the athletic complex. Bounding down the stairs, he dashed into the boys' locker room and looked up and down the rows of lockers. Dirty socks, backpacks, half-empty water and sports drink bottles, soiled bandages, and miscellaneous abandoned athletic equipment were strewn on the benches and floor. Simon checked the bathroom. The stalls were vacant, or at least he couldn't see any sneaker-clad feet when he peeked under the doors. The shower room was empty, too.

He swallowed hard. He knew where Bobby's father was.

Simon pulled the hood of his sweatshirt over his head to conceal his face and crept down the narrow corridor leading to the basketball court. He hid behind the propped open door. The team was on the court, and a new Bad Bunny rap blasted from the gym's audio system. Basketballs flew in all directions, some swooshing through the nets, but most hitting the rims and bouncing to the floor. Bobby set up behind the free-throw line on the north side of the court.

"Make it twelve in a row!" a man's voice roared. Simon recognized the deep, nasal tone. Just as he'd suspected, Bobby's father was in the gym with the team.

Bobby hitched up his baggy basketball shorts, and, bending his knees, dribbled the ball twice and stared up at the basket. Rising on his toes, he fully extended himself, stretched his right arm above his head, and released the ball with a downward flick of his wrist. It made a high arc before cleanly dropping through the net.

Bobby's father pumped his fist in the air. "Way to go, son!" He stripped off his jacket and flung it towards the bleachers. "Make it thirteen!"

Simon's heart pounded, about to explode from behind his sternum. Now was his chance to get the jacket! Breathing hard, he stepped out from behind the door and, stooping low, darted under the bleachers, careful to avoid the discarded wads of gum, candy wrappers, empty chip bags, and soda cans. He hunkered down and peered through the spaces between the slats of benches. Bobby's father had moved over to the sideline to stand next to Coach Decker.

"That's our boy," Bobby's father shouted over the noise on the court, slapping the coach across the shoulders. "If he plays half this good against St. Fran, he'll be MVP."

Simon crept closer to the jacket . . . and to Mr. Tate and the coach.

"I've made a few calls," Coach Decker said. "Bobby shouldn't have trouble playing in the Ivy. Yale, maybe." He chuckled. "Especially with Smithson out of the way."

Simon's heart lurched. *TheIvyYaleSigmaOmegaEpsilonSmithson . . .* The words flew through his brain.

"Are you sure he's gonna be okay in math now?" Bobby's father said. "I don't want any more obstacles. Bobby's going to the NBA, come hell or high water."

"No sweat. Now that he's in Ms. Goldman's class for good, I'll make sure he passes with flying colors." Another chuckle from Coach Decker.

Simon was horrified. Could Bobby's father have murdered Mr. Smithson to make sure his son played basketball in college and then the NBA? That seemed like a weak motive, but people had killed for less, like the crazy cheerleader mom in Texas who had made certain that her daughter made the varsity squad. Or the parents who paid scam artists to take their children's college admissions tests.

"It would be a shame if he doesn't get that scholarship." Bobby's father turned and glared at the coach. "Know what I mean?"

"Don't worry," Coach Decker said, backing away. "It's a done deal."

The sleeve of Mr. Tate's jacket dangled between two slats of bleachers about ten feet to Simon's right, its white stripes beckoning like a flashing neon sign. He crept toward it. A half-full Doritos bag crunched under his foot. Simon froze, waited a few seconds, and then, inching forward, reached up to grab the sleeve.

"Hey, Bobby, I'll meet you outside after practice." Mr. Tate's voice boomed in the cavernous gym. "I'm going for a run."

Simon's left ventricle skipped a beat. Bobby's father was strolling toward the bleachers. With a nanosecond to act, Simon yanked the dangling sleeve and pulled it under the bleachers.

"What the heck?" Mr. Tate yelled.

Gripping the jacket against his chest, Simon crouched low to avoid smashing his head on the metal supports of the bleachers as he scurried under them toward the gym door. He tripped over an empty soda can and stumbled forward, but he didn't go down. He dashed out from underneath the bleachers and ran full-speed down the corridor toward the locker room.

"Hey, you! Come back here!" Coach Decker shouted.

Not on your life! Simon raced out of the athletic center, skidded around the east side of the swimming pool, and bolted toward Hart Stadium.

"Stop, you little—"

"Dude, he's fast!" This time is was a boy's nasal voice. Bobby's. "You better run!" he shouted at the disappearing figure.

"If I catch you, you're road kill!" Mr. Tate yelled.

Sprinting across the football field, Simon had no idea where he was headed but knew that he'd be pummeled if they caught him. He glanced over his shoulder. Bobby, his father, Coach Decker, and about half the basketball team were a hundred yards behind but closing fast. Simon estimated that he was running a five-minute mile but quickened his pace as he cut through the tennis courts. He hadn't run like this since those bullies had chased him around the playground every day in fourth grade.

Suddenly, Simon knew where he'd hide. The catacombs! Mr. Smithson had given the Math Club a tour of the secret tunnels that had been dug under the campus a hundred years ago to hide the huge pipes carrying steam to heat the classrooms and water to the restrooms and kitchen. He back-tracked toward Hartford Hall and launched himself down a steep flight of cement stairs at the east side of the building. Bracing his left foot against the wall, he gripped the rusty handle with both hands and yanked open the heavy metal door guarding the entrance to the tunnels. *Please God, help me,* he thought, praying that his pursuers hadn't heard the door clang when he slammed it shut behind him. Sealing himself inside, Simon pulled his phone out of his pocket and plunged into the dark passageway.

OneTwoThreeFourFiveSixSeven . . . He counted his steps as he raced down the tunnel, pausing only to recover his balance when his sneakers slipped on the wet, slimy sludge beneath his feet. Simon slid around a sharp left turn and rocketed down another corridor. The phone's flashlight illuminated only a few yards in front of him, but he had memorized the maze-like pattern of the catacombs during his tour with Mr. Smithson. *Fifty-fiveFifty-sixFifty-seven . . .* Simon was underneath the quad. A furry ball the size of a miniature terrier dashed in front of him, its red eyes blazing as it vanished into a tunnel that veered off to his right. The critter was either a small opossum or an extra-large rat, and he didn't even want to think about the crunching sounds under his feet. *Periplaneta americana.* Cockroaches, probably. And what was that putrid, rotten-egg smell? Hydrogen sulfide with a hint of methane.

NinetyNinety-oneNinety-two . . . Another sharp left. Simon clutched his chest, convinced his heart *and* lungs were about to explode. Slipping again in the disgusting ooze, he glanced over his shoulder, half expecting to see Darth Vader himself. Even if Bobby and his father had followed him into the tunnels, he wouldn't be able to hear them over the roar of blood surging through his ears. If they caught him, *his* body would be the next one found.

But Simon also knew that in another sixty-seven steps, he'd be underneath Weatherly Hall and on his way to safety.

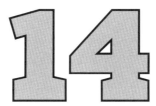

yearbook: *a book published annually to celebrate the past year of school*

A FEW MINUTES LATER

Marcus and Laurel were hunched over a yearbook when Simon skidded into room 102. Startled, they whipped around and stared. Simon pulled the door shut with a loud snap and clicked the dead bolt to lock it. Ducking, he peered into the hallway through the door's observation window. He ripped the sweatshirt hood off his head and brushed the damp, stringy bangs off his forehead.

"M-Marcus. And L-Laurel," he said, struggling to catch his breath. "Th-thank God you're here."

"Are you okay?" Marcus asked. Seeing no blood or obvious injuries, he flipped to another page in the yearbook.

"You smell like a swamp creature," Laurel said, sniffing the air. Simon's shoes were covered with green, slimy, stinking muck. "Ever heard of deodorant?"

"Why didn't you text back?" Simon asked, looking at Marcus. "I tried to detain Dr. Welton but—"

"You did great," Marcus said. "I found the yearbooks. I almost got caught but—"

"Look what I got." Simon held up Bobby's father's jacket.

"Cool," Laurel said. "You have a new jacket."

"No. It's not mine. It belongs to—"

"You're not going to believe what we found," Marcus said. He spun an opened yearbook toward Simon and pointed to a photo. "Recognize him?"

Simon shoved the yearbook aside and thrust the jacket at Marcus. "I said, look what I got."

"Man, what's up with you?" Marcus said, taking a step backwards. "What's going on?" He had never heard Simon raise his voice.

"Caffeine overload, maybe?" Laurel muttered, grabbing another yearbook.

"We need to compare these fibers to the ones Laurel found twisted in the screw," Simon demanded.

Marcus rubbed the fabric between his fingers. "This feels like polyester, definitely not cashmere. Laurel, what do you think?" He already knew the answer, unless Adidas had tapped into the cashmere market.

She felt the jacket. "Yup. Definitely not goat. Can I get back my literature?"

Marcus gave Simon a puzzled look. "Where did you get this?"

Simon drew a deep breath and exhaled slowly. He stood up straight, squared his shoulders, and looked Marcus in the eye. "I stole it. From Bobby's father."

"When?" Marcus looked stunned. "How?"

"Why?" Laurel said, abandoning the yearbook.

"I saw Bobby's father fighting with Mr. Smithson in the parking lot the day before he died. He threatened him. Took a swing at him, actually. Mr. Tate was wearing this jacket." The words flew off his tongue. "I followed him to the gym and grabbed it when he took it off. He and Coach Decker ran after me. Bobby and most of the team, too. But I out ran them and hid in the catacombs."

"The catacombs?" Laurel asked. "They really exist?"

Simon nodded. "Underneath the quad."

"I'll never picnic on the lawn again," Laurel said, shuddering.

"You ran faster than Bobby Tate?" Marcus asked. "*You*?"

"Yes. And his father."

"You're kidding, right? Mr. Tate?" Marcus said. "He's a marathon runner. Finished third in the Boston or something like that."

"And Coach Decker, too," Simon added.

"Coach Decker lettered in cross country in college!"

Simon sank into the nearest seat and wiped the remaining drops of sweat off his forehead with the sleeve of his sweatshirt.

"Dang, Simon," Laurel said. "Have you been taking Mr. Smithson's Cardiotalis?"

"I-I never knew I could run so fast," Simon replied.

"Maybe Bobby's dad *was* fighting with Mr. Smithson," Marcus said. "Who knows what that was about? Probably something to do with Bobby's grades." He started stuffing the jacket inside a large evidence bag. "Maybe Laurel can look at this later. But first check out the photo on page ninety-eight." He handed Simon the 1989 edition of *Knight Time.*

In the bottom left-hand corner of the page was a photograph of Mr. Smithson with his advisory group, according to the caption. "I think it's a copy of the missing photo from his classroom," Marcus said.

Simon adjusted his glasses and studied the photo. "I'm surprised that Pinehurst doesn't have an online archive of yearbooks." Another example of the school's reluctance to change traditions and embrace technology. "I think . . . Yes, I definitely recognize one of the students. The one with Mr. Smithson's hand on his shoulder."

Marcus let out a low whistle. "I'm with you, buddy. That's him all right."

"Who?" Laurel asked.

"Jason Hart," Marcus said. "We saw him Monday. He was the star attraction at the dedication ceremony for the new stadium. You were there, right?"

* * *

After the students had assembled in the stadium's new bleachers, Jason Hart joined the headmaster at the podium. Marcus couldn't tell if Hart's tan was natural or one of those spray-on jobs. Given the slightly orange hue, though, the money was on canned tan. More than six feet tall and medium build, Hart towered over the headmaster, his thick, dark brown hair a sharp contrast to Dr. Welton's thinning thatch of gray. Maybe Hunt's hair color came out of a can, too. Impeccably dressed in a tan linen suit, a white dress shirt, and brown tassled loafers that screamed success, the congressman flashed his trademark toothy smile and waved at the varsity football team, who flanked the stage in rows of folding chairs lined up on the artificial turf. Marcus sat in the second row, squeezed between Manny Santana and Bobby Tate. At least Bobby had tossed the napkin hat he'd worn while marching across the table in the dining hall earlier that morning.

The headmaster grasped the sides of the podium and cleared his throat. "Today we honor a special guest," he said in his slight New Jersey accent. Crackles of feedback screeched from the audio speakers, and he stepped back from the microphone. "It is my pleasure to present a former captain of the football team and one of Pinehurst Academy's most distinguished graduates. The future U.S. Senator from California, Congressman Jason Hart."

Eight hundred students, faculty, and staff, most of them crammed into the bleachers on the home side of the field, stood and exploded in applause and cheers. Manny let out a piercing whistle, and Bobby barked and pumped his fist. "Woof! Woof! Woof!"

Marcus cringed, imagining Laurel seeing him sitting next to Nasal Dog Boy. That is, if she was here at all. Odds were she probably ditched the ceremony. Who cared if she'd skipped out? Marcus tried to focus back on the hoopla. The student jazz band, assembled in the middle of the football stadium at the fifty-yard line, blasted the opening bars of the school's fight song while the Pinehurst mascot, a medieval knight in a helmet and body armor, pranced along the sidelines waving a plastic sword. The pep squad performed a series of back-flips in front of the board of trustees and other VIPs sitting on the stage.

Jason Hart gave a slight bow and removed his mirrored aviator Ray-Bans. "Thank you for the gracious introduction, Dr. Welton," he said, adjusting the microphone to his level. His voice was deep, his words clear and crisp. He raised his arm, signaling the crowd to sit back down. His gold watch glittered in the sun.

Hart waited for silence. "It is a privilege to return to my *alma mater*," he said. "It seems like I graduated thirty days ago, not thirty *years* ago. I sweated through calculus and AP bio just like you." He flashed another toothy smile and chuckled. "Never could understand the difference between the Kreb's cycle and the Calvin cycle."

"He got that right," Bobby said, squirming in his seat. "Man, it's a friggin' sauna out here."

The sun blazed down on the football field, its heat absorbed by the artificial turf. Despite the temperature, the headmaster insisted that the football team wear their varsity jackets, and Marcus's polo shirt underneath was drenched. Bobby had stripped off his jacket and stuffed it under his chair.

Jason Hart took a sip from a bottle of water and loosened his tie. "Next year Pinehurst Academy celebrates its hundredth anniversary, and it has evolved into one of the finest college preparatory schools in America." He nodded at the headmaster.

Hart turned back toward the bleachers. "I graduated valedictorian and headed to New Haven for college, where the winters were cold and long, certainly not warm and sunny like San Diego."

Another burst of cheers from the crowd.

"After law school," he continued, "I earned a coveted clerkship with the Supreme Court, and now . . . well, you know the rest. I was one of the youngest persons ever elected to the United States Congress. If I can do it, you can do it."

Wow, Marcus thought. He'd never have a resume like Hart's unless he solved the mystery of the Bermuda Triangle.

"He sure likes to brag about himself," Manny whispered.

"The guy's a loser," Bobby mumbled.

"I owe it all to your school," Hart continued, "and it's a privilege to give back to Pinehurst what Pinehurst gave to me. Unfortunately, my father, who funded Hartford Hall years ago, has been ill and can't join us today. But it's an honor for us . . . "

"His dad probably paid for his diploma," Bobby said under his breath.

Jeez, Marcus thought. *Show some respect.*

" . . . to give Pinehurst this new football stadium," Hart said.

"Now we're talking," Bobby said.

The crowd stood, their cheers and applause deafening. Marcus took the opportunity to peel off his jacket, hoping the headmaster wouldn't notice.

Dr. Welton rejoined Hart at the podium. "Thank you, Congressman, for all you've done for this school. First Hartford Hall, and now a new football stadium." The headmaster pulled a handkerchief from the pocket of his blazer and blotted his forehead. "Refreshments are available on the quad." Bobby bolted out of his seat. "But before I dismiss you, we have one more treat." Bobby groaned and sat back down.

Dr. Welton pointed toward the west end of the field. The gigantic scoreboard exploded with colorful digital fireworks as red lights spelled out HART STADIUM in huge letters on the screen while a couple rounds of sparklers launched from behind it. Beneath Jason Hart's name was a mock score, HOME 28, VISITORS, 0.

"Woof! Woof! Woof!" More barks from Bobby.

Manny jabbed Marcus's ribs with his elbow. "Too bad we have to wait another six months to light up that baby for real!"

Marcus tried to share his friend's enthusiasm. "Yeah, too bad." How would he tell his teammates that once basketball season was over, he was trading in his varsity jacket for a lab coat? It was hard enough for him to get excited about b-ball these days. Getting crushed by linemen was at the bottom of his wish list. One concussion playing tackle football was one too many.

But as much as Marcus didn't want to be a jock forever, he was still on the team.

"Don't forget my offer to help," he said to Bobby. "You know, with math."

"Nah. It's all good." Bobby chomped and smacked on a piece of bubble gum.

It's all good? Had Bobby forgotten what Mr. Smithson had said, or was he really that dense? Marcus watched his teammate saunter off the field, his arm draped across the shoulders of the head varsity cheerleader. If he skipped the snacks, he could head over to the gym early and practice some free throws. If he couldn't get out of it, he might as well get into it.

But first he had to go back to the lab. It shouldn't take long to analyze the white powder he had found in Ms. Mason's laptop case while processing the mock crime scene.

* * *

Laurel grabbed the yearbook out of Simon's hands. "I know who Jason Hart is. Pinehurst's most famous graduate. Unfortunately, I was forced to sunbathe in the bleachers. My advisor took attendance. Probably got skin cancer."

She stared at the photo. "I don't know. The faces are really blurry." She handed the yearbook to Marcus. "Even if it is him, so what?"

"*So* I don't know yet." He flipped to the index at the back of the book.

"Hart has, like, twenty other photos. He must've been really popular," Laurel said. "Go to the Senior Legends section."

"Yes, ma'am." Marcus located the pages of the yearbook highlighting the senior class. A Pinehurst Academy tradition, each graduating student created a personalized page with a formal photo taken in their cap and gown and several casual ones with friends and family. Some included favorite quotes, poems, song lyrics, and even thank-you notes to favorite teachers. They studied Jason Hart's Senior Legends page.

"Wow. That's harsh," Marcus said.

"A-awful," Simon stammered.

Laurel for once was speechless.

In the center of his Senior Legends page, Jason Hart posed with a teammate, their football helmets tucked under their arms and their uniform pants streaked with dirt. The number 7 was emblazoned on the front of Hart's mesh jersey, and the player next to him, Derek Cross, according to the caption, wore number 12. With broad smiles plastered on their faces and longish hair grazing the tops of their eyebrows, they were two fresh-faced, innocent-looking SoCal boys. Marcus read aloud the caption under the photo.

Derek, you'll always be my co-captain.
RIP in the big stadium in the sky.

No one spoke for several long seconds until Marcus said, "I can't imagine my best friend dying."

Simon closed his eyes. "I can," he whispered.

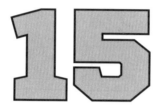

Nancy Drew: *fictional teenage detective known for her intelligence, independence, and sleuthing skills*

LATER THAT EVENING

"Mom? Dad? I'm home." Laurel's voice echoed in the cavernous foyer of the Tuscan-style villa overlooking the beach. "Anybody here?" She draped her book bag over the upraised arm of the huge bronze statue of Artemis her parents had shipped over from Greece last summer. The thing was hideous. The goddess of the hunt needed to go back to Athens or wherever she came from.

Laurel kicked off her shoes and glided across the marble tile in her fishnet tights. "Marta? Are you in the kitchen?" The housekeeper was never around. Laurel picked up the new issue of *Gossip* from a stack of mail on the countertop, glanced at the cover story, and tossed the magazine back on the pile. Who cared about *The Teens of Tennessee*? That show was *so* last season.

Donatella crept out from underneath the kitchen table and arched her back. The silver bell on the cat's Swarovski crystal collar jingled. "It's just you and me for dinner again," Laurel said, stroking the underside of the animal's chin. She poured a cupful of Fancy Feline into a crystal bowl and twisted the top off a bottle of Voss water for the cat. She opened a can of diet cola for herself, not in the mood for healthy.

Laurel handed the delivery guy two twenty-dollar bills, slammed the door, and alarmed the security system before he could ask if she needed change. Donatella dashed in front of her as she trudged up the staircase, causing her to trip. *Oops!* A little bleach should take care of the drops of marinara sauce on the white carpet. Settling in her bed, she picked up the remote for the TV and dove into her thin-crust lobster and truffle pizza with fat-free mozzarella. Ten minutes later she had eaten all but one slice. She should call her mother, but instead she rolled over on her back and, hands behind her head, glanced around the room. Purple walls, purple carpet, purple curtains. Maybe it was time to switch to lime green or orange, but she wasn't really into citrus. Tropical was too San Diego, and she had visited Kauai and Oahu more times than she could count. Perhaps something more exotic. Art deco, maybe.

Laurel dug a new sheet of economics problems out of her bag. She skimmed over it, frowned, and shoved it back in the bag. Maybe writing her *Gatsby* essay would be more motivating. She deleted several attempts at a thesis sentence—the obvious "money doesn't buy happiness" theme was so cliché. How could she put into words the connection she saw between herself and Jay Gatsby, each dreaming to escape the loneliness of their material worlds? Frustrated, she tossed her laptop to the other side of the bed.

Flipping through the TV channels, boredom gave way to inspiration.

Laurel opened the forensic science notebook Ms. Mason insisted each student have. The jury was still out on the teacher's claim that writing by hand improved learning, but so far Laurel had aced every test. She turned to a blank page and squiggled three vertical lines and labeled the four columns in big, bold letters: **SUSPECT, MOTIVE, MEANS**, and **OPPORTUNITY.** She would find out who hated Mr. Smithson, had access to Cardiotalis, belonged to that weird frat, and was able to sneak into his classroom before school and bump him off. Once she had that information, she would go even more old school and make a crime board on her bedroom wall.

For obvious reasons, Bobby Tate was the first name on Laurel's list of suspects. But did that loser have a connection to Yale? *Doubtful,* she thought. According to Simon, his father had threatened Mr. Smithson about something, though. She jotted Mr. Tate's name under his son's. Ms. Goldman was next on her list. Under the column labeled **MOTIVE**, Laurel wrote, *Smithson's evaluation would've ruined career.* Ms. Goldman also taught in Hartford Hall; she could've murdered Mr. S. and been back in her classroom before homeroom. Laurel jotted that info under **OPPORTUNITY**. Ms. Goldman was smart enough to have gone to Yale, but where would she have gotten Cardiotalis? The chemistry lab? Doubtful.

Laurel hesitated before adding a fourth name: Simon's father. Was she the only one to see a connection? Mr. Musgrave had been a member of Sigma Omega Epsilon, so the cuff link could belong to him. The idea of him as a suspect seemed far-fetched, if not demented, but his wife had access to a lab. Laurel was pretty sure Simon's mother was a chemist at a pharmaceutical company. Or was it biotech? Maybe the university. Regardless, Simon's dad could've gotten Cardiotalis from her. That gave him **MEANS.** But why would Simon's father murder a teacher his son had idolized? That would be sick, really sick. She wrote down his name anyway.

Staring up at the ceiling, another name popped into her head: Jason Hart. She added his name to her list. Hart had been in Mr. Smithson's advisory group in 1989, the group in the missing photograph. Had he mentioned in his speech where he'd gone to college? For once she should've been paying attention. Laurel vaguely remembered him wearing a tan linen suit at the ceremony for the football stadium. It had been too hot for a cashmere sweater.

Laurel put down her pen, and, leaning back against the headboard, closed her eyes. As she gently stroked her cat's belly, Ms. Mason's anthem echoed in her head. *Follow the evidence. Follow the evidence.* She mentally listed the pieces of evidence they had collected, beginning with the cuff link. *Follow the evidence. Follow . . .* Laurel tossed Donatella off her lap and, scrounging under the bed pillows, found her cell. She was about to punch in a number when it rang. She looked at the display, then raised the phone to her ear.

"I know who murdered Mr. Smithson," she said.

HableHablesHablemosHablem . . . The words on the page of the Spanish book blurred together. Marcus hated conjugating verbs. He stuffed another handful of potato chips into his mouth and, rocking back in his chair, stared at the poster of the Warriors NBA champion-ship team tacked above his desk. *Time to give it to Timmy,* he thought. His little brother was more obsessed with Steph Curry than he was with LeBron. Marcus's basketball days would soon be history. But he couldn't blame sports for his inability to concentrate on Spanish. His schoolwork had gone down the toilet, and he expected that any minute Coach Decker would kick in his bedroom door and drag him to practice in handcuffs. The sooner he could figure out what happened to Mr. Smithson, the sooner he could get his life back on track.

But first he had another bit of business. He took a deep breath and picked up his phone.

The call went directly to voice mail. "This is, uh, Marcus. Your, er, son," he said. He resisted the urge to press the 'end' button, but why prolong the agony? "We, uh, need to talk. Yeah. Bye." *Gosh, that was lame.* He shouldn't have to introduce himself. He tossed his phone onto his bed, disgusted just to be holding it. How would he ever find the right words, and the guts, to tell his father about his college plans? *Uh . . . yeah . . . uh . . .* Pathetic. But then, it probably wasn't the words that mattered, anyway. What mattered was to duck when the crap hit the fan.

Marcus snapped his Spanish book closed and swapped it for his forensic science notebook. The shiny dark blue cover always reminded him of the ocean just down the street from school. He'd fallen in love with that ocean—and the freedom of the open sea—the minute he'd moved to San Diego from Philly when he was in the fourth grade. Despite the danger for wildfires, he'd trade an icy Nor'easter any day for Santa Ana winds blowing in from the desert. He turned to a fresh page in his notebook. *Okay, what would Grissom do?* He thought a moment, remembered Grissom's rules, and then wrote **FOLLOW THE EVIDENCE** across the top of the page and began drawing a small crime board. He scribbled for several minutes until his diagram looked like a food web in an ecosystem. Staring at the page, an image materialized. It had been hot, like a sauna, during the dedication ceremony for the football stadium.

And Jason Hart's gold cuff link had sparkled in the afternoon sun.

No way, he thought, trying to shove the visual aside. Jason Hart didn't belong on his list of suspects. The man had been a scholar and football star and was now a candidate for the U.S. Senate, for crying out loud. But . . . he *had* been in Mr. Smithson's 1989 advisory group. Another memory exploded in Marcus's head. Hart had said in his speech that he'd gone to college *where the winters were long and cold.* In New Haven. New Haven, Connecticut.

Yale was in New Haven.

Marcus's heart raced. He didn't like where the evidence trail was leading but remembered what Sherlock Holmes had said in *The Sign of Four* about the improbable. About it leading to the truth. He punched another number into his phone. This time he wouldn't hesitate.

Laurel picked up on the first buzz. "I know who murdered Mr. Smithson," she blurted without so much as a hello.

"Wait, Laurel, I—"

"No, you wait. And listen." Then words tumbled out of her almost faster than he could process them. Interrupting was impossible. How could she sputter so many sentences without taking a breath?

Finally, he couldn't take it anymore. "Are you crazy?" he shouted over her. "You want to do *what*?"

She barely paused. "No, I'm *not* crazy. But clearly you're deaf. This time, *listen*." More words spilled from her. He tried a few *but . . . but . . . buts,* then finally gave up and just listened until she said, "You know I'm right."

"Are you done?" Marcus said.

"Yeah."

"Is it my turn?"

"Yeah."

"Good. Now *you* listen. I hear what you're saying." Marcus studied his ecosystem-like crime board again. He and Laurel had come to the same conclusion: The evidence trail pointed to the man at the top of the food chain. "It has to be him. The thing is, what do we do now?"

Pacing around his bedroom, Marcus listened to what she had in mind. "No way! We can't do that!" He picked up a dirty polo shirt and a crumpled pair of uniform pants and tossed them in the laundry basket along with several pairs of socks. "Isn't Hart's office in Sacramento? My parents will kill me if we drive up there. And flying to D.C. is *really* out of the question." Knowing Laurel, she probably had access to a private jet.

Laurel checked Google. Jason Hart had another office in downtown San Diego at the commercial real estate business he and his father owned. According to the firm's website, Congressman Hart was scheduled to be the guest speaker at a fundraiser tomorrow evening at the Hotel Del, so she was betting he was staying in town. "I'll make sure Hart's there," she said.

"Oh, right. And you're going to pull that off *how*, Nancy Drew?" He imagined her gritting her teeth.

"Just leave it to me, okay?"

"No, okay. Tell me."

Marcus's head began to throb as she outlined her plan. It was risky. *Way* too risky. And if they got caught, they would get expelled as surely as the Warriors would win another championship. Not playing in the St. Francis game would be the least of his troubles; he could kiss off any chance of going to college and becoming a forensic scientist. Laurel's plan was nuts. Totally nuts.

It was also brilliant.

* * *

While Marcus and Laurel were plotting their next move, Simon's fingers were flying over the keyboard. *Both Isaac Newton and von Liebnitz deserve credit for defining the modern calculus.* He paused, then punched the 'delete' key. He needed a thesis worthy of Mr. Smithson, but his mind was on Greek, not calculus.

He had tried several search engines on the Internet but found no references to Sigma Omega Epsilon. Was it a secret society like Skull and Bones? Why hadn't his dad ever mentioned that he had belonged to a fraternity in college? Simon had no choice but to ask him about Omega, but not tonight. He had a more important homework assignment.

He flipped open Mr. Smithson's old ledger.

```
1000D93   35000
1000E93   36000
2000F93   38000
2000G93   40000
```

Code-busting wasn't his strongest talent, but it had numbers, so how difficult could it be? Simon fiddled with the numbers for several minutes, erasing as much as he scribbled, until finally he crumpled up the paper with his equations and tossed it toward the trash can. He didn't notice the clean shot. *What's wrong with my brain?* he thought. His parietal cortex was usually dependable. It should be a breeze to figure out the code. It wasn't multivariable calculus. He turned to another page.

2000D96　118000
2000E96　120000
3000F96　122000

After struggling with the numbers for a few more minutes, Simon put down his pencil. He had solved far more difficult problems, but tonight he was incapable of performing any calculations, distracted by what he had done after school. What if Bobby's father had recognized him before he'd disappeared into the catacombs? Theft had serious disciplinary consequences at Pinehurst. The headmaster wouldn't excuse him for collecting evidence for a crime that only he, Marcus, and Laurel were convinced had happened.

Trying to focus, Simon stared at his chess board. *What? That's not right.* When had he moved the white rook to h5? How could he have made such a simple mistake? He moved the black knight, captured the rook, and put the white queen in jeopardy. He was about to move her out of danger when his phone buzzed. "Hello?"

Listening to Marcus's instructions, the sick, hollow feeling in Simon's stomach returned with a vengeance. He was already a thief. Now he'd be a liar, too.

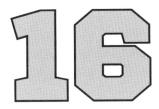

polygraph: *a machine used to detect if a person is lying*

THURSDAY MORNING

"Dad, tell me about Sigma Omega Epsilon," Simon blurted at breakfast the next morning.

Startled, Martin jerked, and drops of orange juice sloshed out of his glass and landed on the sports section of *The San Diego Tribune.* He must be the only person who still read a print newspaper. "Let's go, son," he said, dabbing the spots with a dish towel. "You don't want to be late for school." He picked up his laptop case, tucked the newspaper under his arm, and headed for the garage. "Our boys signed a new outfielder. Stole him from the Dodgers. Maybe this year the team will get to the Series. With this guy's batting average . . . "

Oh, great. Baseball again. There'd be no bringing his dad's mind to another subject now. Simon choked down the rest of his cheese omelette and headed for the car. The marine layer along the coast was less thick than it had been the previous few mornings, and streams of sunlight filtered through breaks in the clouds. Traffic was light on Del Mar Mesa Road but became congested as they neared the on-ramp to the interstate. As usual, his father tuned in his favorite classic rock channel, and they drove without speaking through Carmel Valley. Shoving aside thoughts of the Yale fraternity, Simon pondered the columns of numbers in Mr. Smithson's ledger, trying to make sense of them.

As he pulled off the interstate, his father turned off the radio. "Okay, son. What do you want to know about Omega?"

He did hear me. Simon perked up. "Everything, actually. I couldn't find much information except that it's a Yale fraternity. We talk about college a lot, but you never mentioned that you belonged to a Greek." Simon could recite *verbatim* his father's curriculum and had even calculated his GPA—3.98. *Summa Cum Laude.*

"You never asked," Martin said as they drove past the sprawling campus of the university.

"Is it a regular fraternity, or some kind of secret society, like Skull and Bones?" Simon asked. "Or Key and Scroll? Maybe even Wolf's Head. Did you get tapped?"

"Tapped? How do you know so much about—" His father shook his head. "Of course. The Internet. Google, huh?"

"Some societies are so secret that members are forbidden to talk about them."

"That's Hollywood nonsense. Do you really think Yale would tarnish its reputation by condoning these types of groups? Harvard, maybe, but not Yale."

"Then why won't you talk about Omega?"

"It's nothing exciting, I promise," Martin said. "I wanted to meet new friends and wasn't much of a party guy. I heard about some small groups—clubs, really—based around a common interest. Sigma Omega Epsilon was one of them. It wasn't a *real* fraternity like they have at the U. We met for dinner every Wednesday night at the University House and discussed current events. And, no, we didn't select new members by tapping them on the shoulder or anywhere else."

"Does Omega still exist?"

"No," Martin said, shaking his head. "Several years after I graduated, a few members were involved in a cheating incident. Something about collusion on an astrophysics test." He paused. "Or was it biomolecular engineering? Regardless, the Greek Council suspended Omega's charter. It's embarrassing. That's why I never talk about it."

His father was right. Other than the cheating scandal, Sigma Omega Epsilon sounded boring. Certainly nothing like fraternities Laurel had described, with wild behavior like jumping into fountains. After listening to her stories, Simon was almost afraid to go to college.

They joined the line of cars trickling into Pinehurst's front parking lot and pulled up behind the sleek black SUV unloading the Parker triplets. How could he have thought his dad had belonged to a secret society? Simon's life felt uncomfortably out of sync. First Mr. Smithson dying, then Simon stealing the jacket, then distrusting his father. And he'd add lying to his list by the end of the third period.

"It's a shame that a few bad apples ruined Omega's reputation," Martin said. "We were just a bunch of nerds who sat around on a Wednesday night debating politics."

Simon's hand froze on the seat belt buckle. "Politics? You're a tax attorney. I thought you majored in economics."

His father smiled. "You'll change your mind a hundred times about what you want to do for a living. For a while I was serious about joining a rock band. Had the long hair, ripped jeans, and everything. I can still play a mean guitar, you know. I dabbled in ancient history and even biology—that's when I met your mother—ran track and played a little baseball. The coach said I had a pretty good arm, but . . . "

Simon wasn't thinking about his career path. The Omegas were interested in politics. Jason Hart was a politician—a congressman and now a candidate for the U.S. Senate. He had gone to Yale and law school, like Simon's father. Hart was a few years older than his dad. Could he also have been a member of Sigma Omega Epsilon? What were the odds of these coincidences? Simon mentally made the calculations: astronomical.

"Do you know if Congressman—" Simon hesitated. No, it was crazy. The last thing he needed was his dad questioning his sanity. "Never mind." He would find another way to see if Jason Hart had belonged to Sigma Omega Epsilon. Maybe he could . . .

"How 'bout we play that new video game *Zombies from Zenon* when you get home?" his father asked. "Chess maybe? You know . . . to take your mind off things."

"Huh? I mean, sure," Simon replied, grabbing his backpack of the backseat. *Right, Dad,* he thought. *A game.* As if that would get his mind off Mr. Smithson's murder.

* * *

Laurel strutted out of the girls' bathroom in the student center. It was mobbed with tall, blonde, and tanned SoCal girls adjusting their looks until they resembled the cloned celebutantes in *US Daily.* She headed over to the bathroom in Hartford Hall where she could work in private. The wannabes avoided the math building.

She brushed a thick layer of translucent face powder on her cheeks and blotted off her ruby lip gloss. More pale than usual was good if she was going to pull off the "worst headache of my life" scenario. Just as she finished smudging another layer of kohl to the purple shadow she'd rubbed under her eyes, the door swung open, and Ms. Goldman walked in, her heels clicking on the tile.

*Holy sh—*Laurel cleared her throat and coughed, sounding like her cat hacking up a fur ball. "Good morning, Ms. Goldman," she rasped.

The teacher backed away. "Are you okay, Laurel? You sound terrible." She set her purse on the counter next to the sink and pulled out a small bottle of hand sanitizer. "Can you please watch my bag? I hate to take it into the stall. Germs, you know."

Is she kidding? Laurel thought. *She might as well hand her purse to me on a platter.* "No problem." She blew her nose and roughly rubbed it with a piece of paper towel until it was redder than that reindeer's. "I can't believe how bad I look," she said, staring into the mirror. "I hope I don't have a weird virus or something." She coughed again, sounding like Donatella choking up *two* fur balls.

"Feel free to use the sanitizer." Ms. Goldman disappeared into the stall at the end of the row and slid the latch into place.

Laurel picked up Ms. Goldman's purse—a soft black suede clutch—turned the clasp, and rifled through it as quietly as she could. Since Ms. Goldman would definitely notice if her wallet went missing, Laurel would have to find something else and discovered it at the bottom of the bag. The lipstick tube had to be covered with fingerprints.

Ms. Goldman flushed the toilet.

In one quick gesture, Laurel dove into the purse and picked up one end of the lipstick with her index finger and thumb like a bird plucking a seed with its beak. Careful not to smudge it, she dropped the tube into the pocket of her hoodie, set the purse back on the counter, and prayed that Ms. Goldman didn't need more gloss.

Keeping a safe distance, Ms. Goldman tucked her bag under her arm as she washed her hands twice and then rubbed in several large drops of sanitizer past her wrists. "I hope you feel better, Laurel. Maybe you should go to the nurse's office. You don't look well."

"You wouldn't believe awful how I feel." Laurel stared in the mirror. With pasty skin and dark smudges under her eyes, she looked like an extra from the set of *The Walking Dead*. Perfect. She could fool her own doctor—unless he took her temperature.

* * *

While Laurel pretended to have bronchitis, Marcus was faking something else. His mother's signature looked like the real deal. He passed the note to the receptionist in the attendance office and flashed a smile. "Have a great day," he said and dashed out of the office before she could ask any questions. If his luck held out, the receptionist wouldn't call the orthodontist to confirm his appointment.

"Hey, dude, what's up?" Bobby said, jogging up behind him with a surfboard under his arm. "The waves rocked this morning!"

Marcus continued walking toward Weatherly Hall. "Sorry, but I can't talk. I don't want to be late to homeroom."

Bobby stayed at his heels. "Why haven't you been at practice? Decker's getting really pissed." Slurping an energy drink, he flung his hair around like a wet mop.

"My . . . uh . . . my ankle's been acting up. The trainer talked to Coach D," Marcus said, adding a slight limp to his gait. "It's no big deal. I'll be there today."

"You'd better be." Bobby took another swallow. A dribble of blue ran down his chin and onto his polo shirt before he swiped it away with the back of his forearm. "We're running plays without you, but Carter sucks. *You're* our center, man." He let out a huge belch.

"No worries. I'll be ready for St. Fran—" Marcus halted, whipped around, and almost smacked into the surfboard. "Do you hit the waves every morning?"

"Yeah. My truck's in the stupid shop, so I had to bring the board to school."

"Did you surf on Tuesday?" Marcus almost added, "When Mr. Smithson was killed," but caught himself.

"Tuesday?"

"You know, two days ago." The guy was clueless.

"Me and Carter haven't missed a day in months."

"See anybody else from school?" Marcus said, trying not to wince at Bobby's grammar. He was probably close to failing English, too.

"What's it to you?" Bobby tossed his empty can toward a trash can. It bounced off the rim and rolled to a stop under a bird-of-paradise.

"Nothing. Maybe I'll join you sometime." Marcus playfully punched Bobby's shoulder. "I'll catch up with you. We're going to blow St. Fran out of the water." He probably should add learning to surf on his list of things to do.

"Later, dude," Bobby said. "Gotta see a teacher." Despite the school's "not noon, no grass" tradition—the origin of which Marcus never understood—Bobby took off across the quad toward Hartford Hall. "Ms. Mason saw me," he yelled over his shoulder. "She was taking a run on the beach."

Bobby had an alibi—a good one. Could he have taken care of his "problem" with Mr. Smithson and *then* gone surfing? He doubted if Bobby would be that clever in covering his tracks. Nor did he seem like a murderer. Marcus mulled over another question as he headed to his locker: What teacher was Bobby going to see at zero hour?

Marcus did an about-face, retraced his steps, and bagged and tagged Bobby's empty energy drink can. Ms. Mason had said that saliva was a good source of DNA. And who slobbered more than Bobby Tate? The slimy can was gold itself.

* * *

"Achoo!" Laurel blew her nose into a crumpled Kleenex. "Thanks, Mrs. Mullins. I just need a Tylenol or something." She tucked the hall pass into her pocket but had no intention of visiting the nurse's office.

Period one had begun, and with students tucked away in their classrooms, the upstairs hallway of the English building was deserted. Laurel's source had told her that old issues of the school newspaper were stored in the journalism office, not the archives of the library. She crept down the hall and quietly tapped on the door of the office. No answer. Glancing around, she knocked again, this time a little louder. Still no sound from within. Her heart started beating a little faster, but not from the caffeine in her morning mocha. Now she knew how Marcus must've felt breaking into the headmaster's office. One final knock, and Laurel slowly counted to ten, turned the doorknob, and peered in.

The journalism office was empty—of people—but filled with piles of the school newspaper. Bundles of *The Knightly News*, most bound together with twine, were stacked everywhere—on the floor, on the six rectangular tables, and on the dozen or so plastic chairs. *Jeez.* Maybe it was time to update to a digital format—or at least recycle. Several abandoned laptops, iPads, batteries, and power cords were haphazardly strewn on the tables, adding to the chaos. *No wonder the tuition's so high,* Laurel thought. A large calendar was tacked on a bulletin board, and newspaper clippings covered an entire wall. Three large wooden cupboards took up another.

She yanked open the first cupboard. It was crammed from top to bottom with old newspapers. "Achoo!" This sneeze wasn't fake. She stood silent for several minutes in case someone had heard. Confident that the hallway was still deserted, she pulled an issue from the top of the pile, brushed off the thick layer of dust, and, stifling another sneeze, looked at the date. June 4, 2002. Too recent. She flung it back on the stack. Rifling through the next cabinet, she discovered newspapers from 1997 to 2001. She chucked them to the floor. Nobody would notice a few extra papers tossed about the already messy room. The next cupboard's door was stuck, and she nearly dislocated her shoulder wrenching it open. *I'm not getting paid enough for this,* she thought as she pulled a newspaper from the middle of the stack. October 2, 1994. Closer.

Laurel glanced at the clock on the wall. The period was almost over, and she should check into French before Madame Jolie called the nurse's office to confirm her whereabouts. The woman must've been a prison guard at the Bastille in a previous life. Nothing slipped her attention. Laurel also needed to search the lost-and-found box for a new uniform before catching up with Marcus and Simon.

She opened the last cupboard and bit her lip to keep from shrieking. *No No No . . .* A fuzzy brown spider the size of a cotton ball dangled from the web that hung like a circus trapeze over the stack of papers. *Don't freak. Don't freak. Don't freak.* She rattled off several choice curse words. *Dang Marcus!* She must've been crazy to listen to that CSI-wannabe. Why had she let him drag her into this? It was his fault if this thing bit her. Maybe it was a tarantula, for heaven's sake. Or a scorpion. It was also his fault if . . . She thought about Mr. Smithson's cold, dead body sprawled over his desk, and then looked at the spider. It really wasn't *that* big, was it?

Taking a deep breath, Laurel dove in, grabbed a newspaper near the top of the stack, and slammed the closet door shut. She glanced at the date at the top of the paper, and her eyes dropped to the headline. "Oh, no," she said, this time aloud.

FOOTBALL STAR DIES IN DRUNK DRIVING ACCIDENT
Jason Hart Almost Killed by Best Friend

undercover operation: *an investigation performed while avoiding detection*

LATER THAT MORNING

Who is this girl?

Marcus almost hadn't recognized Laurel when she picked up him and Simon in a sleek black Mercedes by the tennis courts on the far side of campus. The thick eyeliner and spidery clumps of mascara were gone, her nails were bare, and pale coral lip gloss replaced the usual magenta. A burgundy velvet headband with a small bow held her hair out of eyes, hiding the pink stripe, and tiny pearl studs dotted her earlobes. She wore a navy wool blazer with the school's crest on the pocket, and her plaid uniform skirt skimmed the top of her knees. Even her black-and-white saddle shoes looked new. She was all that she said she despised—the perfect Pinehurst Academy student, *circa* 1952. She actually looked kinda . . . cute. Marcus shook off the thought.

"Nice ride," Marcus said, rubbing his hand over the leather seat.

"It's one of my dad's," Laurel said. "Your legs would never fit in my two-seater. Buckle up." She handed him the old copy of *The Knightly News*. "Read this on the drive downtown. Just don't get carsick."

"I'm Laurel Carmichael," she announced to the scarlet-lipped young woman behind the reception desk. "Lawrence Carmichael's daughter. We're here to see Congressman Hart."

The name worked like magic. "Oh, Miss Carmichael. Welcome to Hart, Winston, and Hart." Laurel's father's name was practically the key to the city. The woman's smile was brilliant, like a toothpaste ad. "I'm Celeste Montgomery, one of Mr. Hart's assistants. Please make yourselves comfortable." In her black patent four-inch heels with red soles, she was nearly as tall as Marcus. With her gray pencil skirt and purple-and-black striped silk blouse clinging to every curve, she strutted down the hallway like a runway model—or a star of *Suits*—and disappeared behind a pair of doors at the end of the corridor.

Marcus glanced around the lobby, terrified to sit on the overstuffed cream-colored leather couch. It likely had been handmade in Italy or France. *And probably costs more than our whole house,* he thought. The rich, green wallpaper was flecked with gold, and Marcus was sure the lamps were real crystal, not bottle glass. For a minute he thought he was in the lobby of a five-star hotel.

Laurel pointed to a large, colorful painting of what looked like a woman and child hanging above the couch. "That's a Picasso. An original," she said. "From his cubist period."

Marcus's eyes widened. "Really? How do you know?"

The look on her face said she couldn't believe she knew such an idiot. "My dad built the MOMA. Museum of Modern Art," she said. "I know a Picasso when I see one."

"Pardon me, Professor," Marcus said. "It might be art, but it looks like anime. *Bad* anime."

Simon stifled a giggle behind them. He was still standing at the door, as if he'd set off some kind of alarm if he stepped on the marble tiles. Marcus gestured to the couch, then sat down next to him. Both barely perched their butts on the edge. Laurel plopped down on the far end, settled in, and, straightening her skirt, crossed her legs and began shaking her foot impatiently.

"How did Hart make so much money?" Marcus whispered.

Laurel whispered back, "Commercial real estate, mostly. Doesn't own as many buildings as my dad, but maybe a close second. Hart's father started the company decades ago."

Marcus picked up a copy of *San Diego Weekly* from a stack of magazines on the coffee table in front of the couch. Jason Hart was on the cover, flashing his trademark toothy grin. The magazine's teaser read "A Man After Our Own HART: Can California's Rising Star Resuscitate Washington?"

"Miss Carmichael?" a familiar man's voice said. "I'm Jason Hart."

Startled, Marcus banged his knee on the edge of the table as he sprang up. *Great*, he thought. *Way to make an impression.* Wincing, he pulled Simon up beside him and carefully placed the magazine back on the stack.

Laurel crossed the room and offered her hand. "Thank you for seeing us, Congressman," she said in the polite, girly voice she had used with the headmaster's assistant while Marcus was borrowing yearbooks from Dr. Welton's office. "We know how busy you are."

"Anything for the editor of *The Knightly News*," Hart said, flashing his trademark toothy smile. "And Lawrence Carmichael's daughter."

The cliché is right, Marcus thought. Money talks. Just like they had read about in *The Great Gatsby.*

Hart stared at Marcus, his smile less warm. "Have we met before? Maybe it's the varsity jacket. I have one myself."

"Marcus Jackson, sir. I, uh, was with the football team at the dedication ceremony for the stadium."

"Ah. I knew you looked familiar." Hart shook Marcus's hand, nearly crushing his fingers. "I rarely forget a face." Marcus consciously forced himself not to shake out his fingers. There was such a thing as taking a firm handshake too far.

"Marcus is the captain of the football *and* basketball teams," Laurel said. "Runs track, too. And writes the sports column for *The Knightly News.*"

Marcus swallowed hard. How easily the last lie had rolled off Laurel's tongue. Why was she building him up so much?

Hart nodded. "Impressive." He turned to Simon, who was half-hidden behind Marcus. "I know we haven't met before."

"Simon Musgrave," Laurel said. "I'm trying to recruit him for the newspaper staff. He's an excellent photographer."

Don't shake his hand! Marcus warned silently. Luckily for Simon, Hart didn't even bother to extend his hand. Looking like he'd rather be anywhere on the planet but here, Simon fussed with the strap of the Nikon camera hanging around his neck.

"We don't want to take up much of your time, Congressman," Laurel went on. "We know how busy you are with the campaign."

"Nonsense. Follow me." He glanced a his assistant. "Ms. Montgomery, please hold my calls except for the governor."

"Of course, Mr. Hart," she said, flashing another blinding smile.

The governor? Hart was kidding, right? Marcus studied the assistant to see if she laughed at the joke, but she just nodded like he told her this all the time. Marcus's mouth went dry. *Man, what're we doing here?* He glanced toward the exit as if planning an escape route through the defensive line.

Instead of bolting, he followed Hart toward the doors at the end of the corridor. "How is your father, Laurel?" Hart asked. "I haven't seen him since the fundraiser at the Regency last summer."

"He sends his regards," she said. "Maybe you can join us for dinner sometime."

Jeez, Marcus thought. Now she was acting as if Hart was a close family friend.

"I'd be delighted to. I'll ask Ms. Montgomery to set something up." Hart opened his office door and gestured for them to enter. "After you."

Marcus stood in the doorway and stared, his mouth gaping. Hart's office made the headmaster's look like a mouse hole. An L-shaped mahogany desk took up at a least a quarter of the room. As seen from the bank of tinted windows, the views of the marina, Petco Park baseball stadium and the Coronado Bridge were overwhelming. The lamps, paintings, sculptures, and other accessories belonged in a museum— or the Oval Office. Marcus's feet sank into the plush carpet as he followed Laurel across the room. His grandmother would've scolded him for not taking off his shoes if she had known.

Hart gestured to the two wing-backed chairs in front of the desk. "Please have a seat." Marcus and Laurel settled into the thrones, and Simon tucked himself into a smaller accent chair by the fireplace.

"What can I do for you?" Hart said, pouring himself a glass of ice water from a frosted crystal decanter. "May I get you anything? Sodas?"

Heck, yeah! "I'll take a—" Marcus began.

"No, thank you," Laurel said, taking her iPad from her bag. "We had something on the way over."

Marcus stared at the water pitcher. How could Laurel look so relaxed when his mouth felt as dry as Death Valley? She could be a real, experienced newspaper reporter on an ordinary assignment.

"Pinehurst students would like to learn more about their most distinguished graduate," she said. "I hope you don't mind, but I've prepared a few questions to save your valuable time."

"Ask away," Hart said, loosening his tie. He rocked back in his large, leather desk chair and took a long swallow of water.

Laurel consulted her iPad. "What was your favorite class when you were a student?"

"Math," he said without hesitation. "I've always had a knack for numbers."

"Ah, math," she said, as if she cared deeply. And she did. They'd chosen these questions very carefully. Ms. Mason had said to look for links between suspect and victim. They knew Mr. Smithson had been Hart's homeroom advisor, but had he also been his math teacher? And the code in Mr. Smithson's ledger? That was all about numbers. Laurel jotted down Hart's reply.

"Besides sports, what other extracurricular activities were you involved in?" Laurel asked.

Hart glanced at Marcus. "As Marcus knows, football didn't leave me with much free time. However, I was on the student council during my junior year and president of the senior class. I was also captain of the Quiz Bowl team."

"Quiz Bowl? *I'm* on the Quiz Bowl team," Simon blurted from across the room before catching himself. Laurel shot him a dirty look. His instructions had been to observe, not to speak.

"Really?" Hart looked amused. "Small world, Sam." Simon sank back into his seat.

"Was Mr. Smithson the team's sponsor back then?" Laurel asked. "I'm sure you heard about his death."

"I did. A terrible loss for Pinehurst. Such a brilliant man and an exceptional teacher." Hart paused. "I rearranged my schedule so I'll be able to attend his memorial service next week."

Marcus filed the congressman's answer in his mental notes app. Would Hart dare return to the scene of the crime if he was guilty of murder? How could he—

Hart's response to Simon's outburst interrupted Marcus's thoughts. "Douglas—I mean, Mr. Smithson—was indeed the faculty sponsor for my Quiz Bowl team. Sponsoring the team was quite an accomplishment for a relatively new teacher."

Laurel scrolled to the next question. "Why did you choose Yale? I'm sure you had many options."

"My family has a long history with Yale. A legacy. I couldn't disappoint my father, grandfather, and great-grandfather. Had I bothered to apply, I'm sure I would've been accepted to Harvard, Princeton, and Stanford. Even Cal and UCLA. USC as well. Occidental is a bit too small."

Yeah, Marcus thought. *Money talks. I'll be lucky if I can afford state college.* Especially after he talked with his father. His mind wandered again. Tonight he'd call his dad once more and leave another message. Hopefully this time he wouldn't sound like a total idiot. Maybe his dad would understand . . . As if hypnotized, he stared at the gold fountain pen Hart was twirling between his fingers.

"Marcus's father played basketball at Georgetown," Laurel said. "Maybe you've heard of him. Jeremiah Jackson."

Huh? Marcus glared at Laurel, the spell broken. The question was not in their script.

"Of course I've heard of him. Played for the Lakers," Hart said, grinning widely. "*That's* why you look familiar! I definitely see the family resemblance now. And, if you play basketball like him, well, what could be better?"

"Everybody says that," Marcus said. Before Hart knew who his father was, he probably thought Marcus was a nobody trying to make it in the clichéd world of the rich and famous. Now Hart would want to be his best friend. Anything to get more campaign money.

"You played football at Yale, right?" Laurel asked.

"Yes. Quarterback for the Bulldogs until I tore up my knee. ACL."

"Anterior cruciate ligament," Simon mumbled from his chair across the room.

Hart sighed. "I was headed for the NFL. The Chargers and Colts had expressed interest."

"That's, uh, too bad." Marcus struggled to sound sympathetic. *The poor guy, stuck being a stinkin' rich businessman and congressman instead of a professional football player. Life's tough.* Marcus's intense reaction caught him by surprise. Why did this man make him feel so self-conscious?

"I had to pass on a football career and went to law school instead," Hart added.

Laurel glanced back at her iPad, but both she and Marcus knew what the next question would be. "Were you in a fraternity at Yale?" Laurel asked. "High school students are fascinated with the Greek system."

"I was. Not a popular one, though. I wasn't much into partying."

Yeah, Marcus thought. *Nothing like a drunk driving accident to spoil somebody's fun.*

"Sigma Omega Epsilon wasn't your typical frat," Hart said. "A club, really." He pointed toward the fireplace.

Marcus twisted around. From across the room he recognized the three Greek letters. ΣΩE. *Bingo!* Hart's pledge certificate was displayed next to a photo of him with Jerry Brown, one of the state's former governors. Congressman Hart might dine with celebrities, but if he had murdered Mr. Smithson, "California's Rising Star" was about to implode.

"*The Knightly News* prides itself on writing quality articles. We don't just publish gossip or letters to the editor complaining about the food in the cafeteria," Laurel said, glancing at Marcus. *Here it comes,* he thought, taking a deep breath. *The big one.*

"One of the concerns of the administration is alcohol abuse by teenagers." She paused and looked directly at Hart. "Weren't you involved in a drunk driving accident your senior year?"

Hart uncrossed his legs and, swallowing hard, sat up straighter in his chair. "You've certainly done your homework, Miss Carmichael." His eyes darkened as he opened his desk drawer and took out a package of gum. He unwrapped the gum slowly. Very slowly. Marcus heard Simon fidget in the corner. "We beat Marshall West, our biggest rival, that night," Hart finally said. He shook his head sadly. "Derek Cross kicked a thirty-five yard field goal with two seconds left on the clock to win the game. It felt like we had won the Super Bowl." He popped a stick of gum into his mouth. *Man, the guy's cool,* Marcus thought.

"We drove to Jimmy's house in Rancho Santa Fe to celebrate," Hart continued. "My car was at the dealer for an oil change, so I hitched a ride with Derek. We couldn't stay long because we had to take the SAT in the morning. I grabbed a couple slices of pizza—pepperoni, I think—and watched the videotape of the game downstairs in the den. Derek stayed upstairs. I didn't know he had consumed a couple of beers. Had I known, I never would've risked letting him get a DUI—or worse." Hart took a lengthy sip of water.

"It was raining on the ride home. I must have dozed off because the next thing I remembered is feeling something warm and sticky running down my face. My own blood. Derek took a curve too fast on Ocean Crest Road. The truck slid off the wet road, jumped the curb, and crashed into a light pole. My head hit the dash." He stroked the faint but visible scar on his forehead. "I still see the pole directly in front of us. I was lucky I wasn't killed."

Nobody spoke for several long seconds.

"And Derek died," Marcus said quietly.

Hart nodded. "At the hospital. All I want to remember about that night is the grin on his face after he kicked that field goal."

Marcus stared out the window. A fog bank was stalled several miles off the coast, its dark gray clouds a sharp contrast to the turquoise of the Pacific. Something didn't feel right. Hart's story sounded rehearsed, as if he had told it a hundred times. *Intuition,* Ms. Mason had called it. Grissom's Rule Number Seven. That little voice inside your head. *Listen to it.* What was wrong with Hart's story?

The answer hit Marcus like a solid pass from Manny Santana. How could Hart have seen the light pole directly in front of him if he'd been *asleep?*

Laurel stood and smoothed her skirt past her knees. "We've taken up too much of your time, Congressman, and we need to get back to school. Marcus has basketball practice, and I've got tons of homework." She picked up her bag. "Pinehurst, you know."

"Of course," Hart said. He tossed his gum into a small trash can behind his desk.

"But before we go," she said, "can Simon take a photo of you to go along with the article? Perhaps one with you sitting under the Picasso in the foyer?" She looked at her iPad again. "Marcus and I will make sure we've covered everything."

"The painting is one of my favorites," Hart said. "Wait here. Sam and I will be right back. Before you leave, I'll grab a few campaign buttons for you."

"Get several good shots, *Simon*," Laurel instructed, emphasizing his name. "This is your big chance to show off your talent."

"Come along, Sam," Hart said, leading Simon out of the office and closing the door behind them.

"Quick!" Marcus said, jumping out of the seat. He pulled several plastic evidence bags from his jacket pocket and tossed a pair of nitrile gloves to Laurel. "Don't leave your prints on anything."

"Worry about your own naked fingers, Sherlock," she snapped.

"Toss me the iPad." He clicked a photo of Hart's fraternity certificate. Turning to toss the iPad back, he caught Laurel picking up Hart's fountain pen. "What are you doing? Put that back."

"It's like the one I found at the mock crime scene Ms. Mason set up. That's a coincidence, don't you think?"

"He'll notice if it's missing," Marcus said. *And probably accuse us of stealing it.*

"We can use it to compare Hart's fingerprints to the one on the cuff link."

Marcus shook his head. "Too risky. Leave it here. We'll find something else."

"Whatever."

The first piece of evidence Marcus collected was the wad of gum Hart had discarded in the waste basket. It was still slimy with saliva and a good source of DNA.

Next Marcus opened Hart's coat closet. Smelling of cedar, it was packed with a neatly organized collection of not only coats, but business suits and more casual blazers, sweaters, and long-sleeved dress shirts draped in plastic from the dry cleaner. Several pairs of highly polished shoes, both brown and black, were lined up on the floor, their toes precisely pointing forward.

He froze, sure he'd heard the doorknob rattle. Was Simon done with the photos already? When the sound didn't repeat, he dove back in his search.

Laurel rifled through Hart's desk drawers. "Not much in here except campaign propaganda. Bumper stickers and stuff. Maybe I should slap one on my dad's car," she said, chuckling.

"Hey, look what I found," Marcus said. He held up a clothes hanger with a black-and-white sweater draped over it. The sweater felt soft, like cashmere. He plucked off several fibers and sealed them in a small evidence bag he had pulled out of his backpack.

"Check this out." Laurel held up an invitation. "It's for a fund-raiser breakfast at La Bella Mar Hotel the morning Mr. Smithson—"

"Shh!" Marcus said, pausing again, this time at the sound of distant voices getting closer. "Simon and Hart are coming back." He tossed the sweater back in the closet, closed the door, and crossed the room in five quick strides. He snatched the invitation out of Laurel's hand and shoved it under his varsity jacket along with the bag of fibers.

They plopped back in their chairs a second before the office door opened.

"Sorry we took so long," Hart said. "Sam had to use the bathroom and locked himself in. Ms. Montgomery had to search for the key."

"Freshmen," Laurel apologized, shooting Simon a killer look. She stood, picked up her bag, and, hunting through it, fished out her car keys. Taking Simon by the shoulder, she turned him and pushed him toward the door. "Thank you so much for your time, Congressman, but we really need to get back to school."

"Yeah. Bye, sir," Marcus said, practically tripping on Laurel's heels.

"Not so fast," Hart said firmly, rooting around in his desk drawer.

All three of them froze in the doorway. *Holy crap!* Marcus slowly turned around. He kept his arms folded across his chest to protect the evidence hidden underneath his jacket. *Isn't my life supposed to flash before my eyes now?* "Yes, sir?"

Hart stepped forward and handed each of them several campaign buttons and bumper stickers. "The slogan's clever, don't you think?" he said.

"Yes, sir," Marcus said, exhaling. "*Hart Attack* is pretty catchy."

Hart pointed a firm finger at Marcus's chest. "Remember to ask me for a personal recommendation when you apply to college, young man," he said, flashing his toothy smile. "I have contacts at Yale." He gave Marcus a jolly slap on the shoulder. "Pinehurst . . . football . . . we're practically brothers."

Marcus nearly fell over with the slap. "I, uh, yes, sir. Thank you, sir . . . ."

Laurel grabbed the back of Marcus's jacket and tugged. "Thank you for your time, Congressman," she said, pinning a campaign button on her school blazer. "Good luck with the election. If I was eighteen, I'd vote for you."

Hart's phone rang. "Duty calls. I'm sure you can find your way out. Give my regards to your fathers." He gave a little wave before answering the phone. "Ah, Governor. Good to hear from you. About that new proposition for tax rebates. What if we . . . "

"Simon," Simon mumbled as they walked into the hallway. "My name is Simon."

"Shh," Laurel said. She gave Ms. Montgomery a little wave as they passed by her desk.

"Like I'm going to ask a murderer for a letter of rec," Marcus said as they descended in the elevator to the parking garage.

"As if I'd vote for him." Laurel ripped the campaign button off her blazer. Except for one that she tucked into her pocket, she tossed the handful of bumper stickers in the recycle bin.

"Hey, guys," Simon said. "When I was looking for a roll of toilet paper—"

"Spare us your personal hygiene story," Laurel said. "By the way, locking yourself in the bathroom was a genius move to give us more time to search his office. Well played, *Sam*."

"*Hart Attack.* I thought I was going to have a heart attack when he was digging around in his desk drawer," Marcus said. "And then when he—"

"When I was looking for a roll of toilet paper," Simon continued, shutting them up with his persistence, "I found this." He pulled a plastic amber medicine vial out of his camera case. "Read the label."

"Cardiotalis!" Marcus exclaimed. "Two-hundred-fifty microgram pills."

Laurel snatched the vial out of Simon's hand. "Hold on. The prescription's not for Jason Hart. It's for *Gareth* Hart."

"His father!" Marcus said. "Don't you remember? Hart said at the dedication ceremony that his father couldn't make it because he was sick. We have means."

"See?" Laurel said, poking him in the ribs with her elbow. "Wasn't this worth a detention for ditching?"

"I hate to admit it, but—"

"And we have this." Laurel pulled Hunt's fountain pen out of the pocket of her blazer.

"You took it! I told you to leave it," Marcus said.

"Yeah, and my mom told me never to wear flip-flops to the White House. It's evidence." She dropped it back into her pocket.

Well, what was done was done. Nothing he could do about it but to go forward. And he had just the evidence to top off the mission. "I also got this," he said, holding up a small evidence bag. "Hart's gum. *Bubble* gum. And it's loaded with DNA."

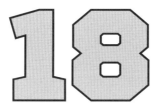

alibi: *a verifiable claim that one was elsewhere when a crime was committed*

TWO HOURS LATER

"Make it fast, please. I'm in a hurry," Laurel said to the new barista behind the counter at the Coffee Mug. "And throw in a double shot of espresso."

After stopping for lunch at The Taco Truck on Pacific Coast—at Marcus's insistence—the drive back to school from downtown had taken nearly an hour in the afternoon traffic, and it would take at least that long to process the evidence they had collected from Jason Hart's office. Longer if the barista didn't speed it up. The bell over the door jingled. An older man wearing what looked like a custom-made gray business suit strolled in, and through the bay window, Laurel saw Ms. Mason and Ms. Goldman crossing the street toward the café.

"Great. Just what I need," she said under her breath. She hadn't ditched the nerdy uniform, and the teachers would likely notice. Everyone at Pinehurst was familiar with her unique style. To make matters worse, she supposedly had gone home sick. She had to hide, but where? The businessman had gone into the single bathroom. The bell over the door jingled again. Laurel grabbed a hard copy of *The Wall Street Journal* from the rack next to the pastry counter, plopped into a chair behind a impressively large display of coffee mugs, and hid her face behind the sports section of the newspaper.

"I'll have my usual," Ms. Mason said to the barista. "A caramel macchiato, no sugar added, with soy milk, please. My friend will have a double cappuccino, non-fat."

"With foam," Ms. Goldman chimed in.

The teachers sat at a small table on the other side of the grab-and-go snack display. Laurel hunkered down and pulled the newspaper closer to her face. She couldn't see the teachers, and doubted if they could see her, but she could hear them just fine.

"Okay, Audrey," Ms. Mason said, "spill it. Where were you Tuesday?"

"Good grief, Kathryn. You don't give up, do you?" Ms. Goldman said. "I'll tell you because you're my best friend, not because it's any of your business." She paused, probably to take a sip of coffee. "I drove up to Orange County after school on Monday and stayed overnight."

"Tell me you didn't take a day off to go to Disneyland."

"The Magic Kingdom is the last place I'd go." Ms. Goldman's tone was serious.

"Well?" Ms. Mason asked. "Are you going to tell me or not?"

Ms. Goldman seemed to take a deep breath. "Douglas Smithson made it clear that my days at Pinehurst were over. The evaluation he wrote would've destroyed my career. He said, and I quote, 'Audrey Goldman's teaching is not up to par with our school's standards. She is unqualified to chair the department'."

"What? Surely, you must have misunderstood," Ms. Mason said. "You're an excellent teacher, one of the best. Look at how many students come to you for extra tutoring. You can turn any one of them into Einstein. And what about your STEM girls? You're such a great role model."

Laurel peered over the top of the newspaper. Ms. Goldman shook off the compliments. "Smithson obviously didn't feel that way. I refuse to stay at a place where my accomplishments aren't appreciated."

"What's in OC?"

"I made a few calls, and a former college friend invited me to visit Newport Prep. One of their algebra teachers decided to go back to grad school starting this spring, so there's an opening in the math department."

"Did you accept the position?"

"They made a generous offer, but now that Smithson's dead, I have no reason to leave Pinehurst," Ms. Goldman said. "In fact, I expect the headmaster will appoint me to chair the department after all." She gave a throaty laugh. "Poor Douglas. He had no idea that by dying, he gave me what he didn't want me to have."

"Miss?" the barista said in a loud voice, addressing Laurel. "Your drink's getting cold."

Startled, Laurel rustled the newspaper. Couldn't he see that she was busy? Pretending to read the paper, she waved him off.

"Oh, no. The time," Ms. Mason said. "Let's go. I'm going to be late for a meeting."

"I recommend the new Marriott the next time you're in Newport Beach," Ms. Goldman said. "The spa is to die for."

Peering over the top of the newspaper, Laurel watched the teachers dart across the parking lot and disappear into the campus. She tossed the newspaper paper back on the rack and grabbed her mocha, tossing a five-dollar bill into the tip jar. Time to get to work.

* * *

Marcus had already swapped his varsity jacket for a lab coat when Laurel strutted into room 102 with a coffee cup in one hand and an evidence bag in the other. She hadn't changed out of the Patty Pinehurst get-up, and she looked ridiculous. Laurel Carmichael wasn't meant for uniforms.

"We won't have to dust this for fingerprints," she said, holding up Ms. Goldman's lipstick. "Before you open your mouth, don't. You might accuse me of *stealing*." She tossed the lipstick on the lab counter with the other evidence they'd bagged and tagged. "Ms. Goldman's got an alibi. The most she's guilty of is breaking into Mr. Smithson's desk to retrieve her evaluation."

"How do you know?" Marcus said.

"I overheard her and Ms. Mason at The Coffee Mug. Before you ask, no, they didn't see me. Anyway, Ms. Goldman drove up to OC for a job interview. She stayed at the new Marriott, which, by the way, apparently has a spa to die for. That explains the phone conversation

I overhead. You know, the one where Ms. Mason asked somebody where they were when Mr. Smithson was murdered." Laurel took a sip of mocha. "I can call Newport Prep and pretend I'm looking for a teaching position. You know, to confirm her story."

"Let's assume Ms. Goldman was telling the truth." Laurel pretending to be a newspaper reporter was one thing, but a teacher? Her acting skills weren't *that* good. Marcus glanced at his watch. "Simon started a TLC on the pills he found in Hart's bathroom. It should be finished in a few."

"Where is Simon?" Laurel asked, looking around.

"His dad picked him up early. I told him to keep working on the code in Mr. Smithson's ledger."

"What're you doing?"

"I'm trying to pull Hart's fingerprints off the fountain pen you took from his office and compare them to the print on the cuff link." He tossed her an evidence bag. "Here are the fibers from Hart's sweater. Run them."

"Aye, aye, *Captain*," she said, saluting.

"Sorry. I shouldn't tell you what to do. It's just that—"

The door opened suddenly and Ms. Mason strode in. She nearly skidded to a stop when she spotted them. "What are you kids doing in here? You can't work in here without supervision."

They were too surprised to answer.

"I'm especially surprised at you, Marcus. You usually follow the rules. I hope Laurel's not a bad influence." Ms. Mason peered at Laurel over the frame of her glasses. "Didn't you sign out sick?"

Laurel recovered first. "We, uh, had to finish a lab," she said. "You know, to study for the midterm. I went home and took a nap. I'm feeling much better." She placed her hand on her forehead. "See? Fever's gone."

"The door was unlocked," Marcus added before Laurel could embellish her lie even more. "We thought you were at a faculty meeting. You know, still at school in case, uh, we needed you."

"You should've checked with me if you wanted to work late," Ms. Mason said. "Wrap it up. I've got to get over to the U. I'm subbing this evening for a friend."

"But we only need a few more minutes," Laurel said. If they left now, Simon's chromatography would be ruined because the solvent would run off the top of the plate and evaporate. "Please? We want to ace the test."

"I wish I could help you out," Ms. Mason said, grabbing her laptop, "but I'm already late."

"Can't Dr. Gladson—" Marcus began.

"Not this time, Marcus." Ms. Mason said. "He's already gone home. C'mon, out."

Before they could protest further, Ms. Mason ushered them out, locked the classroom door, and hurried down the hallway. "By the way, Laurel," she said over her shoulder, "I like your new look. A different hairstyle, right?"

* * *

They stood on the steps outside Weatherly Hall. "Let's hope Simon saved enough sample to run another TLC," Marcus said. "This one's ruined." There had been only three pills in Gareth Hart's prescription bottle. "If not—"

"We're toast," Laurel said.

Gazing out across the quad, Marcus wondered what it would be like taking calculus behind bars if Jason Hart discovered what they'd taken from his office. The school at juvie wouldn't be anything like Pinehurst. He shook off the terrifying thought. "There's nothing we can do about it now. Let's just go." If the TLC was ruined, they'd have to make sure the other evidence nailed Hart, if in fact he was guilty. He pulled his phone out of his pocket.

"Who're you calling?" Laurel said.

"My mom. I missed the late Pinehurst bus, and the next city one isn't until six. She worries if I'm late."

"Bus?" She grimaced like she had tasted something disgusting. "Where's your car?"

"It's in the shop. Porsches are so high maintenance."

"Porsche?" Laurel said. "I'm impressed. Thought you'd be the hybrid type."

"Actually, I don't have a car. I'm, uh, saving up to buy one." *Saving up?* How lame was that? His father probably had a fleet in his garage. Not that he ever saw his father's garage.

"I can drive you home," Laurel offered.

"Oh, I don't know." Marcus craned his neck, like he could see the bus coming. The last thing he wanted was Laurel Carmichael driving him home. "What about your parents? Won't you be late for dinner?" He doubted if his house was on the route to wherever she lived.

"They were supposed to get home three days ago, but their flight from Paris was canceled," she said. "Then a blizzard hit New York, then . . . never mind." Shivering, she hugged the old-fashioned uniform blazer close.

Marcus snapped up his jacket. The fog bank had moved inland, hugging the coast with a thick, gray mist and dropping the temperature by several degrees.

"Do you want a ride or not?" Laurel asked.

"It's out of your way . . . "

"I wouldn't have offered if it was too much trouble. C'mon." She started walking down the steps.

Marcus hesitated. Was he ready for Laurel to meet his family? Did he want to wait around for the next bus when he could get home early and start studying?

"C'mon, it's getting dark. Are you going to make a girl walk by herself?" she called over her shoulder. "Some gentleman you are."

Like she couldn't kick the tar out of anybody who tried to stop her. He bet she wasn't afraid of anything. He slung his backpack over his shoulder and jogged to catch up. "Thanks," he said, slipping the phone back into his pocket.

Laurel wrapped the blazer tighter across her chest. "If it wasn't so cold, I wouldn't be caught dead in this hideous thing. It even smells weird, like a wet dog."

"Wool, probably," Marcus said. "You know, the fiber evidence lab."

They cut across campus to the front lot where Laurel had parked her father's Mercedes, the one she had driven to Jason Hart's office. The red, white, and blue HART ATTACK bumper sticker stood out against the car's highly polished black exterior. Laurel giggled. "My dad hates bumper stickers." She rubbed a loose corner before letting them into the car. "A nice touch, though, don't you think?" Settling into the plush leather interior, she activated Sirius XM. "Any preference for music?" They had been too nervous to listen to music during the round-trip drive to Jason Hart's downtown office.

Marcus shook his head. "Whatever you listen to."

Academy Drive was a narrow, two-lane road with groves of pine and eucalyptus trees on each side and canyons below, but few houses and no street lamps or sidewalks. The curves could be sharp. As they descended down the hill away from campus and toward Ocean Crest, Laurel kept glancing in the rearview mirror.

"Anything wrong?" Marcus asked.

"There's some freakoid behind us without his headlights on."

Twisting around, he looked out the rear window. Despite the car's climate control system, the window was covered with a thin layer of mist, making it difficult to see. "Man, the fog's really bad," he said.

Laurel kept checking the mirror.

Marcus looked back again. "He's right on our tail."

"Tell me about it." Laurel tooled down the slick road with both hands on the wheel as she steered around the curves. The twists tested the Benz's suspension, but the car hugged the road.

The other vehicle was drawing dangerously close. "Maybe he's just following our taillights. You know, because of the fog," Marcus said. "I remember that from driver's ed."

"Not this close. The guy's a maniac." She mumbled a few cuss words.

Marcus peeked at the speedometer. "Aren't you taking this road a little fast?"

Laurel gripped the wheel tighter. Her knuckles were white. "What's wrong with this psycho?" The other car was only a few yards away from the Benz's back bumper. "Any closer and he'll activate the collision warning system."

"Try braking. That should get him to back off," Marcus said. "Just slow down!"

A clearing in the mist broke directly in front of them, and Marcus caught a glimpse of the stoplight at the bottom of the hill before their car lurched into another fog bank. The vehicle behind them sped up, crossed the double-yellow line, and started to pass on the left.

Laurel jerked the wheel to the right.

"Holy crap!" Marcus shouted, bracing himself against the seat. "He's going to run us off the road!"

Trees loomed dangerously close to the side of the car. The tires of the Benz skidded on the sandy shoulder of the road, and gravel pinged off the underside of the car. Something larger, probably a small rock, bounced off the windshield. Marcus held his breath and waited for the inevitable impact into a tree—or light pole. Just when he thought they would fly off the road and plummet to the canyon below, Laurel jerked the wheel to the left and stabbed the brakes, fishtailing the car as the other vehicle cut in front of them and nearly clipped their left bumper. She held the wheel tight, barely controlling the skid as the other car's taillights disappeared into the fog down the hill.

Straightening the car in the lane, Laurel let fly with an impressive set of cuss words this time.

Marcus's heart pounded, and his face was streaked with sweat. "Man, that was close! That guy could've killed us! What was he thinking?"

Staring straight ahead, Laurel loosened her grip on the steering wheel. Marcus heard her breathe deeply.

"I thought we were going to end up like Derek Cross," he said, his pulse slowing to the strains of Coldplay's "Swallowed by the Sea."

"And you were gonna take the bus," Laurel joked weakly. She breathed deeply again. "Thank God this is a really good car." She patted the dashboard. "But so was that one. An S-Class Benz. Top of the line."

"He should invest in some driving lessons."

"Did you get a look at him? I was too busy keeping the car on the road."

"No," Marcus said, shaking his head. "The windows were tinted."

"Too bad. I've got words for that jerk."

"But I got the license number," he said.

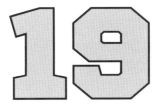

misconception: *a wrong conclusion, often based on incorrect evidence*

LATER THAT EVENING

The mist had turned into a heavy drizzle, and it took Laurel an extra thirty minutes to drive to Marcus's neighborhood. SoCal drivers freaked out in any type of rain, and two fender-benders had turned the interstate into a parking lot. After exiting at Mission Bay, she pulled onto the narrow residential street lined on both sides by palm trees and older model cars and mini-vans and parked in an empty space along the curb in front of the house Marcus pointed at. *Is this where Marcus lives?* she wondered. She was surprised he didn't live in an exclusive area of La Jolla or Del Mar. Didn't professional athletes like Jeremiah Jackson make millions? Surely he had saved some of it for retirement.

"Check the DMV records," Marcus said, speaking into his phone. "I'm sure you can hack . . . I mean, access them." His phone beeped, signaling a low battery. "Later."

He ended the call and sat for a second. Laurel kept the car's engine running. "Well, uh, thanks for the ride home," he said.

"No problem."

Marcus unbuckled his seat belt. "I'll see you tomorrow then. In the lab."

"Actually," she said, "I . . . " *Jeez, could this get any more awkward?* "I really need to, uh . . . pee." All the caffeine, adrenaline, traffic, and the psycho driver made her feel as if she would burst. She'd never make it back home, and no way did she want to pop into the nearest In-N-Out. "Can I use your, er, bathroom?"

"Bathroom?" he asked.

"Yeah. You know, the room with the shower—and usually a toilet."

"Uh, sure. C'mon," Marcus said. "Just don't tell my mom about the tailgater. She'll freak out."

Laurel switched off the ignition. "I'll make it quick." She peered up and down the poorly lit street. Maybe she should've taken that pepper spray her dad had offered her last month. She grabbed her bag off the backseat and activated the Benz's alarm system.

"Don't worry. We haven't had a car stolen here in a couple of days," Marcus said, reading her mind.

"Very funny." She pressed the car's alarm button a second time just to make sure and stuck close to him as he trudged up the driveway. He *was* kidding, wasn't he?

Marcus's house was a one-story, Spanish-style bungalow with a faded red tile roof. A pink tricycle was tipped on its side under a skeletal, nearly leafless tree, and a basketball hoop hung above the garage door. Laurel caught her heel on a garden hose sprawled across the walkway.

"Sorry," Marcus said, grabbing her elbow to steady her. If she'd been in her stilettos instead of the saddle shoes, she would've gone down for sure. "One of the kids forgot to roll it up." He quickly rolled up the hose and shoved it under a shrub by the front door.

Kids? Plural? she thought. *What the heck am I doing here?* The light over the front door was on, and a shadow flickered behind the drapes. "Maybe I should just go."

"What are you gonna do, stop at a gas station? Have you seen those restrooms?"

Unfortunately, she had. *I'd rather pee my pants*, she thought, shuddering.

Marcus rapped twice on the front door, opened it, and ushered her inside. With one big swing, he heaved his backpack onto a brown tweed couch near the door, bouncing a gold and red pillow onto the floor. Matching end tables at each end of the couch were topped with lamps whose shades were slightly lopsided. A vase of artificial yellow tulips and a neat stack of magazines rested on the coffee table, and a large gray tabby was curled up underneath it. Several toy trucks and cars, crayons, coloring books, and a headless Barbie were strewn across the carpet along with several children's books, including a well-read copy of *Where the Wild Things Are*. Despite the clutter, the rug looked as if it had been vacuumed recently and the tables dusted. And what was that delicious smell wafting out of the kitchen?

"Hello, people," he called out.

A small girl with two blonde, straight pigtails wrapped with pink bows jumped out of the recliner facing a flat-screen HDTV that just about took up half the wall. "You're home!" she shrieked. The cat bounded out from underneath the coffee table, leaped over the couch, and disappeared behind it. The girl wrapped her arms around Marcus's shins and glared up at him with her big, blue eyes. "You're late."

Marcus struggled out of his jacket and tossed it on the couch beside his backpack. "Way to go, Ashley. You scared Taz."

A young boy who looked like he was about eight or nine sat cross-legged back on the floor in front of the TV, tossing a ball back-and forth between his bare right hand and the baseball glove on his left. "Hey, Timmy," Marcus said, "what're you watching?"

"*Jeopardy!*" he mumbled without looking up.

A child identical to the squealing girl, but a boy with a crew cut, raced into the living room. He skidded to a stop. "Who's that?" he said, pointing at Laurel.

Marcus ruffled the boy's hair. "Justin, meet Laurel. Laurel, meet Justin, my other brother."

"Hi there . . . I . . . " Laurel carefully stepped over piles of Legos. Somebody had attempted to build a miniature city, but it looked like a tornado had ripped through it. Nearly doing the splits, she stuck out her hand. "Nice to meet you." The boy looked at her like she was an alien. *What, you've never seen saddle shoes before?* She turned to the little girl. "And who are you?"

"Ashley," she replied with a slight lisp. "I'm Marcus's sister." It came out 'thister.'"

Ashley suddenly let go of Marcus's legs, and, throwing her hands on her hips, glared up at Laurel. "Are you his girlfriend?"

"No! No, I'm not his girlfriend. I'm his—" *His what?* Laurel thought, glancing at Marcus. "I'm his . . . classmate."

"I'm four. How old are you?" Ashley demanded.

"Old," Laurel said. "Sixteen."

"Do you have a cat?" Taz had resettled himself on the end of the couch.

"I do. A calico. Her name's Donatella."

"Why does she have such a funny name?" Ashley said.

Enough with the questions, Laurel thought. *She's really cute, though.*

"Calicos are pretty rare," Marcus said. "We studied them last year in biology. They're usually only females because one of their X chromosomes is—"

"Is that your real hair?" Ashley asked, pointing at Laurel's head. "Why is some of it pink?"

Now we're talking. Stepping out of the awkward split pose over the Legos, Laurel knelt next to Ashley. "Can you keep a secret?" she whispered, placing her finger over her lips.

Ashley nodded.

"Only the pink's real," Laurel said, winking.

Ashley's eyes widened.

"Ah, she's just messing with you," Marcus said. He pointed to his right. "The, uh, bathroom's down the hall."

Laurel remained in the center of the room. "Maybe I can wait."

"Hey, Timmy," Marcus called to the boy watching TV. "Come meet Laurel. She can help you answer Final Jeopardy."

She glanced at the screen. "Hockey History isn't exactly my category. I'm not really into sports." What kind of little kid watched TV game shows in the first place?

"Marcus, you're finally home. I was getting worried." A woman who was at least a foot shorter than Marcus walked into the room, wiping her hands on a blue striped kitchen towel. She stopped in mid-stride and looked at Laurel. "And you've brought a guest."

Marcus bent over and kissed her cheek. "Sorry I'm late, Mom."

Marcus's mother was dressed casually in dark-washed jeans, a black turtleneck, and zebra-striped fuzzy slippers. Her blonde hair was twisted into a knot on top of her head, with several loose sun-streaked strands framing her heart-shaped face. Her complexion was flawless, clean of makeup except for a light dusting of amethyst eye shadow. A pair of tortoise-shelled eyeglasses accentuated her teal-blue eyes. *She's Heidi Klum beautiful,* Laurel thought. Marcus had inherited his mom's unique eye color.

"Mom, this is Laurel," Marcus said.

She smiled. "Nice to meet you, Laurel." She glanced at the toys littering the carpet and blushed. "Sorry. I haven't had a chance to straighten up. Timmy had Little League right after school until it started raining, traffic was terrible, the cable guy was late, then the vet called about Taz, and—"

"Nice to meet you, too," Laurel said. "I hope I'm not intruding."

"Of course not." She pointed at Laurel's uniform. "I'm assuming you go to Pinehurst?"

Laurel thanked every god she could think of that she was still wearing the Patty Pinehurst costume and not her unique version of the school uniform. "Yes, I do."

"We're in forensic science together," Marcus said.

"Please stay for dinner, Laurel. Nothing fancy, but it's hot and—"

"Actually, Mom," Marcus interrupted, "Laurel just dropped in to—"

"I really can't stay," Laurel said. "But thank you for the invitation."

"I've made Marcus's favorite. Turkey meatloaf," his mother said. "Feel free to take off your blazer. It looks scratchy." She looked down at Laurel's feet. "Your saddle shoes, too, if you'd like."

"Where's Dad?" Marcus said. "His car's not in the driveway."

"It's Wednesday, remember? He teaches a lit class tonight."

Literature class? Had she heard correctly? Jeremiah Jackson was a former basketball star, not an English teacher. Talk about a career switch! *What's going on here?* Laurel thought. She glanced over her shoulder at the front door. Maybe the restroom at In-N-Out wasn't such a bad idea.

Then she looked at Marcus's mom and the children. Justin had curled up next to Timmy in front of the TV and, wearing his older brother's baseball glove, repeatedly slapped a baseball into the pocket. "It . . . it smells wonderful, Mrs. Jackson."

"Please call me Cindy. I haven't been Mrs. Jackson for quite some time."

"I'm sorry," Laurel fumbled. "I just assumed—"

"I'm starving," Marcus said. "Tim, Mom said to turn off the TV." He swung Justin over his shoulder like a duffel bag.

Ashley trotted over to Laurel, gripping the headless Barbie.

"What happened to your doll?" Laurel asked. "Where's her head?"

"I don't know. I'm still—" Ashley looked up at Marcus. "What's the word you use when you're trying to figure out a crime?"

Surprised, Laurel stared up at Marcus. "Don't tell me you discuss crime scenes with—"

"An *investigation*," Marcus said. "That's what you do when you try to figure out how something happened. You investigate."

"I'm *in-ves-ti-gat-ing* what happened to Barbie," Ashley said, drawing out the syllables, her lisp taking the word to a whole new realm. "I found fingerprints near her house and some broken glass." She skipped in front of them. "Blood drops, too."

"You're sick!" Laurel whispered to Marcus. "I can't believe you discuss stuff like that with a four-year-old. Is she helping with your squirrel experiment, too?"

"It's a chipmunk," Ashley said over her shoulder.

"Cute, Marcus, really cute," Laurel said, ditching the blazer. "Where's the bathroom again?" Another minute and she'd need a diaper. He pointed to his right. She practically sprinted down the hallway.

Six chairs were crowded around the kitchen table. Ashley had saved the seat next to hers for Laurel. The kitchen was small and cluttered, the sink full of pots and pans, but the countertops, appliances, and floor sparkled. A pair of crisp peach voile curtains framed the single window. Marcus helped his mom with the platters of turkey meatloaf, macaroni and cheese, and green beans.

"This looks delicious, Mrs. Jack—I mean, Cindy," Laurel said.

Marcus passed her the platter of meatloaf. "Would you like some ketchup?" he said, rapping the bottom of the bottle of Heinz.

"No, thank you," Laurel said. She'd never eaten any kind of meatloaf before, with or without ketchup.

"Look!" Justin said. He had stuffed black olives on the tips of his fingers. "Justin!" Marcus's mom said. "Where are your manners?"

"Sorry." He picked off the olives one-by-one and popped them in his mouth—all except the last one. Just before he got to it, Marcus grabbed his finger and ate the olive off. "Hey!"

"Marcus!" His mother's cheeks were bright red. "Sorry," she said, looking at Laurel. "I don't know what's gotten into them."

Laurel scooped a forkful of macaroni to keep from smiling. She had a feeling she was going to like turkey meatloaf.

"You have a nice family," Laurel said as they walked outside. "Ashley's adorable. So sassy. I've never been asked to a slumber party by a four-year-old before. She sure asks a lot of questions, though."

Marcus grinned. "Yeah. Like somebody else I know."

"Who?"

"She'll never take off the bracelet you gave her," Marcus said. "Are you sure you want her to keep it? It must be expensive."

"I'll send her a couple more tomorrow," Laurel said.

"No!" Marcus blurted. "I mean, you don't have to do that. One diamond bracelet's more than enough."

"How can you be so dense?" Laurel said. "It's CZ. Cubic zirconia." As if she'd wear real diamonds with the hideous uniform. "Don't worry. I'll try not to corrupt her," she said, digging around in her bag for her keys, "even though you're teaching her about crime scenes."

"Speaking of crime scenes," Marcus said, pointing, "your car's gone."

"What?" Her head whipped up.

"Just kidding," Marcus said, grinning. "It's still here."

"Very funny." Laurel unlocked the car and tossed her bag on the front passenger seat. "Well, then, I guess I'll meet you in the lab in the morning. We've got a ton of evidence to process." She started walking around to the driver's side.

"Wait," Marcus said, gently grabbing her elbow. She didn't shake him off. "I . . . I should explain a few things about my family." He dropped her arm and, crossing his legs, leaned against the car.

"You don't need to—"

"Yes, I do. I saw the surprise on your face when you saw my house and met my mom and the kids." She looked down at her shoes, ashamed. Marcus smiled weakly and pulled his jacket tighter.

"Timmy, Justin, and Ashley are my half-siblings." He stared down the street.

"Please. You don't need to explain." Shivering, Laurel stuck her hands in the pockets of the blazer and met his gaze.

"I want to," Marcus said. "Jeremiah Jackson's my father, but he's not my *dad*. There's a difference. He met my mom when they were in college at UPenn, and they got married after graduation. Then I came along. Jeremiah was drafted into the NBA by the Sixers, made lots of money, and, well, you can guess the rest. Same cheesy ending. He took off when I was two."

"I'm sorry," Laurel said quietly, her eyes not moving from his.

"I'm not." He didn't sound bitter. "Mom went to nursing school, and she married Bob when I was nine. Then we moved out here from Philadelphia so I could be closer to Jeremiah when he started playing for the Lakers. My stepdad teaches English at Scripps CC and the U. I may have Jeremiah's last name, but Bob's my dad. He's always there for me. For all of us. Jeremiah only sees me as a jock—his clone. I got his size, and I can dribble a ball, but that's about it."

He stared down the deserted street. "I've got to tell him that I want to be a CSI, not a pro athlete like him. He'll never understand. He pays my tuition and sometimes gives me a gift, like the TV. He probably feels guilty or something." Marcus raised his chin towards the house. "We're not rich like most Pinehurst families, but we've got it going on. Know what I mean?"

Laurel nodded. She knew exactly what he meant.

"It's late," Marcus said, standing up straight again. He tapped the roof of the car. "Drive safe."

Laurel got in the car and started the engine. Before pulling away from the curb, she lowered the passenger-side window. "Thanks for dinner."

He shrugged. "It was just turkey meatloaf."

"The best meatloaf I've ever had." She raised the window and pulled away from the curb. It wasn't just meatloaf. She'd take mac-n'-cheese any day over tortellini alla Bolognese. She dreaded going back to her parents' lonely old villa. She hoped Marcus appreciated how lucky he was.

Her shame deepened as she drove back to La Jolla. Had she learned nothing from Ms. Mason about jumping to conclusions without evidence? Forensic scientists worked to dispel misconceptions, not contribute to them. She had always despised people who stereotyped others, and now she was one of them. Marcus wasn't just the son of a rich athlete. He was so much more.

Marcus watched the car's taillights fade away. What had he just done? Laurel would probably spread his business all over the school. *Stupid, stupid move.*

His mom was fast asleep on the couch with a copy of *Women's Health* resting on her lap. She stirred as he draped a fleece throw over her and switched off the TV. Careful not to wake her, Marcus went into the kitchen and poured himself a glass of milk and grabbed a handful of chocolate chip cookies out of the jar. He crept back into the living room and picked up his backpack and jacket. As he headed toward his bedroom, his jacket vibrated. Strange. He thought the battery on his phone was dead.

The text was from Simon.

DAWGS93 belongs to JH

Marcus wasn't surprised. He'd already guessed that the car which had almost run them off the road was registered to Jason Hart. Hart had graduated from Yale in 1993, and the university's mascot was a bulldog.

gel electrophoresis: *a laboratory procedure in which DNA frag-mentsare separated from each other in an electrical field*

FRIDAY MORNING

Laurel looked like Laurel again.

Almost.

From three rows over Marcus could see wisps of magenta sticking out from underneath a crystal hair clip, and she had replaced the old-fashioned uniform with her usual tight polo shirt and short Pinehurst plaid skirt. Her purple glittery shoes sparkled under the classroom's lights. But today her eye makeup didn't look so raccoon-like. He almost missed the thick black eyeliner.

When she turned his way and caught him looking, he whipped his eyes back down to his notebook. The last thing he wanted was to talk to her, or interact with her in any way. He still felt embarrassed about last night. Not about Laurel meeting his family—he was glad she had because they meant everything to him—but about running his mouth off. What an ungrateful punk he was. Without Jeremiah's money, he wouldn't be able to attend Pinehurst. He was lucky just to have that.

"Dr. Gladson's out sick today," Ms. Mason said, "and I have to help his substitute with a dissection this period. It's your lucky day, but use the time wisely. Remember, we have an exam next week." She picked up a box of nitrile gloves. "Now, please clear the lab. As you know," she said, looking directly at Marcus, "you can't work in here without supervision."

As soon as she left Bobby grabbed his backpack and sprinted out of the room, followed by the other students. Only Marcus, Laurel, and Simon lingered.

Laurel strolled his way. "Hey, Mr. Basketball, I—"

"Quick! We need to finish before Ms. Mason gets back." He had no idea how long the dissection would take. "I'll lift the prints off Hunt's fountain pen." He rushed over to the cabinet and fumbled with a microscope. "You take the fibers again."

"Oh. I see." He saw Laurel cross her arms over her chest out of his peripheral vision. "You invite a girl to dinner and then . . . never mind. Maybe you should just go dribble or something."

That's not such a bad idea, Marcus thought. "Simon, you'll have to run another TLC on the pills."

Simon looked confused. "I'm certain I used the right solvent." He scurried over to the fume hood.

"You did," Marcus said. "I had to leave before it was finished. It's my fault the solvent ran off the top of the plate."

Plugging in the microscope, Marcus glanced in Laurel's direction. She was rifling through her bag like an archaeologist digging for lost treasure, and he was acting like a jerk. "Listen, about last night," he said, walking over to her and keeping his voice low. "Jeremiah's not such a bad father. He's just—"

"Give this to Ashley." She thrust a small turquoise box from Gems by James at him. "A girl can't have too many."

Marcus peeled off the delicate silver ribbon and cautiously opened the box. A tiny bracelet glittered under the overhead lights. He wasn't too familiar with diamonds, but this looked like the real deal, not CZ. Cubic zirconia. "This is, uh, really nice, and I know she'll love it, but—"

"And about Barbie? You know, the headless one?" she said, turning and grabbing her lab coat off the hook. "Tell Ashley to investigate Ken." She popped in her earbuds and began removing the bottles of chemicals from the *Fabric Analysis Kit.* "It's always the boyfriend."

"I will." Marcus zipped the box in his backpack. "Thanks for the bracelet." He doubted if she heard him.

He started dusting Jason Hart's fountain pen—the one Laurel had stolen from his office—for fingerprints, then stopped when he remembered Mr. Smithson's traveler's mug. How could he have forgotten that? He unlocked his lab drawer and withdrew the plastic evidence bag with the mug. A small puddle of brown liquid pooled in the bottom of the bag. "Simon, can you see if there's anything in this tea besides tea?"

"Some Cardiotalis, perhaps?" With his head under the fume hood, Simon's voice was slightly muffled.

"You got it." Using a small brush, Marcus spread a thin film of charcoal powder on Hart's fountain pen. As if by magic, three prints appeared. He lifted each with gel tape, prepared three separate slides, then put the first under the microscope and adjusted the magnification. "Hey, Laurel, come check this out." *Nothing says "I'm sorry" more than a fingerprint*, he hoped.

She didn't answer but was looking in his direction. He pointed to his ears. "What?" she said, tugging out the right earbud. "I'm busy."

"The right thumb print from Hart's pen has a central tented arch, like the one on the cuff link." The odds were probably a trillion to one that the rare print on the cuff link *didn't* belong to Hart.

"See? I was right about him," Laurel said. Using a pipette, she drew up several milliliters of sodium hypochlorite from a small plastic bottle. A bleach-like smell permeated the air.

"Whew! That stuff stinks," Marcus said, waving his hand under his nose. He almost added, "Maybe you should work under the fume hood with Simon," but caught himself. At least she was speaking to him. Sort of. Before he could say a word, Laurel trotted over the fume hood.

With Laurel and Simon focused on their tasks, Marcus had a little piece of business in the prep room behind the lab. He had never done a DNA fingerprint before—according to the syllabus, learning that technology was next week's curriculum—and if he screwed up, he'd likely owe the science department a nice chunk of change for supplies. Instinct told him that the bubble gum stuck to the bottom of the desk in Mr. Smithson's room belonged to Jason Hart, not Bobby, and he was going to prove it. He opened his lab manual to "Lab 32: Snared by Spit" and skimmed the introduction.

*Inside each human cell are strands of genetic material
called chromosomes that contain nearly 100,000 genes
arranged like beads on a string. Genes carry information
for traits, such as hair or eye color. Each gene is composed
of a large, complex molecule called deoxyribonucleic acid or DNA . . .*

Hundreds of hours of watching *CSI* had taught him that a molecule of DNA was made by linking together nucleotides, or units consisting of a sugar, phosphate group, and one of four nitrogenous bases—adenine (A), thymine (T), cytosine (C), and guanine (G). He kept reading.

*. . . two strands of nucleotides coil together to form a
double helix, or twisted ladder. The four-letter
A, T, C, and G alphabet makes up the genetic code . . .*

Blah, blah, blah. Marcus had learned all this in middle school. He skipped the rest of the introduction and flipped to the step-by-step procedure.

Mimicking Ms. Mason's demonstration, he gently swabbed what he hoped were cells off the wads of gum he had collected from Jason Hart's office and Mr. Smithson's classroom. He also swabbed the lip of Bobby's energy drink. He placed the swabs into separate test tubes and added three milliliters of SDS, some kind of cell detergent stuff, and several drops of cold ethanol. A few minutes later, small white fibers resembling wisps of cotton candy which he assumed were DNA appeared in the tubes. There also was stuff in the tubes that looked like snot. Next he prepared an agarose gel. According to the lab manual, agarose was a polysaccharide—complex sugar—that functions as a filter. When solidified, it resembles Jell-O.

While waiting for the liquid gel to solidify, Marcus dug around in the freezer and randomly selected small vials of *EcoRI* and *HindIII*, two of several restrictions enzymes Ms. Mason had stored. Acting like chemical scissors, the enzymes cut DNA at specific nucleotide sequences, producing fragments of different lengths. Marcus didn't understand all the details, but from what he could understand, the enzymes would cut DNA from different sources at different places, producing fragments of varying sizes. He turned the page and got to work.

"What are you doing?" Laurel said, strolling into the prep room. She peered around his shoulder. "Is than a gel electrophoresis box?"

"Yup."

"And you made what I think is an agarose gel?"

"You got it."

She glanced at the open lab manual. "But we haven't learned how to do a DNA fingerprint yet," she said.

"We have now." Marcus pointed at the page in the manual. He wasn't sure if he could do a gel electrophoresis without running a polymerase chain reaction first. Without duplication by PCR, would the DNA samples be too small to get anything useful? Running PCR was out of the question—for now. They didn't have a thermal cycler. Besides, he wasn't targeting a specific gene or segment, just DNA in general. He had no idea if this was going to work, but he had to give it a shot.

"Are you sure you know what you're doing?" Laurel asked.

He sighed. "I hope so." *Or I might have to pawn Ashley's bracelet to pay for supplies,* he thought. Marcus carefully placed the agarose gel inside the electrophoresis box.

With Laurel looking over his shoulder, his hand trembled as he manipulated the micropipette and loaded the miniscule 20-microliter DNA samples he'd treated with the restriction enzymes into small, hollow, comb-like wells in the gel. He turned on the power box and set the current to 100 volts. "Okay, electrophoresis, do your thing."

"I haven't skipped ahead like you, CSI Man," Laurel said, "so how's this supposed to work?"

Marcus read aloud from the lab manual. "It says, 'When subjected to an electrical field, DNA fragments, called RFLPs, or restriction fragment length polymorphisms, move through the gel and separate from each other according to charge and size. Smaller fragments migrate farther and faster than larger fragments. The resulting pattern, called a DNA fingerprint, resembles a bar code like on a package at the grocery store. For a control, use . . . '"

Crap! Marcus thought. He had forgotten about a control. *Oh, well. Too late now.* The electrophoresis was already running. Grissom would never have screwed this up.

"Sounds simple enough," Laurel said, "except for the RFLP part." Like Marcus, she pronounced the acronym as "riff-lip."

"DNA from the same person produces the same bar code," Marcus translated, covering his mistake. "So unless Jason Hart has an identical twin or is a chimera or something—"

"The DNA from the gum I found stuck under the desk will match the DNA from the gum you took from Hart's trash can," Laurel said.

Unfortunately, separating the DNA fragments would take an hour or more. "What about the fibers from Hart's closet?" Marcus asked. "Goat or sheep?"

"Goat. Hart's sweater is cashmere."

Simon walked into the prep room holding a chromatography plate. "Cool. You're running a gel electrophoresis. Just a suggestion, but I'd drop the voltage for better separation of the DNA fragments. It will take longer, though."

Marcus lowered the current to 50 volts. "Better?" Simon nodded.

"Oh, Simon," Laurel said. "FYI. I tested the fibers from Bobby's father's jacket. They're cotton with some polyester mixed in."

"That rules him out," Marcus said. "What did the TLC show?"

"From the screening test, the pills from Congressman Hart's bathroom are chemically identical to the pill I found in Mr. Smithson's classroom," Simon replied. "There's also Cardiotalis in Mr. Smithson's tea. A lot of it."

Poison! *Oh, man. This is crazy!* Hart had dumped a bunch of his father's pills into Mr. Smithson's tea! Marcus's heart raced from excitement—and fear. It was one thing to speculate, another thing altogether to *know.* Mr. Smithson had been murdered. And they were sure who'd done it.

Now what? Intuition had given him the means of Mr. Smithson's murder before science had supported his hunch. The evidence trail had led to a dangerous place—to Pinehurst's most distinguished graduate. But was he willing to go down that road? To risk his future? College?

What if nobody believed them? They were just kids working in a high school lab. What if . . .

The chimes rang just as he made his decision.

"You two can't be late to class. You don't need problems with the dean," he said. "I'll wait until the electrophoresis is finished." If he had to ditch Spanish and maybe even math to solve a murder, he was willing to take the consequences. He'd have to make up an excuse when Ms. Mason asked why he will still in the lab.

"Let's meet back here during lunch. Simon, how close are you to figuring out the code in Mr. Smithson's ledger?" All the lab tests in the world meant nothing without a motive. There must be a clue to Hart's motive in that code. It was too weird and illogical that someone would bother writing in code in the first place. It had to mean something.

"I'm going to try one more algorithm," Simon said. "Dr. Marley's at a conference, so I don't have AP chem, and then—" He looked at Laurel. "Sorry. I'm off on a tangent again."

"We're not supposed to be in here during lunch," Laurel said, picking up her bag. "But what's one more rule to break?"

"I'll ask Ms. Mason if we can study in here," Marcus said. "She should be okay with it if we don't do any lab work."

This time he wouldn't have to lie. It was the truth. Their lab work was almost finished.

"Hey, Laurel," he called out before she stepped into the hallway. "Thanks for the bracelet. Ashley will love it." He'd figure out another way to pay for the gel electrophoresis supplies besides pawning the bracelet.

hypothesis: *a tentative explanation for an observation or phenomenon*

LUNCHTIME

"Who's guilty of sticking gum under the desk?" Laurel asked, strutting into the lab prep room with a mocha in her hand despite the *No drinks or food in the lab* sign on the door outside room 102. "Bobby or the Congressman?"

Marcus showed her the DNA fingerprint pattern from the finished gel electrophoresis. "It's pretty obvious."

Gum classroom	| ||| | ||| |||| |||
Bobby's drink	| ||| |||| | ||| || ||
Gum JH office	| ||| | ||| |||| |||

"So it worked. I'm kinda shocked," Laurel said. "Wow."

As Marcus had suspected, the fragment pattern showed that Jason Hart's DNA, not Bobby's, was on the wad of bubble gum Laurel had found in Mr. Smithson's room.

"What was Hart thinking?" Laurel asked. "You'd have to be living on Jupiter not to know about DNA."

"He probably just stuck the gum under the desk out of habit," Marcus said. "Or he figured no one would find it. Students have been sticking gum under their desks for centuries."

"He should've just swallowed it and worried about his liver later."

"You do know that's a myth, right?" he asked. "Chewing gum isn't rerouted to the liver, although—"

Laurel held up her hand like a traffic cop. "Stop. You're starting to sound like Simon."

They took their usual seats in the classroom area, and Marcus opened his notebook. "Here's what we've got. Simon saw Hart's car hauling tail out of the parking lot the morning he found Mr. Smithson—the same car that tried to run us off the road. The license plate confirms the car is registered to Jason Hart. The cuff link, Cardiotalis pills, gum, and cashmere threads place Hart in Mr. Smithson's classroom. We've got opportunity."

"But the fountain pen from Hart's office is identical to the one I found in *here*, at the mock crime scene," Laurel said. "Mr. Smithson's room is in Hartford Hall, not Weatherly."

Marcus turned to a clean page in his notebook and wrote, *Why would Jason Hart have been in Ms. Mason's room?*

"Add the invitation to your list," Laurel said. "The purpose of the breakfast was to raise funds for Hart's campaign."

"But did he actually attend the breakfast the morning Mr. Smithson died? That would be a pretty solid alibi." La Bella Mar was located just a few blocks from Pinehurst. The former Prince Harry and his family had stayed there a few months ago.

"Everyone would recognize 'California's Rising Star'." Laurel's voice dripped with sarcasm.

Marcus scribbled in his notebook. "Let's move on to means. Hart slipped some of his father's Cardiotalis in Mr. Smithson's tea. The overdose poisoned him."

"This is like *Clue*," Laurel said. "But instead of Professor Plum in the study with a candlestick, we've got Congressman Hart in the classroom with the pills."

"Yeah, but this is no game," Marcus said, "and we still don't have motive."

"I've got it!" Simon skidded into the classroom clutching Mr. Smithson's ledger, a single sheet of notebook paper, and a calculator.

"What? You've got motive?" Marcus nearly toppled over the desk as he sprang out of his seat. "You know why Hart murdered Mr. Smithson?"

Simon looked really confused. "N-no. I deciphered his code."

"Oh. Is that all?" Laurel said.

"Is that all? When was the last time you cracked a hexadecimal code?" Simon handed Marcus the ledger. "Take a look."

Marcus scanned the sections Simon had tagged with yellow Post-its.

1000F89 1000
1000G89 2000
1000H89 3000

1000E934 9000
2000F93 50000
2000G93 52000

3000F96 123000
3000G96 126000
3000H96 129000

"Sorry, Simon," Marcus said. "I don't get it."

"Can't you see the pattern?"

"I'm not even good at Skribbl."

"I'll give you a hint: World Bank," Simon said.

Marcus examined a page more closely. "The numbers in the right column could be amounts of money." He handed the ledger to Laurel. "What do you think?"

"The numbers in the left column could be years," she said. "For example, 93 could be 1993."

Simon nodded. "You're both correct."

"And the letters?" Marcus asked.

"Mr. Smithson used an alphanumeric substitution, where A equals 1, B equals 2, C equals 3, and so forth," Simon explained. "January is the first month of the year, so A—the first letter of the alphabet—represents January. Thus, B represents February, the second month, and C—"

"Is March," Marcus finished. "I get it."

"This seems too simple. A sixth-grader should be able to figure it out," Laurel said. "Are you sure?"

"One-hundred percent." Simon showed them the sheet of legal paper covered with equations. "Here's a sample of the same sections decoded. Now it's obvious."

$1,000	June 1989	$1,000
$1,000	July 1989	$2,000
$1,000	August 1989	$3,000
$1,000	May 1993	$49,000
$1,000	June 1993	$50,000
$2,000	July 1993	$52,000
$3,000	June 1996	$123,000
$3,000	July 1996	$126,000
$3,000	August 1996	$129,000

"So in June 1989, Mr. Smithson started receiving a thousand dollars a month," Laurel said, "and two grand in June 1993. The three grand beginning in 1996."

"For a total of fifty thousand. Simon, let me see your calculator," Marcus said, holding out his hand. He punched in several numbers. If Simon was right, Mr. Smithson had received more than a half-*million* dollars by the end of 2004. By now . . . Wow! Did Jeremiah and LeBron make that much money as professional athletes?

"A simple alphanumeric substitution. You're right, Laurel, this shouldn't have fooled a sixth-grader. I should've been able to decode it at first glance." Simon slumped behind a student desk. "The code was so simple that I missed it. I . . . I expected something more extraordinary from Mr. Smithson."

"Sometimes less is more," Marcus said. "Mr. Smithson said that all the time."

"Why does it start in '89" Laurel asked. "When did Mr. Smithson start teaching here?"

Marcus scratched his head. 1989. Why was that year so familiar?

"Maybe Mr. Smithson was keeping track of his retirement fund in his own weird way," Laurel said. "If so, he had one impressive 401K when he died."

"No, Pinehurst teachers don't have salaries that high, even if they have been here for years like Mr. Smithson," Simon chimed in. "My dad is a tax attorney, and he doesn't make—"

"The yearbook!" Marcus blurted. "The 1989 photo of Mr. Smithson's advisory group is missing from his classroom. That's the year Hart graduated from Pinehurst."

"Along with a hundred other students," Laurel said.

"Check it out," Marcus said, running his index finger down the column of numbers. "After Pinehurst, Hart went to Yale. That's another four years. 1993. Most graduations are in May or June."

"The E or F in Mr. Smithson's code," Simon explained, perking up.

"Then Hart went to law school for another three years. 1996."

"This code's about Jason Hart?" Laurel asked.

"Yup." Marcus continued flipping through the pages in the ledger. "This is gonna sound crazy and awful, but I think I know what it means."

"Do tell, Mr. Holmes," Laurel said, lounging back in her seat, her arms crossed over her chest.

Marcus took a deep breath. "Mr. Smithson was blackmailing Jason Hart."

"No way," Laurel said.

"B-blackmail? Impossible," Simon stammered, sitting up straight. "Not Mr. Smithson." He shook his head. "Laurel's right. N-no way."

"How did you get from graduations to blackmail?" Laurel asked.

"Think about it. Every time Hart reached a milestone of some kind, Mr. Smithson started receiving more money. Pinehurst . . . Yale . . . law school . . . "

"Give me that." Laurel grabbed the ledger and opened it to another section. "If you're right, Mr. Smithson started receiving ten thousand dollars a month beginning in *November* 2004, not May or June. Why?"

"That's when Jason Hart was elected to Congress." Simon took off his glasses and rubbed his eyes. "Blackmail. I can't believe Mr. Smithson would do something like that." His lower trembled, and his eyes began to tear. "The Mr. Smithson I knew would never do anything dishonest. We must be wrong."

"I hate to dampen your enthusiasm," Laurel said, passing the ledger back to Marcus, "but we're still back to motive. *Why* would Mr. Smithson blackmail Jason Hart, if indeed your hypothesis is correct? What bad thing did Hart do that Mr. Smithson knew about?"

"That I don't know," Marcus said. "Out of motive, means, and opportunity, motive is always the hardest thing to figure out. Let's get back to opportunity. We need to confirm if Hart attended the breakfast at The Bel."

"Easy," Laurel said, taking her phone out of her bag. "My dad built the place."

Marcus and Simon kept studying the list of evidence and adding questions while Laurel called the hotel and waited patiently for the operator to direct her to the concierge.

"Thank you very much. You've been very helpful," Laurel said, speaking into the phone. She turned and gave a thumb's up. "I'm sure my parents will be coming in for dinner soon."

"Well?" Marcus asked. "Did he or didn't he?"

"The concierge confirmed that Hart was at the breakfast—"

"Darn!" Marcus said, slumping in his seat. "We're wrong. He's got an alibi."

"—but he arrived twenty minutes late," Laurel finished.

"Yes!" Marcus high-fived both her and Simon. "Hart had time to come to school before zero hour, meet Mr. Smithson, drop some Cardiotalis in his tea, and then head over to The Bel."

"But why did Mr. Smithson have the prescription bottle in his hand when Simon found him?" Laurel's questions as devil's advocate were annoying, but she was making sure they covered all bases.

"Hart could've put the bottle in his hand to make it look like an accidental overdose," Marcus said. "You know, like that actor last year."

"Which one?" Laurel said, shuddering. "That's sick. Hart sat in a desk and watched Mr. Smithson die. His sweater got caught on the screw, like mine did."

"Don't forget DAWGS93. Hart's college team. The Yale Bulldogs," Marcus added.

"Hart was fleeing the scene of his crime when he almost crashed into my dad and me," Simon added. "He was driving out of the parking lot like a maniac."

"Somehow after our visit to his office he knew that we were on to him. That's why he tried to run *us* off the road," Laurel said, looking at Marcus.

"We've got means and opportunity," Marcus said, "but still no motive."

"Okay," Laurel said, "back to what I asked. What dirt did Mr. Smithson have on Hart to blackmail him with?"

Marcus stuffed himself behind a desk and start scribbling in his notebook. After several minutes, he put his pencil down. "I think I know."

"We're listening," Laurel said, nodding at Simon.

"What could Hart have done in high school that was *so* bad, if the truth was found out years later it would ruin him?" Marcus asked. "Destroy his reputation, his career, and even his family. Remember, this was before we had cell phones, texting, Facebook, Instagram, SnapChat, and maybe even the Internet."

"Lots of things," she said. "Cheating, plagiarism, drugs—"

"Worse," Marcus said. "What's the worst thing either of you could do?"

"Stealing," Simon answered.

"Much worse."

"Lying?" Simon guessed again.

"Uniform violations?" Laurel asked.

Marcus shook his head.

"I don't know, Sherlock," Laurel said. "Killing someone?"

"Bingo, Miss Drew," Marcus said, his tone serious. "Jason Hart killed Derek Cross."

"What? Where's that coming from?" Laurel said, nearly toppling out of the desk. "You read the article in *The Knightly News*. Derek was drunk, and he was driving. Hart could've died, too."

"What if *Hart* was driving?" Marcus asked.

"But how could he—"

"Listen to what I'm thinking." Marcus climbed out from behind the desk and started pacing in front of the whiteboard. "Hart said that he had to take the SAT the morning after the football game, so I doubt if he'd been drinking."

"The article in *The Knightly News* says that only Derek had been drinking. The cops tested their blood alcohol levels," Laurel said.

"If Hart knew that Derek had been drinking, what would he—a responsible person and Derek's best friend—have done?" He whipped his head around. "Simon, what would you have done?"

"I would have driven," he whispered.

"Exactly."

"Hello, the newspaper said *Derek* was driving," Laurel said. "Hart waited for help with blood all over his face. You saw the scar on his forehead. It wasn't Hollywood makeup."

"He could've cracked his head from the driver's seat," Marcus said. "Picture this: Hart drives because Derek was drunk. Derek sits in the passenger seat but doesn't buckle his seat belt." Marcus paced faster. "It's late, and they're tired from the game. Derek falls asleep. Beer can do that, you know."

"But—" Laurel said.

"Hart gets behind the wheel of Derek's truck. It's raining, and the roads are slick. Hart takes a curve on Ocean Crest too fast and BAM!" Marcus smacked his hand on a desk, causing both Laurel and Simon to jump. "He slams into the light pole. It almost happened to us. And it wasn't raining as hard as it was that night."

"I always can check the meteorology archives," Simon said, "in case you want to know precisely how much rain had fallen in San Diego that night in 1989."

"But the paramedics found *Derek* in the driver's seat, not Hart," Laurel said. "And wouldn't the airbags have exploded?"

"Let me finish," Marcus said. "Derek's old truck probably didn't have airbags."

"The 1973 Oldsmobile Tornado was the first car with a passenger airbag," Simon added. "So if Derek's truck was older—"

"God, how do you know this stuff," Laurel asked. "The newspaper article said that Derek's truck was a '67 Ford F100. Classic."

"Okay, no airbags. But Hart, always Mr. Responsible, wears his seat belt," Marcus said.

"And Derek?" Laurel asked.

"Derek, who's *not* buckled in, slams into the dash on impact and—"

"The rest is history," Laurel said.

"In the rain, they didn't need to be driving *that* fast to slide off the road," Marcus added. "Especially on Ocean Crest."

Marcus took a seat and stretched his legs out in front of him. Lost in thought, nobody spoke for several long seconds until Laurel broke the silence. "Your theory works, but you haven't answered my question: How did Derek wind up in the driver's seat if he started off in the passenger seat?"

"Hart panics," Marcus said. "Derek's unconscious, and he's too heavy to carry. Hart drags him around the truck, puts him in the driver's seat, and buckles him in."

"The cops didn't notice the drag marks because the rain washed them away," she said. "And, there probably were lots of tire tracks in the mud. Their clothes were already wet because it was raining when they left the party."

Marcus nodded. "Hart's head hit the steering wheel because—"

"Because the seat belt held back his body, but not his head," Simon explained. "Newton's first law of motion. To paraphrase, an object in motion stays in motion until acted upon by an external force."

"That's one reason they invented airbags," Marcus said.

"I don't know," Laurel said, looking at Marcus. "How did you come up with this hypothesis?"

"Hart told me," Marcus said.

"Hart? What? When?" She looked at him like he should be admitted to a psychiatric hospital.

"When we interviewed him. You heard it yourself. We all did. Laurel, you can check your iPad notes. Hart said he still sees the light pole directly in front of the truck. How could he have seen it if he was *sleeping* in the passenger seat? That's what Hart said, that he had fallen asleep. But if he was *driving*, he would have seen the pole before crashing into it."

Nobody spoke for several long seconds.

"That's good," Laurel said, nodding. "Really good. I can almost buy it. Why didn't Hart just own up to it? It was an accident, not a crime. He wasn't drunk."

"He tampered with evidence when he made it look like Derek was driving. Obstruction of justice or something like that," Simon explained. "That is a crime. California Penal Code, section—"

"Who knows what Hart was thinking?" Marcus said. The man had left his gum behind! "He panicked. Maybe he thought he wouldn't go to Yale, that his life would be ruined. His classmates would hate him because he killed one of Pinehurst's own."

"How does Mr. Smithson fit in?" Laurel asked.

"Hart knew he did something wrong. *Very* wrong. The guilt was probably killing him." He leaned forward over the desk and dropped his voice. "If either of you did something really bad and were afraid to tell your parents, who would you talk to, especially if you didn't want your friends to find out?"

Laurel shrugged. "My therapist?"

"Simon?" Marcus asked. "Who would you talk to?"

"My . . . my advisor," he said quietly after several long seconds.

"Checkmate," Marcus said. "Hart talked to the person he knew he could trust. His advisor. He told Mr. Smithson the truth about what happened."

For a moment, Marcus hoped his hypothesis was wrong. Simon sat motionless behind his desk, staring straight ahead. Mr. Smithson had been Simon's advisor, too.

Marcus knew how much Simon idolized the math teacher. Telling him about the blackmail scheme was like confessing to his sister, Ashley, that the tooth fairy wasn't real.

"Hart murdered Mr. Smithson," Marcus said, "and then took the photo of the advisory group from the classroom. Probably to hide how close he and Mr. Smithson had been." He crawled out from behind the desk and stretched.

"If Mr. Smithson had blackmailed Hart for thirty years, why murder him now?" Laurel asked.

"I'm thinking the stadium," Marcus said. "Mr. Smithson thought that if Hart could give Pinehurst millions to build a new football field, he should get more—a lot more. Hart was running for the U.S. Senate. Mr. Smithson figured Hart would pay anything to prevent the truth from becoming public."

"A scandal like that would've ruined him," she said. "Remember that mayor last year? All he did was rack up a few speeding tickets. Don't even get me started on the golfer or movie producer."

"Mr. Smithson asked Hart to meet him," Marcus said. He rifled through his backpack and pulled out an evidence bag. "Remember this note? The one I found at the mock crime scene?"

"Ah, that note," Laurel said, reading it. "*Meet me in 102. Bring the money*."

"Mr. Smithson wrote it," Marcus said. "He was old-fashioned. No emailing or texting for him."

Marcus pulled out several crumpled pieces of paper from his bag. "Here's my calculus test. I'm no handwriting expert, but the *B* in *B+* looks like it matches the *B* in *Bring*." Both letters slanted to the right and had the same small ending loop. He bet the other letters would match names in Mr. Smithson's grade book, which was still tucked deep in his backpack.

"Ms. Mason set up the fake crime scene, not Mr. Smithson. How did the note get in here? Laurel asked. "And what about the fountain pen I found? The one I'm sure belong to Hart, not Ms. Mason?"

"Who knows? Hart could've dropped it when he was writing out a check," Marcus said.

"A check? Who writes checks anymore? He should've brought a duffle bag full of cash," Laurel said. "Doesn't he watch TV?"

"What I can't figure out is why they met in *here* and not in Mr. Smithson's classroom," Marcus said.

"I know," Simon said, his voice strong. "Mr. Smithson's classroom is in Hartford Hall *now*. In 1989 it was in here—room 102. Weatherly was the math building before Hartford was built."

Still an outsider, Marcus had a lot to learn about the school's history. Simon had added the final piece to the puzzle. "Mr. Smithson wanted to meet Hart in familiar territory—the place where Hart had confessed."

"And now the forensic science lab," Laurel said. "Shakespearean irony doesn't get better than this."

"Without knowing it, Mr. Smithson and Jason Hart became part of Ms. Mason's *mock* crime scene," Simon added.

"Okay, we've got motive, means, and opportunity," Laurel said. "But who's going to believe us?"

Marcus leaned against the SMART board and chewed his lip as he pondered her question. "Who's going to believe us?" he repeated. "Who can we . . . " *Of course! Who else?* "I'll be right back," he said before dashing out of the room.

evidence: *any material object that proves a fact*

FIVE MINUTES LATER

Marcus returned with Ms. Mason trailing at his heels. "I hope you have a good reason for dragging me away from lunch. Fish tacos, especially mahi-mahi, are my favorite. And today's pineapple and mango salsa is to die for," she said, glancing around. "I thought I made it clear that you can't be in the lab without supervision. I don't see Dr. Gladson—unless he's the Invisible Man."

She peered up at Marcus over the frame of her glasses. "Well? You're apparently the ring leader. Spill it. What's so important?"

Marcus breathed deeply. Not only was Ms. Mason his teacher, she was also his advisor. He could tell her anything. Even the worst. "We think Jason Hart murdered Mr. Smithson."

"Marcus!" Ms. Mason cried, taking a step backward. "What are you talking about? Mr. Smithson had a *heart attack*. You can't accuse people of murder."

"Mr. Smithson did have a heart attack, but it wasn't a *natural* heart attack," Marcus explained. "Hart poisoned Mr. Smithson's tea with digitalis."

"Cardiotalis, actually," Laurel said.

"Two-hundred-fifty milligram tablets, to be precise," Simon added.

163

"What are you kids talking about? You're mistaken. Impossible," Ms. Mason said, shaking her head. "Mr. Smithson had an arrhythmia. An irregular heartbeat. He told me so years ago."

"We followed the evidence," Marcus said. "Just like you taught us."

"What evidence? You're supposed to be reconstructing *my* crime scene, not trying to make up a real one."

"We found some stuff in Mr. Smithson's classroom that didn't belong there," Marcus said. "Not only Cardiotalis pills, but a cuff link with Greek letters, a fingerprint with a central tented arch, a blob of gum with Hart's DNA, threads from a cashmere sweater we took from his office—"

"His office? You went to Congressman Hart's office?" Ms. Mason asked, her face blanching.

"Hart even tried to run us off the road with his car," Laurel said. "He could've killed *us*, too."

"What? Are you okay?" Ms. Mason checked them over as if expecting to see blood.

Marcus nodded. "Luckily, Laurel's dad has a really good car. And," he said, looking at Laurel, "she's a pretty good driver. It definitely shook us up, especially when Hart almost clipped the front bumper."

"The same vehicle almost crashed into my dad's Tesla the morning I found Mr. Smithson," Simon said.

"Are you sure it was Congressman Hart's car?" Ms. Mason said.

"I-I hacked . . . I mean I got information online how to run the license plate through the Department of Motor Vehicles records. The Mercedes with the tag DAWGS 93 is registered to Jason Hart. You know, for the Yale Bulldogs. He also has a 1966 classic Corvette with the license plate KNIGHT7, a 2019 Audi Q7 SUV with plate 1ERC380, and a 38-foot sailboat with—"

"We get the picture," Laurel said.

Ms. Mason sank behind a student desk and took several deep breaths. Color slowly returned to her cheeks. "Start from the beginning," she said. "And don't leave anything out."

Marcus took the desk next to hers. "It began thirty years ago," he said, "on—pardon the cheesy phrase—a dark and stormy night."

His explanation began with the cuff link, white pill, and missing photograph they had found in Mr. Smithson's classroom. Words spilled out of his mouth. He told Ms. Mason about Jason Hart's connection to Yale and Sigma Omega Epsilon, the yearbook, and the car accident that had killed Derek Cross. He described how he had run a gel electrophoresis on DNA from Hart's gum.

"You haven't learned how to do that! I don't know how accurate it is. This is a high school lab, not a *real* crime lab," Ms. Mason said, stunned. "Do you know how expensive restriction enzymes are?" She glared at Laurel. "Believe it or not, we have a budget."

"I'll pay for the supplies," Marcus said. With his rising debts, he'd be lucky to be able to buy a car before he was a senior citizen.

Laurel talked about Hart's fundraiser breakfast at La Bella Mar, the cashmere fibers, the mysterious blackmail note, and the fountain pen. Simon described, in every miniscule detail, Mr. Smithson's ledger and the math code he had deciphered. Marcus admitted that they had suspected Bobby, Bobby's father, and even Ms. Goldman. The only thing he intentionally left out was what he had discovered snooping through the grade book, especially about the high grade Bobby received. Maybe Mr. Smithson curved everyone's scores, including his.

"So?" he asked. "What do you think?"

Ms. Mason hesitated. "I can confirm Bobby's alibi. He was surfing when I took my morning run. I saw him heading into the water. Ms. Goldman was in Orange County interviewing for a teaching position. The head of school at Newport Prep called me for a recommendation." She shook her head. "I just can't believe—"

"C'mon," Marcus said. "We'll show you the evidence." He bounded out of his seat and, grabbing her elbow, pulled Ms. Mason up, too. "I'll get the fingerprints. Laurel, show Ms. Mason the fibers from the screw and Hart's sweater. Simon, get the TLC plates, the Cardiotalis pills, and the tea."

Ms. Mason spent nearly thirty minutes examining each piece of evidence they had collected. She read *The Knightly News* article about the car accident and studied the photographs of Jason Hart and Mr. Smithson in the 1989 yearbook. She admitted that she had not written the blackmail note as part of her mock crime scene, nor was the Mont Blanc fountain pen part of it. She would've used a cheap ballpoint. Simon described Mr. Smithson's alphanumeric code, and

Marcus, to spare Simon more discomfort, explained to her the connection between the numbers and the blackmail scheme.

"See? We have means and opportunity," Marcus said. "And probably motive." Mason took off her glasses and rubbed her eyes. "You've broken nearly every school rule and probably the law. You've lied, stolen, ditched class, accessed confidential computer records, and who knows what else. Pinehurst has an honor code, you know."

"But—" Marcus began.

"Let me finish," she said, holding up her hand. "I'm impressed with your work. I don't know what possessed you to go into Mr. Smithson's room in the first place, but you found what you found. The evidence—the science—speaks for itself."

Grissom's rule number four, Marcus thought. *But this is real.* "What should we do now? Call the police?" He took out his phone.

"Not so fast." Chewing on her lip, Ms. Mason looked at him, then Laurel, and then Simon. "Come with me. All three of you."

Mrs. Hudson pointed at the couch in the headmaster's office. "Please have a seat. Dr. Welton will be here shortly." She leaned toward Laurel and lowered her voice. "I hope you had a chance to speak with your father about my beach house. I can feel the sand between my toes already!" She closed the door and left them alone in the office.

Marcus squeezed between Laurel and Simon on the small couch. Ms. Mason took one of the two armchairs. The second was reserved for Dr. Welton, unless he preferred to sit behind his desk. Except for the other afternoon when he borrowed the yearbooks, Marcus had been in the headmaster's office only once, after the football team had won the city championship last fall. This would be his last visit. Ms. Mason was right: They had broken the honor code. How was he going to explain the reason for his expulsion to his parents, all three of them? Worse, what about Timmy and the twins? A big brother was supposed to be a role model. And why had he dragged Laurel and Simon into this mess? Laurel could hold her own, but Simon?

The door burst open. "Sorry," the headmaster said. "The meeting with the trustees ran late." He looked at Ms. Mason. "Is everything all right? Mrs. Hudson said it was urgent." His gray tufts of hair were wind-blown, and he was slightly out of breath.

"I think my students should explain," she said, nodding at Marcus. Smoothing his hair, Dr. Welton settled in the chair next to Ms. Mason. "What can I do for you young people?"

Marcus cleared his very dry throat and sat up straight. "Sir, it began thirty years ago when Pinehurst beat Marshall West for the championship . . . " Like he had done with Ms. Mason, he described everything they had discovered, starting with the fountain pen and note they had found while processing the mock crime scene. He finished with, "We think Jason Hart murdered Mr. Smithson to put an end to the blackmail scheme."

The headmaster stared at him for several long seconds, his lips pressed tightly together. "Do you realize the seriousness of your accusations?" he said in a calm but firm voice. His complexion had visibly paled. "To accuse Congressman Hart of murder and Mr. Smithson of blackmail?"

"Yes, sir." Beads of sweat had erupted on Marcus's forehead, and the inside of his mouth felt like the Sahara. "But we followed the evidence," he said, glancing at Ms. Mason. "And there's only one explanation."

Dr. Welton clenched the arms of his chair with white knuckles, and an angry red blush began creeping up his neck above the collar of his shirt. He loosened his tie and cleared his throat. "I assume you know that Congressman Hart is Pinehurst Academy's most distinguished graduate and a well-respected member of not only this community but San Diego and California as well." The angry blush had reached his cheeks. "And to accuse Mr. Smithson of blackmail is outrageous! He was the most honest man I knew."

"I know, sir, but—"

"But nothing!" the headmaster roared. He hoisted himself out of his chair and stomped across the room to his desk and began shuffling through a stack of papers, sweeping several onto the floor. "Congressman Hart would never—I repeat, *never*—destroy his career and family by committing such a terrible crime. Furthermore, Mr. Smithson's record is impeccable."

"But, sir, we have proof—"

Dr. Welton slapped his desk with his palm so sharply that Marcus just about jumped out of his skin. "Mr. Jackson, who do you think you are? I will not let you ruin this school's reputation by making these horrific accusations. You should be ashamed of yourself." He glared at Laurel and Simon, too. "All of you should be."

"Sir, please," Marcus begged, his heart racing. "Just hear us out. We—"

"Not another word!" The headmaster stared at Ms. Mason. "Frankly, Kathryn, I'm shocked and disappointed that you would allow, if not encourage, your students to engage in such nonsense. Investigating *mock* crime scenes is one thing, but pretending to be *real* forensic scientists is another. Mr. Smithson had a heart attack. Period."

"Please don't blame Ms. Mason," Marcus said, standing. "She had nothing—"

"Enough!" The headmaster's face was now a mottled purple-red, and Marcus hoped the man wouldn't have a stroke or something. "Teachers are accountable for the actions of their students. I have a list of teachers who would love Ms. Mason's job."

"Dr. Welton," Laurel said, rising and taking her place beside Marcus. Her skirt crept halfway up her thighs. "You must listen—"

"Miss Carmichael, this is not an episode of *Law and Order*. I don't care how many buildings on this campus your father owns."

The headmaster turned his attention to Simon. "Mr. Musgrave, I sympathize with your grief and understand your fondness for Mr. Smithson." His voice was softer, but not less intimidating. "However, you are intelligent enough to realize the legal consequences of slander. I will not allow this school to be sued by Congressman Hart and Mr. Smithson's family. We could lose our financial endowment and the support of the entire community. Bankruptcy is *not* an option for Pinehurst Academy."

Simon rose and stood between Marcus and Laurel. He looked at the headmaster square in the eye. "Dr. Welton," he said, his voice strong, "Grissom's rule number four: science never lies."

"Who the heck is Grissom?" the headmaster asked.

"Simon's right, sir," Marcus said. "Jason Hart murdered Mr. Smithson, and we can prove it."

"You kids can't prove anything," he said. "This is a high school, not an FBI lab."

Ms. Mason pushed aside her chair and stood beside her students. "With all due respect, Dr. Welton, you need to listen to them. Please. They have motive, means, and opportunity *and* the physical evidence to back up their conclusions."

"Stop! Not another word." The headmaster walked over to the bank of bookcases and selected a tattered volume of Faulkner. "Wait for Ms. Mason in her classroom. All three of you. There will be consequences for your behavior."

"But, sir," Marcus pleaded, "Jason Hart's guilty. You can't just ignore this."

The headmaster closed the book with a snap, turned around slowly, and stared at him with cold, dark eyes. "Have you forgotten that I am the head of this school?" he said softly. "I can ignore anything I want."

Marcus knew better than to argue. The meeting with the headmaster was over.

His shoulders sagged as he, Laurel, and Simon slowly headed back to Weatherly Hall. A fog bank had rolled in, blanketing the campus and adding to the gloom he already felt. "Ms. Mason's going to get fired, and we might as well start clearing out our lockers."

"Maybe we should go to the police on our own," Simon said. "There's a station on Beach Street. The 7900 block."

"As if they'll believe three high school kids," Laurel said. "It's over, Marcus."

As they walked past the chapel, Marcus glanced up at the steeple and then, pausing, gazed across the quad. "I'm going to miss this place."

"Strange as it sounds," Laurel said, "I was actually enjoying writing my *Gatsby* essay."

"I hope my new school has a Quiz Bowl team," Simon said. "And a Math Club."

"I do, too, Simon," Marcus said, sighing. It was finally sinking in that he'd never have a chance to learn the Spanish subjunctive from Señor Martinez nor fetal pig anatomy from Dr. Gladson. No more championship trophies, either. He could kiss the Ivy good-bye. He'd run a thousand extra laps for Coach Decker if it meant he could stay in school.

"I can ask my dad to build a new dance studio," Laurel said. "Or upgrade the IT lab."

"A new building isn't going to save us," Marcus snapped. "You can't buy our way out of this one. We're going to get expelled." He shook his head. "And maybe even arrested."

slander: *making a false spoken statement damaging a person's reputation*

TWENTY MINUTES LATER

"I really screwed up," Marcus said, slumping down behind a desk. "What was I thinking?" The headmaster was right. This wasn't some stupid TV show, and he wasn't Grissom or Gibbs any of those other fake CSIs. With an expulsion on his record, he could kiss the FBI Academy good-bye.

"It's not your fault," Laurel said. "We're in this together." She took her water bottle out of her bag and took a long sip. "Pacific High won't be so bad. It's a public school. Look how much money our parents will save."

"I'll be grounded for life," Marcus said. How would he explain this to his fathers? He'd been stressing about how to tell Jeremiah that he didn't want to play basketball anymore. Now this? He would never understand. His mom would be equally disappointed, and so would his stepdad. What about Ms. Mason? Would the headmaster really fire her? She was a single mom with two kids. Could she afford to lose her job?

Simon started fiddling with his calculator. "I never got to finish my research paper for calculus."

"Consider yourself lucky," Laurel said "What's the title? Something like 'Geometry in the Middle Ages'? Could that be any more boring?"

Marcus stared at Simon. He might be a genius, but he was only thirteen. A kid not much older than his brother Timmy. Marcus should've been looking out for him. Instead he had dragged him down with him. A sick, sinking feeling gnawed at his stomach, like he had dropped the ball in the end zone or missed a game-winning shot at the buzzer. "I'll talk to your parents, Simon," he said. "I'll make sure they know that I'm responsible for all this." Maybe Simon could skip the rest of high school and go directly to college.

Simon held up his calculator. "I reconfigured the Rf values for the Cardiotalis tablets. The chromatography was accurate. The pill from the floor had twice—"

"You—and we—got it right," Laurel said, "but if nobody believes us—"

"Somebody's got to!" Marcus said, slapping the top of the desk. "We followed the evidence. Hart murdered Mr. Smithson."

"I'd be very careful about your accusations, Mr. Jackson. Defamation, otherwise known as slander, is a crime," a deep familiar voice from behind him said.

Marcus whirled around. His heart lurched.

Jason Hart stood in the doorway with his left hand propped against the door frame and his right tucked in the pocket of his suit jacket. "Are you surprised to see me? You shouldn't be. I'm Pinehurst's most distinguished graduate, remember? I'm always welcome on campus. Drove right through the front gate. The security guard even showed me where to park."

Hart looked at Laurel like a wolf eyeing its prey. "Ah, Miss Carmichael. You're out of proper uniform. I almost didn't recognize you. Especially with the pink hair. You could win an Oscar for your performance the other day. For a moment I believed you were the editor-in-chief for *The Knightly News*." His toothy smiled disappeared. "Too bad you won't be awarded your diploma."

His loafers squeaked as he stepped into the classroom. "One of you needs to learn how to properly hang a sweater, especially a cashmere one." Marcus remembered the cedar smell in Hart's closet—like the inside of a coffin.

Hart stared at Simon, his eyes narrowed. "You disappoint me the most, Mr. Musgrave. You're smart enough to know not to toy with me. My IQ far surpasses yours. I was valedictorian. Pinehurst Academy, class of '89. But you already know that, don't you?" He took a step toward Simon and held out his hand. "You have something that belongs to my father. The Cardiotalis tablets you took from the bathroom in our office."

Simon swallowed hard and scrunched down in his desk while Marcus started to unfold himself from behind his.

"Sit down, Mr. Jackson!" Hart snarled. "Now."

Ignoring the command, Marcus stood and pushed the desk aside, his hands curled into fists. *He* was in charge here. The lab was his turf, not this psycho's. He took a step toward Hart.

"You're already in trouble with the headmaster," Hart said. "You don't want to add to your rap sheet. Think of the headline: *Son of NBA Star Arrested for Assault Against Future Senator.*" He chuckled. "Jail, not Yale, for you."

Marcus rose to his full height and squared his shoulders. He refused to be intimidated, especially by an arrogant jerk. The ball was in his court, and the shot clock was running down. "You murdered Mr. Smithson," he said, his voice firm despite the jackhammering in his chest.

"Don't be ridiculous," Hart scoffed.

"We've got evidence," Laurel said, standing.

"You've wasted your time."

"We found your DNA on bubble gum and a cuff link with your fingerprint on it in Mr. Smithson's classroom," Marcus said, taking another step toward him. "Your right thumb has a central tented arch. Very rare."

"Five-percent. About 350 million out of the world's seven billion people," Simon piped in. He crawled out from behind his desk, too, and began plugging numbers into his calculator. "If you want the *exact* figure—"

"We also found your Mont Blanc fountain pen in Ms. Mason's lab," Laurel said. "Room 102."

"You belonged to Sigma Omega Epsilon," Marcus said. "The frat's inscription is on the cuff link."

Hart shrugged. "So what? I was on campus for the stadium dedication ceremony and stopped by to see my old math teacher. We took a little tour to see the new buildings. Dropped my pen, and one of my cuff links came loose." He sniffed. "It was an expensive one, of sentimental value. A reminder of my days at Yale." His eyes grew cold, like chips of ice. "I could always say it was *stolen* by one of the students. You, perhaps," he said, staring at Marcus. "I'm sure theft still is against the honor code."

"And murder isn't?" Laurel said.

Hart opened his palm. "The cuff link, Mr. Jackson. And the pen."

Marcus took another step forward. "We found a pill from your father's prescription bottle on the floor in Mr. Smithson's classroom."

"Smithson had a bad heart, just like my dear old father. Cardiotalis is a common drug."

"Mr. Smithson had digitalis in his *tea*," Marcus said. "You poisoned him."

"You arrived late to the breakfast at La Bella Mar," Laurel said. "You had plenty of time to meet Mr. Smithson before zero hour."

Hart's face was expressionless and slightly gray, like a slab of granite, but his upper cheeks were flushed. The vertical creases between his eyes seemed carved into his flesh. "Smithson was getting senile. He probably thought he was putting artificial sweetener in his tea."

Marcus took a deep breath and slowly exhaled. Enough with the two-pointers. It was time to play hardball.

"You killed Derek Cross," he said. "*You* crashed into the light pole in the rain and made it look like he was driving." He took another step toward Hart, narrowing the gap between them. "The guilt ate away at you. You had to tell someone you trusted. You told your advisor. Mr. Smithson."

"Derek almost killed *me*." Hart rubbed the scar on his forehead and winced.

Marcus ignored the theatrical gesture. "The only thing good you did that night was not letting your friend drive because he'd had some beers at the party. Then you made one bad decision after another."

Now it was Hart who took one step closer. Marcus held his ground.

"Instead of advising you to do the right thing, to tell the truth about the accident, Mr. Smithson decided to blackmail you." Without breaking eye contact, he reached behind him and picked up Mr. Smithson's ledger from the pile of evidence on the lab counter. "He protected your reputation and got some extra cash on the side to keep quiet. Mr. Smithson did something he shouldn't have, but he didn't deserve to be murdered."

Hart's pupils were dilated, like an animal assessing danger. He took another step closer.

Marcus tapped the ledger with his finger. "It's all in this book. All the numbers. Why shouldn't Mr. Smithson have nice things, too? Like everybody at Pinehurst."

"You've got it wrong." Hart's voice was calm, but his jaw muscles were clenched. He grabbed for the ledger, but Marcus pulled it back. "Give me that!"

"You've been giving Mr. Smithson money for thirty years, but he finally asked for too much," Marcus said.

"Who are they going to believe?" Hart was practically shouting. "The adolescent son of a washed up athlete, a spoiled debutante brat, and a geek?" he said, looking at each one of them. "Or me?" He jabbed his chest with his index finger. "A future U.S. senator."

Simon took several steps backwards toward the fume hood, but Marcus and Laurel held their ground.

"Mr. Smithson felt that if you could give Pinehurst enough money to build a new football stadium, he deserved a lot more," Marcus said. "How much did he ask for this time? A hundred grand? Five hundred?" Simon had calculated that Mr. Smithson had accumulated several million dollars over the years.

Marcus stepped forward until only a meter separated him from Hart. It was time for the kill shot. "How much did he want when enough was enough and you decided to murder him?"

Hart's face was red with fury. "I'm going to say this one more time. Give me that book!" His breath reeked of peppermint. "I should've run you off the road when I had the chance."

Marcus held the ledger high above his head. "Come and get it."

Hart made several swipes to snatch the ledger out of Marcus's fingers, but it was well out of his reach. Backing away, Hart slowly pulled his right hand out of his pocket. The small silver revolver shimmered under the florescent lights.

"Marcus, watch out!" Laurel screamed. "He's got a gun!"

Before Marcus could react, Simon whipped around and grabbed a chromatography jar filled with solvent from under the fume hood and flung it sharply toward Hart.

"Aaaghhh!" Hart shrieked as the jar impacted in the center of his chest, and drops of solvent splashed upwards toward his face, releasing a pungent odor like the scent of a hundred permanent markers. The jar shattered on the floor, and shards of glass scattered across the linoleum. Arching his body backwards, Hart wildly waved his arms as if stung by a swarm of killer bees and swiped at his face. The gun flew out of his hand, slid across the floor, and came to rest behind the recycle bin in the corner of the lab.

Lunging forward, Marcus wrapped his arms around Hart's chest and tackled him to the ground. *Crack!* The back of Hart's head smacked against the linoleum. The lab floor was much harder than artificial turf, and Marcus had sacked the former all-star quarterback. Still clutching Mr. Smithson's ledger, he knelt across Hart's lower legs and pinned his arms.

Hart writhed in the puddle of solvent and struggled to break Marcus's hold. "Get off me! It's acid. It's burning!"

Marcus couldn't let the solvent blister Hart's skin, could he?

Hart screamed again, this time more loudly.

"Oh, don't be so dramatic, Congressman." Laurel's heels clicked on the linoleum as she strutted over to them. "This isn't Oz. You're not going to melt." She twisted the top off her bottle of water. "A little aqueous sodium citrate *whatever* probably never hurt anybody. But just in case—" She splashed water on Hart's face and chest, soaking his clothes. "As Ms. Mason always says, never be too far away from a safety shower." She tossed the empty bottle in the recycle bin. "Simon, open a window. It stinks in here."

Hart stared up at Marcus through the strands of wet hair plastered against his forehead. "In-in my p-pocket," he sputtered. "G-get my wallet. I've got money. Credit cards. Cash. Take it all. Buy yourself anything you want. A new car."

"What kind of car?" Laurel asked. "Hmm. A Porsche, maybe. Think about it, Marcus. You could stop saving up."

Marcus increased his weight on Hart's arms and legs. He'd buy his own car, thank you very much.

"Stop!" Hart begged, "You're breaking my legs."

Marcus eased up. Just a little.

"Yale. What about Yale? One call from me, and you're in. A full scholarship. I'll make sure you're a starter on the basketball team. Football, too, if you'd like. Wide receiver, right?"

Marcus fought the urge to slam his fist into Hart's face.

"Take the money," Hart pleaded. "Nobody will know. It'll be our little secret."

Marcus hesitated for a nanosecond and then said, "Laurel, you know who to get. Now, please."

For once she didn't hesitate to follow his order and ran out of the room.

motive: *a reason for doing something*

ONE MINUTE LATER

Jason Hart, still pinned to the ground by Marcus, looked up at the headmaster, who was standing in the doorway with Ms. Mason peering over his shoulder. "You're here, Welton. Help me up," Hart sputtered, breathless. He tried wiping the water off his face. "This young punk—"

"Marcus, please let Congressman Hart go," the headmaster said. He walked the rest of the way into the room, with Ms. Mason, Laurel, the school's security guard, and two uniformed police officers following. The older of the two police officers was unhooking a pair of handcuffs from his utility belt. Marcus scrambled to his feet.

"Dr. Welton, you've gotta listen to us," Marcus said. The headmaster was going to let a killer go. It was *Marcus* who was going to jail. "Please—" he begged.

"Get Congressman Hart off this campus before he does any more damage," the headmaster said, directing his order to the police officers. "He's no longer welcome here."

"What?" Marcus asked, stunned. "You believe us?"

"Ms. Mason convinced me that science never lies." The headmaster glanced at Simon and then back at Marcus. "As you reminded me,

178

I am head of this school. I could not ignore what you had discovered. I had already notified the police before Laurel informed Mrs. Hudson."

"We'll take it from here." The cop slapped the handcuffs over Hart's wrists and used his bulging biceps to hoist him to his feet.

"What're you doing? Let me go!" Hart shouted, struggling to wriggle free. He looked at Dr. Welton. "Please. You seriously can't believe these kids." The cop tightened his grip. "You've got it wrong."

"Believe it," Laurel said. "This is oh-so-happening."

The younger female officer picked up the gun, careful not to smudge any fingerprints. "Can I have one of your evidence bags?" she said to Marcus. "We'll send a crime scene crew over. You can show them the evidence you tagged and bagged."

"Huh? You're kidding!" He was going to help *real* CSIs. "I mean, no problem," he said, clearing his throat. "No problem at all."

"You can't arrest me!" Hart said, glaring at the officers. Drops of saliva flew out of his mouth. "I'm the next senator from California. I . . . I have immunity." With his wet hair plastered against his skull, he no longer resembled the handsome candidate in the photo on the magazine cover. California's "Rising Star" had imploded.

"I'm disappointed in you, Jason," the headmaster said. "You've brought shame and dishonor to this school. Fortunately, you will never sit in the Senate Chamber. You should never have been in the House."

"This is harassment! I'll sue. I'll call the governor. And the president." His shoes slipped on the wet linoleum as the officers dragged him out of the lab and into the hallway. "What about Hart Stadium?" he yelled over his shoulder.

"The board of trustees will find a more appropriate name for it," the headmaster said.

"What about Hartford Hall? My father used to be president of the board. He . . . " Hart's vice faded as the officers escorted him down the hall.

"We'll rename Hartford Hall as well," Dr. Welton said, loud enough for Hart to hear. "Nor more Harts of any kind on this campus."

* * *

The headmaster closed the classroom door and turned toward Marcus, Laurel, and Simon. "Please take your seats," he instructed, taking a deep breath. "You, too, Ms. Mason." He waited until they had settled into their student desks. "You have broken nearly every rule at Pinehurst—and a few laws. Have you heard of search warrants? You deserve to be at least suspended."

"Yes, sir," Marcus said. "We, um, definitely made some mistakes." He glanced at Ms. Mason, who had taken a seat next to Simon.

That was an understatement. He was relieved that they weren't going to get expelled, but if the headmaster suspended them, he couldn't play in tomorrow's league championship game. Did it really matter? Did he even want to play basketball anymore? He had accepted the possible consequences days ago, but was this how he wanted to end his high school athletic career—by getting thrown off the team?

The headmaster pulled over a desk and sat in front of them, closing his eyes. After several awkward seconds that seemed like hours, Dr. Welton broke the silence. "I sat in a seat like this once. Seems like a century ago. We didn't have classes like forensic science, though. Just like on TV." He glanced at Marcus. "I'm going to check out this Grissom person."

"We're . . . we're pretty lucky, sir," Marcus said. He'd been given an opportunity for a great education and had almost blown it.

"Despite your questionable behavior, I am proud of all of you. You were determined to seek truth and justice despite the consequences for your actions. You represent the highest expectations of students and faculty alike—especially headmasters like me," he said.

Dr. Welton paused. "There's one thing you got wrong: Mr. Smithson did not blackmail Jason Hart." The headmaster had never sounded so serious, even when he had informed the student body and faculty about the math teacher's death. "At least not blackmail in the traditional sense."

He briefly closed his eyes and then took a deep breath. "After you left my office, I started thinking. If it's true that the evidence—the science—never lies, you found what you found." He looked at each of them, his expression turning more serious, if that was even possible. "However, I discovered a major flaw in your investigation."

"But, sir—" Marcus interjected, sitting up straighter.

"Please." The headmaster waved him off. "Let me finish." Marcus settled back into his seat. "Even I know that scientists have to be good observers. Did you find anything in Mr. Smithson's room to lead you to conclude that he was spending the money on himself?" He paused. "I was Mr. Smithson's colleague for more than thirty years and had never known him to be extravagant."

"That's true," Laurel said, nodding. She looked at Marcus and Simon. "I pointed out his old stereo system and lack of modern tech tools. The Tiffany lamp on his desk is cracked and probably not worth much now. And that old desk?" She shuddered.

"His Rolex had two scratches on its face," Simon chimed in.

"And his clothes were a bit outdated," Marcus added.

"Mr. Smithson's Volvo was several years old," Ms. Mason added, "but he took really good care of it."

"When I was hiding in his closet," Marcus began, looking at Dr. Welton, who raised his eyebrows, "I, uh, noticed that his gym duffle bag was from the eighties."

"Mr. Smithson was a bit old-fashioned and quirky, but he was never particularly impressed by wealth despite the affluence of many Pinehurst parents," Dr. Welton said. "He was very frugal. His philosophy was to buy good, but buy less. Make things last. He rarely dined out, and that car of his must have a couple hundred thousand miles on it. I remember how proud he was when he first drove it into the faculty parking lot a decade ago. He drove it everywhere, even on cross-country vacations. No business class flights for him."

Dr. Welton smiled and paused, as if reflecting on the thirty years he had known Mr. Smithson. "Shortly after Jason Hart graduated from Pinehurst, an anonymous donor established a scholarship fund in Derek Cross's name. This mystery person has regularly contributed thousands of dollars to the fund, and the money has allowed students from all over San Diego to attend Pinehurst. Not just the children of millionaires." Dr. Welton paused. "This same donor has provided funding for ADA, our anti-drug and alcohol program."

"Do you think that Mr. Smithson was the anonymous donor?" Marcus asked.

"I do now. The donor has never come forward nor been identified."

"Is it still blackmail if Mr. Smithson didn't spend the money on himself? You know, for personal gain?" Laurel asked, looking at Ms. Mason.

"Probably so," Ms. Mason replied, exhaling. "Mr. Smithson took money from Jason Hart to cover up what really happened the night of the car accident. That's a crime."

"Jason Hart is everything I said he was at the dedication ceremony for the football stadium," Dr. Welton said. "Thousands of students have graduated from Pinehurst since I've been headmaster, and Jason stood out as the best of the best. He was an honor roll student, valedictorian, captain of the varsity football team, and president of the student council. He—"

"Vice-president," Laurel interrupted. Marcus nudged her with his elbow. "Sorry, Dr. Welton, I don't mean to be rude, that but that's what it says in *The Knightly News*. Hart was vice-president of the student council."

"He was bright, conscientious, responsible, popular, and destined to do great things," the headmaster continued, checking off the list of accomplishments. "Until he made one horrific decision."

"If Jason Hart confessed to Mr. Smithson that he was driving the truck, why didn't Mr. Smithson call the police?" Laurel asked. "It was an accident. Hart hadn't been drinking. The truck slid off the road in the rain and slammed into a light pole."

Marcus chimed in. "Mr. Smithson could've explained that Hart panicked and made it look like Derek was driving."

"Teenagers do stupid things all the time," Laurel said.

Simon, who had remained quiet through this exchange, finally spoke. "I-I know why Mr. Smithson asked for money." He stared down at his lap. "I have a good grasp on how Mr. Smithson thinks." They noticed his intentional use of the present tense.

"Do tell, "Laurel said.

Simon took a deep breath and swallowed hard. "Although his logic was flawed, Mr. Smithson thought he was doing the right thing. He agreed with Laurel about teenagers making poor choices but believed that their 'indiscretions'—his word exactly—should not define the rest of their lives. Derek Cross and the other football players shouldn't have been drinking beer after the game. Jason Hart shouldn't have covered up what he had done, but if he went to jail, his life would be over, too."

Simon paused and glanced at the others. "Mr. Smithson believed in consequences for actions and thought of an appropriate one for Jason Hart—a consequence that would turn the tragedy into something positive but without ruining another life."

The headmaster smiled at Simon. "I couldn't say it better, son." His eyes narrowed. "I am, however, stunned and disappointed by Mr. Smithson's actions. He should have told the truth thirty years ago."

"If he had, he might still be alive," Laurel said.

"By setting up a scholarship fund using Hart's money, Mr. Smithson could help hundreds of kids attend Pinehurst," Marcus said. *Kids like me without a Jeremiah.* "He gave other students the same opportunities Hart had."

"Hart would pay for his 'indiscretion'," Laurel said. "Literally."

"Mr. Smithson would never have taken Hart's money for himself," Simon said, his voice sounding as if he was close to tears.

Laurel reached over and wrapped her arm around Simon's shoulders. "If he had, he would've had a new Rolex every year, not one with a scratched face."

She looked at Marcus who had given her another soft nudge with his elbow. "What? Just trying to lighten the mood in here."

Dr. Welton nodded. "I cannot excuse Mr. Smithson's inappropriate actions, but we all make errors in judgment, including adults. And *his* 'indiscretion', as he would have called it, should not define his legacy at Pinehurst Academy. Mr. Smithson was an exceptional teacher and a fine and generous human being. The scholarship fund has changed the lives of many students. Undoubtedly, our ADA program has saved lives."

"That's true," Ms. Mason added. "Mercifully, not one Pinehurst student has been involved in a drunk driving accident since the night Derek Cross died."

Everybody was quiet for several long seconds.

"This story isn't finished," Laurel said, "Motive. *Why* did Jason Hart murder Mr. Smithson? Why not just keep paying him?" She took a long sip of water. "Hart's been paying for years. Why stop now? Surely he has the money."

"Hart's famous now," Marcus said, "and probably thinks that as a politician he's above the law. He made amends for a stupid thing he did as a teenager by contributing to the scholarship fund. Mr. Smithson was getting older. What if he decided to clear his conscience before retiring? What if he became senile and accidentally blurted out Hart's secret at a faculty meeting? Hart's career would be over, and he'd likely go to prison."

"He's not going to look as good in an orange jumpsuit as he did in the linen suit he wore to the dedication ceremony," Laurel said.

"Hart decided that enough was enough," Marcus said. "No more money. He had paid his debt to society, pardon the cliché. When Mr. Smithson asked for more, Hart snapped."

"All of this is pure speculation," Ms. Mason said. "We may never know what Hart's true motive was. Your evidence trail supports everything you are saying about means and opportunity."

Shaking his head, the headmaster crawled out from behind the desk. "If you will excuse me, I need to notify the trustees about Hart's actions. The media will have a frenzy over this."

"What about our suspensions?" Marcus asked. "You said—ow!"

Now it was Laurel who had given a jab with an elbow.

"I will consider this case closed if you promise to behave yourselves. No more snooping into matters—and closets—that do not concern you. Stick to the school rules because next time I *will* expel you. For homework, I want you to think about the lessons you learned in this room," the headmaster said. "Ms. Mason, I'll leave any disciplinary consequences to you."

"I have a sink full of glassware waiting to be scrubbed. They need to work off the cost of a few supplies," she said. "And, no, Laurel, you can't use a credit card."

As the headmaster started to leave, Marcus said, "Uh, Dr. Welton, about tomorrow's game. Do you . . . do you think you could fix things with Coach Decker? I . . . I really want to play." The bench could be the coldest place on Earth. He owed it to himself and his teammates to finish the season.

"I'll drop by to the gym before I go home. I doubt if we can beat St. Francis without you." The headmaster started walking slowly down the hallway, head bowed and ambling as if he had aged ten years in the past twenty minutes.

"There's one more thing," Marcus said, addressing Ms. Mason. "Do you, uh, think we could get, uh, extra credit for solving Mr. Smithson's murder?"

"Don't even go there," she said. "Although you got the evidence right, you got the motive wrong."

"But Grissom said that figuring out motive isn't the job of a CSI," Marcus protested.

"Grissom isn't in charge here. I am." Ms. Mason smiled. "You may have solved this crime, but you still need to reconstruct my mock crime scene and study for the midterm." She grabbed her laptop case and keys. "Luckily, DNA technology *won't* be on the test. You've got a lot to learn, especially about gel electrophoresis. It's a miracle you got the results that you did."

"Just thought I'd ask," Marcus said sheepishly. He looked at Laurel. "We've also got to crank out those *Gatsby* essays."

"You might," she said. "Mine's finished."

"No way!" Marcus said, stunned.

"Yeah, I'm kidding." She grabbed her bag and followed Ms. Mason out the door. "Or maybe not," she said, glancing over her shoulder.

Man, he thought, running his fingers through his hair. It was going to be a long weekend.

"Don't forget those flasks and beakers," Ms. Mason said as she walked out into the hallway. "See you in here tomorrow. Zero hour."

Marcus turned around. "Simon, do you want to help?" But Simon had already disappeared from room 102.

As Marcus left the building and stared out over the quad, a thought came to him for the second time. Without Jeremiah's money, he might have had to tap into Mr. Smithson's scholarship fund. The headmaster was right: He had a lot to think about. He needed to do the right thing and knew where to start.

Marcus pulled his phone out of his pocket. It was time to make a call.

Gil Grissom: *main character of the original CSI television series and Marcus's idol*

SATURDAY NIGHT

They needed a two to tie and a three to win.

Breathing hard, Marcus wiped the layer of sweat off his forehead with the corner of his jersey. He drained a cup of water in one gulp and asked for another. The team's student manager handed him a lime-flavored sports drink and a dry towel. With fifteen seconds left on the clock, Coach Decker huddled the team together, squatted down on one knee, and began sketching the final play on his clipboard. Students, parents, and teachers—most dressed in blue-and-silver spirit gear—packed the gym and cheered so loudly that Marcus could barely hear the coach's instructions over the noise. The jazz band blasted the school's fight song, and the pep squad was pumping up the crowd by shouting the school's name over and over into their megaphones.

"Pinehurst! Pinehurst! Pinehurst!"

"Knights! Knights! Knights!"

Marcus fought to block out the racket, but the chanting grew louder, echoing off the walls of the gym. Now the students were stomping their feet on the bleachers, shaking them like an earthquake.

"Pinehurst! Pinehurst! Pinehurst!"

"Knights! Knights! Knights!"

The head cheerleader faced the crowd and began Pinehurst's famous roller coaster cheer. Dozens of arms simultaneously raised and began rocking side-to-side, mimicking the motion of a coaster train careening through the twists and turns of the Big Dipper. Four hundred voices screamed "Aaaaa" over and over with each dip.

Marcus glanced up at the stands. As he had predicted, a group of photographers were pointing their lenses toward his father, who was sitting about four rows up, mid-court, in the VIP section. The headmaster, a Pinehurst baseball cap perched crookedly on his head, sat next to him. Marcus looked higher up the bleachers. *No way!* He must be hallucinating. What was *she* doing here? Laurel was sitting with his family about ten rows up behind the team bench, bouncing Ashley on her lap. Both were waving silver pom-poms as they did the roller coaster cheer. Ms. Mason sat with her two children next to Marcus's mom.

"Jackson! Focus!" Coach Decker said. "Quit flirting with the cheerleaders."

"I wasn't—"

"We're down by two, and we're going to win this. We need that three!" the coach shouted. He hated overtime. He drew up a play for Bobby to shoot a three-pointer. "Don't let their eleven get that ball!"

The buzzer rang. Pinehurst had used its last time-out. St. Fran's number eleven was big, and he was fast. Marcus swapped high-fives and fist-bumps with his teammates as they jogged back onto the court. "Let's do it," he said to Bobby.

"Just get me the ball, dude."

On the wing, Marcus caught Manny's inbound, but his man played off him. After a quick move to his left and then back to his right, he saw a clean shot. He could race to the rim, make a two-pointer, and tie the game. But Coach Decker would kill him if he tried the shot and missed. Out of the corner of his eye, Marcus glimpsed an arm in the air. Pivoting, he fired the ball to Bobby who was coming off a screen at the top of the key. Bobby launched a deep three.

The crowd, now on its feet, fell silent.

The ball was on target. Marcus's heart pounded, about to explode out of his chest. *Yes!* he thought. *We're going to the finals.* The ball made a high, looping arc toward the basket—and clanged off the front of the rim and dropped to the floor. A loud, collective groan echoed off the walls of the gym.

Dang! Bobby never missed the three-pointers. He rarely missed free throws.

St. Fran's number eleven grabbed the rebound and raced toward the other end of the court with Manny on his heels. As he tried to pass the ball forward, Marcus flew in and got the steal. He whirled around, and with only three seconds left on the clock, hurled the ball at the basket from near half court. The ball slipped cleanly through the net at the exact moment the final buzzer rang.

Screaming and pumping his fists, Marcus leaped into the air. He had never made a basket from half court. Staring up at the score-board, he realized that this time he wasn't hallucinating. Yellow lights spelled out the final score: *Pinehurst 82—St. Francis 81.*

Manny knocked the wind out of him with a crushing hug. "Awesome, man!" he said, rubbing Marcus's head.

"We did it!" Marcus yelled, a broad smile plastered on his face.

His other teammates cleared the bench and tackled him to the ground.

"Way to go, man!"

"You're the bomb!"

Students and teachers bounded off the bleachers and ran onto the court, their cheers more deafening than the cheerleaders'.

"Pinehurst! Pinehurst! Pinehurst!"

"Knights! Knights! Knights!"

A trio of water polo players hoisted Marcus on their shoulders and, surrounded by photographers clicking away, paraded him in front of the basket. Manny tried to hand him a pair of scissors, but Marcus shook him off. He knew better than to cut down the net. Winning was one thing, but the headmaster wouldn't tolerate them humiliating their opponent.

Coach Decker jogged over, a serious expression on his face. "Lucky for you not taking a two-pointer. If you would've missed, I would've benched you for life," he yelled over the noise. Then he grinned and slapped Marcus a double high-five. "Nice job, Jackson."

The headmaster held out his hand. "Congratulations. This is another proud moment."

"Thank you, sir." Marcus said. He looked toward the other end of the court. Bobby stood alone under the St. Francis basket with a scowl on his face.

"Hey, Bobby, wait up!" Marcus yelled. "We couldn't have won without you."

Bobby raised his middle finger in Marcus's direction and stormed off the court.

Marcus hoped the media guys had missed *that* photo op.

* * *

"You shouldn't have passed to Bobby on the screen. You should've taken the shot yourself," his father said. "I would've." In a charcoal pin-striped suit, yellow tie, and shiny black loafers with tassels, Jeremiah Jackson stood out in the sea of Pinehurst sweatshirts, baseball hats, and denim. At six-feet-ten he towered over everyone.

"Coach told me not to." Taking another swig of sports drink, Marcus wiped his brow with the corner of his jersey, surprised that he wasn't sweating green. "He said to wait for Bobby."

"What does he know? Show me *his* NBA championship ring." Jeremiah tapped the huge one on his right ring finger. It glimmered under the gym's bright lights. *Click!* A photographer leaned in and snapped a close-up of the father-son moment.

Great, Marcus thought. Now his mug would be plastered on tomorrow's front page of the sports section of both the online and print copies of the paper. Why had he invited his dad to the game?

Jeremiah glanced at his watch—a gold thing that probably cost more than a small country's annual budget. "Listen, I've gotta fly. I'm catching the red-eye to Miami."

Yeah, Marcus thought, glancing at the small mob that had gathered a polite distance away. Jeremiah's fan club was waiting.

His father squeezed his shoulder. "You've got game, but if you don't have guts, you'll never play with the pros." He turned to leave.

"Don't go," Marcus said.

"I can't miss my flight," Jeremiah said. "What's up?"

"I, uh—" He didn't want to do this, at least not here, with everyone and all the noise. Jeremiah shrugged and started to turn away again. "Wait!" Marcus grabbed his father's arm and look him in the eye. "We need to talk about college."

Jeremiah waved him off. "No worries. I've already made a few calls. Scouts from Duke and Penn are interested. Yale, too." Marcus swallowed hard at the mention of Yale. "Don't sweat it, I'll have them here for the state finals. They might sign you early." Jeremiah poked a finger in Marcus's chest. "You just worry about cranking it up."

Marcus gestured toward the other side of the gym, and led Jeremiah away from his fan club so that they could have some privacy. "That's what I want to talk to you about," Marcus said. "I'm . . . I'm not going to play ball in college."

His father's smile vanished, and his left eyebrow started twitching. He leaned in. "Come again?"

"One more season, and that's it. Senior year. I don't want to be a pro athlete. I'm going to be a forensic scientist." The words spilled out of him. "You know, a CSI. With the FBI, hopefully."

Jeremiah stared at him for several long seconds, then said, "We'll talk more about this later."

The NBA star strolled away to his adoring fans. With a few short words his father had said it all.

"I've got guts," Marcus muttered under his breath. Hadn't he risked everything to find a murderer? Hadn't he had a gun pointed at him? "I've got guts!" he hollered into the noisy crowd. His father took someone's pen and signed a shirt.

Watching his father give out autographs, Marcus was wondering how he was going to pay for college after Jeremiah disinherited him when someone firmly tapped his back. "I-I'd like you to meet my parents."

Marcus couldn't help smiling. Simon was his dad's clone. Both had the same wiry body frame and eye color. Simon's father's hair, however, was neatly trimmed, and his glasses weren't slightly crooked like his son's. They probably had matching IQs. Despite his scholarly appearance, Mr. Musgrave wore a San Diego baseball jacket, and Marcus imagined that he could throw a wicked fastball—or a chromatography jar.

Marcus wiped his sweaty palms on his shorts before shaking Mr. Musgrave's hand. "Nice to meet you, sir. Simon's told me a lot about you. Especially about—" He checked himself. This was not the time to bring up Sigma Omega Epsilon. "Especially about, er, tax lawyer stuff."

Marcus smiled at Simon's mother. "Thanks for coming, Dr. Musgrave. I'd like to hear more about your research. I want to be a scientist, too." If only she knew how much her information about prescription drugs had helped them investigate the toxic effects of Cardiotalis.

A high-pitched squeal ripped through the gym. Marcus glanced up at the bleachers. Timmy and Justin were chasing Ashley up and down the steps. His sister's head was thrown back, and her tiny hair clips—another gift from Laurel—glittered under the gym lights like the pom-poms she still waved furiously. Laurel was chatting with his mom and Ms. Mason. Cindy tilted her head back and laughed. What had Laurel said that was so funny? They weren't talking about him, were they? His stepdad flashed Marcus a thumbs-up and started rounding up the kids.

Marcus turned back to Simon's parents. "I'd like you to meet my family." He pointed at the section of bleachers behind the team bench.

"We'll introduce ourselves," Simon's mother said, linking arms with her husband. "Simon, we'll meet you outside after you're finished celebrating with your friends." She handed Marcus a business card. "Call me anytime. I'll give you a tour of my lab at the U. You can even sit through a lecture."

Teetering on her heels, Laurel carefully picked a path down the steep bleachers. Tonight she wore a black miniskirt and a purple velvety thing around her shoulders. Her silver stilettos were her only display of school spirit—until Marcus saw that her usual magenta strip of hair was now blue.

"I'm surprised you're here. Why did you bring that?" he asked, indicating the iPad tucked under her arm.

"As you recall, Jason Hart practically confessed as soon as I started asking questions," Laurel said, "so I decided to tap into my talent. I got a job writing for the yearbook and *The Knightly News*. I'm going to make sure the school paper goes digital."

"You barely make it to class, and now you're going to be the queen of extracurricular activities?"

"Then I'm going to ask Simon to help me create an online archive for those old yearbooks. There's a lot you don't know about me, Marcus Jackson."

She's got that right, Marcus thought. Laurel Carmichael was one of the most complicated girls he'd ever met. He doubted if he'd ever figure her out.

She tapped the iPad screen as if she was making notes. "Without my interview skills, we wouldn't have solved Mr. Smithson's murder."

"Really?" Marcus wrapped his arm around Simon's shoulders. "What about us? TLC? DNA?"

"You two were useful," Laurel answered, "but remember who determined that the threads were from a goat."

Marcus took a long swig of his drink. "What're you writing about?"

"You. The game, actually. The only position available was sports writer," she explained.

Marcus choked on the sports drink. He wiped the lime green drops off his jersey. "But you hate sports! Last year in biology you said that jocks were lower than bacteria on the food chain. You called them proto-life. You even said that—"

"Don't say another word," Laurel said, poking his chest with a silver-tipped finger, "or I'll . . . I'll mention your father in my article. I'm sure everybody would love to read about the *real* Jeremiah Jackson."

Engulfed by paparazzi, his father was still signing autographs as he slowly made his way toward the exit. "Did you talk to him about, you know, your career plans?" she asked.

"Yeah. Sort of."

"Well? How did it go?"

"Not so good," Marcus said. He didn't need a magnifying glass to identify the significance of Jeremiah's eyebrow twitch. His father was more disappointed than angry, and that made Marcus feel worse. He'd wait a couple of days and then give him a another call. Maybe he'd come around after the initial shock wore off. He'd offer to give him a tour of the forensic science lab.

"Let's talk about the game," Laurel asked. "How did it feel to make that touchdown?"

Touchdown? In basketball? "Forget about the game. I've got a better story for you," Marcus said. "The whole team's talking about some kid who can run faster than anybody. Bobby couldn't even keep up with him." He looked down at Simon. "That couldn't be you, could it?"

Simon blinked a few times, then straightened his glasses. "Really? They're talking about me? The whole team?"

"Yeah, really," he said, ruffling Simon's hair. "Track practice starts next week. The team could use a 100-meter sprinter, *if* you're not playing baseball, that is. You know, pitching. This time with a baseball, not a chromatography jar."

"Wow." A faint blush began to creep up Simon's neck. "Are you sure?"

Marcus nodded. "I've already talked to Coach. So, what do you say?"

"Wow," Simon repeated. "I mean, yeah . . . sure. It will give me something to do after school besides, you know, solving math problems."

"Who would've thought?" Laurel said, checking Simon out. "A genius and a jock. Just like Mr. Smith—" She caught herself. "You're unique, Simon."

"And, Nancy Drew," Marcus said, staring down at Laurel, "are you sure sodium citrate *whatever* never hurt anybody? Hart was flopping around like a beached dolphin."

"I haven't a clue," she said, shoving the iPad in her bag. "Enough about sports. I'm starving. Anybody up for Sushi Rocks? My treat."

Ashley scampered over to them and wrapped her arms around Laurel's waist. "I want blue hair, too," she said.

"I promised the twins we'd go to In-N-Out," Marcus said. "Why don't you come with us?"

Laurel hesitated. "I don't want to butt in. Are you sure it's not, like, a family bonding thing?"

"I'm sure. C'mon. Where's the carnivore in you? When's the last time you had a burger and fries?"

"Please?" Ashley begged. The little diamond bracelet glittered on her wrist.

"How can I refuse?" Laurel said, smiling down at her. "But I can't stay long. My parents are getting back tonight, and I want to spend some time with them. I even made turkey meatloaf."

"Meatloaf? You?" Of all things, Marcus had never pictured her as a chef.

"Yup. With macaroni and cheese," she said.

"What about you?" Marcus asked Simon. "Your mom and dad, too."

"I'll go ask." Simon deftly dodged around Jeremiah Jackson's lingering fans as he dashed off.

Marcus pointed after him. "I wasn't kidding about the track team." He could smell another championship trophy.

"Oh, I almost forgot," Laurel said. "I sent you a text. Check it out after you shower. C'mon, Ashley. I've got a necklace for you in my car. Did you find Barbie's head? I think Ken might have . . . " Her voice trailed off as she and Ashley strutted hand-in-hand out of the gym.

If someone had told Marcus that Laurel Carmichael would eat with his family twice in one week, he would've said they were crazy. For a second he wondered if she was going to the spring formal, then shook off the thought, shuddering. No way was he going down *that* road.

After a quick shower, he changed into a pair of jeans and a clean T-shirt. Slipping on his varsity jacket reminded him of some unfinished business.

He needed to make peace with Bobby. The guy might be a loser, but five years as teammates since middle school counted for something. He'd almost accused him of murder. Marcus hadn't figured out how Bobby had earned a B in math, but he had a hunch that Bobby was seeing Ms. Goldman for tutoring but was too proud to admit it. Maybe Mr. Smithson had said he was close to failing to keep him on track. Grissom would investigate, but the headmaster's warning about minding his own business was tattooed on Marcus's brain. If he wanted to be a real forensic scientist, first he had to graduate from high school. Even in TV world, some mysteries remained unsolved. It had taken Dr. Watson three years to figure out what had happened to Sherlock Holmes at Reichenbach Falls.

Before closing his locker, Marcus opened the text Laurel had sent containing a news article. His eyes widened as read the headline.

BROKEN HART-ED
Pinehurst Teens Help Catch Killer

"No way!" he said aloud, his heart racing. They'd gone viral! So much for remaining anonymous. What if people started asking him to find their missing cats? He'd never get his homework done. Wait until his father got a load of this. What would Jeremiah think of his son's name on a front page—but not the front page of the *sports* section?

His phone vibrated as he skimmed the first paragraph of the article. Laurel was probably wondering what was taking him so long. She had texted him another story.

Teen Heiress Disappears During School Field Trip

His phone pulsed again. This time a simple question appeared in the text bubble.

Are you in, NU Grissom?

"Yes!" Marcus shouted, a wide grin spreading across his face.
She had called him Grissom. The *New* Grissom.
Now Marcus Jackson was The Man.

Marcus's Dictionary of Forensic Science

Aluminum dust
   fine granules of aluminum used to make **fingerprints** more visible

Aqueous sodium citrate isopropanol
   a solvent used in **chromatography** chosen by Simon to analyze tablets of **Lanoxin**

Arch
   a **fingerprint** pattern

Arrhythmia
   a medical condition in which the contraction of the heart is irregular or slower or
   faster than normal

Bradycardia
   A slower than normal heartbeat, usually less than 60 beats per minute. Well-
   trained athletes like Marcus, however, often have slower resting heart rates.

Calculus
   A branch of mathematics used, in simple terms, to study change. The most
   difficult class Marcus has taken at Pinehurst Academy, but a breeze for Simon.

Cardiac glycoside
   A drug used to treat heart **arrhythmias**. **Digitalis** is one type.

Chain of Custody
   Sequence of procedures and documentation to make sure evidence found at a
   crime scene is properly collected and analyzed. Marcus breaks the chain of
   custody when he removes evidence from a crime scene and stores it in his locker.

Charcoal powder
   fine grains of charcoal used to make **fingerprints** more visible

Chromatography
Literally means "color writing". A lab procedure in which individual components of a mixture are separated from each other. For example, plant pigments can be separated into bands of color.

CSI
Crime Scene Investigation. Marcus's favorite TV show. Forensic scientists are often called CSI's or crime scene investigators.

DNA
Deoxyribonucleic acid. A large, complex molecule usually in the shape of a double helix or spiral staircase that makes up genes and carries inherited information. Each individual has a unique set of genes. Structure was worked out by James Watson and Francis Crick 50 years ago.

Dermis
the inner, thicker layer of skin that contains most of the oil and sweat glands

Digitalis
A medication used to treat heart conditions. Derived from the foxglove plant.

Drew, Nancy
Fictional, female teenaged detective created by Carolyn Keene. Nancy is known for her intelligence, independence and sleuthing skills. Laurel's only hero.

Ehrlenmeyer flask
a type of laboratory glassware with a "neck-like" spout primarily used for storing liquids

Epidermis
the inner, outer layers of skin

-2-

Epithelial cells
Cells that make up certain tissues of the body, like the outer layer of skin (epidermis) or line the inside of the cheeks. A good source of DNA.

Fingerprints
An impression produced when a finger contacts a surface, leaving behind a residue consisting mainly of oil and sweat. Help us get a grip on things. The **friction ridge patterns** are unique for individuals. The basic types consist of whorls, tents, arches, and loops.

Forensic science
The application of scientific techniques to the collection and analysis of evidence found at a crime scene. Marcus wants to be a **forensic scientist**.

Fume hood
A large piece of laboratory equipment designed to prevent a person from exposure to hazardous chemical fumes. Simon wisely works under the fume hood when he does **chromatography** because of the odorous **solvents**.

Gel electrophoresis
A laboratory procedure in which large molecules, such as fragments of DNA, are separated from each other in an electrical field. In the case of DNA, an individualized "fingerprint" is produced, like a bar code on a grocery product.

Gil Grisson
Forensic scientist and chief crime scene investigator in the popular TV show CSI. One of Marcus's heroes.

Graduated cylinder
a type of laboratory glassware used for measuring liquids

Holmes, Sherlock
Fictional detective of the late 1800's created by British author Sir Arthur Conan Doyle. Holmes is known for his powers of deduction and reasoning. Contributed to the development of forensic science. One of Marcus's heroes.

Hypothesis
an "educated guess" to explain scientific observations

Iodine fuming
A technique used to make hidden, or latent, fingerprints more visible. Iodine crystals are warmed in a closed container and the vapor will stick to the oils turning the print orange.

Kastle-Meyer test
Used to identify blood. In the presence of hydrogen peroxide, phenolphthalein reacts with the hemoglobin in blood, causing a pink color. The K-M test can produce false positive results with other substances including horseradish. Marcus bought his K-M kit on eBay.

Lugol's solution
A laboratory procedure in which large molecules, such as fragments of DNA, are separated from each other in an electrical field. In the case of DNA, an individualized "fingerprint" is produced, like a bar code on a grocery product.

Mass spec
Mass spectrometry is a laboratory instrument system that separates and identifies molecules in a compound. Marcus wishes Ms. Mason had one in the high school lab.

Microgram
a metric unit of measurement for mass, equal to 0.000000001 gram—a very small amount

-4-

milliliter

a metric unit of measurement for liquids, equal to 0.001 liter—a very small amount

Myocardium

Heart muscle. Contracts about 70 beats per minute, resulting in a heartbeat

PCR

Polymerase Chain Reaction. A laboratory technique in which small samples of DNA can be copied or duplicated several times.

Peristalsis

alternating waves of contraction of circular muscles that make up the digestive tract, forcing food to move down (usually in this direction) through the tract

SMART board

An interactive white board usually found in a classroom that is connected to a computer and projector. Ms. Mason's favorite pieces of equipment to use during her lectures.

Solvent

A substance, usually a liquid, that can dissolve another liquid, solid, or gas. Most common example is water.

Super Glue fuming

Similar to iodine fuming for fingerprint identification except Super Glue is warmed and vaporized.

Tented arch
   a fingerprint that looks like a spiked camper's tent

Thermocycler
   A piece of laboratory equipment used in PCR to duplicate small samples of DNA.
   Ms. Mason has ordered one for the high school lab.

TLC
   Thin layer chromatography. A form of chromatography used to separate
   components of a mixture. Simon is an expert at TLC.

Watson, Dr. John
   Sherlock Holmes's trusted companion and colleague who is overshadowed by the
   world famous detective. Laurel refuses to be overshadowed.

DISCUSSION QUESTIONS

1. Have you taken a class at school or had a moment in a class that ignited a strong interest in the subject, like their forensic science class did for Marcus, Laurel, and Simon? If so, what was the class, and why did it engage you so much? How much did the teacher influence your enthusiasm for the subject?

2. Marcus Jackson struggles with telling his father that he would rather be a forensic scientist than a professional basketball player. Children often have different interests, talents, and ambitions than their parents, often causing conflict. Have you ever had a similar situation with a parent(s)? How have you resolved these conflicts? Is compromise between parent and child possible?

3. For some students, science and math are dull and difficult subjects. What lab investigations in *CS High* sparked your interest and convinced you that STEM-based courses are engaging, fun, and have real-world relevance? How does the scientific method apply to solving mysteries?

4. At the beginning of the book, Marcus, Laurel, and Simon have little in common except that they attend the same school and are enrolled in the same course. Have you ever forged an unlikely

friendship with someone because you shared a mutual experience? What was that experience? What did you learn about your peer from the experience—and what did they learn about you?

5. If Jason Hart had admitted his role in the accident that killed his friend when it happened, could he have made amends to make a good life for himself without Mr. Smithson? What do you think about Mr. Smithson covering up Jason's negligence despite using the money he collected to save the lives of other students?

6. Ignoring the consequences, which included possible expulsion from school, Marcus, Laurel, and Simon are determined to discover the truth about the circumstances of Mr. Smithson's death. How far would you go to discover the truth and seek justice?

ACKNOWLEDGMENTS

It's been said that it takes a village to raise a child. It takes a continent to write a book.

First, thanks to Carolyn Wheat whose evening class at the University of California at San Diego convinced me I could pick up a pen and write a mystery novel. I have fond memories of our Saturday morning writers' circles. Without YA novelist Deborah Halverson's editing and story-line suggestions, *CS High* still would be in my imagination, not on page.

A shout out to my teaching colleagues, especially Mary Fran Cullen, Ron LaRocca, and Ben Duehr, who pressed me to finish the book. They know kids. Coach Tarantino, you know basketball.

Thanks to my cover illustrator, Tom McGrath, who perfectly captured the personalities of the characters with his brilliant art. Thanks to the many folks at Cedar Fort who made my dream of publishing a book a reality: Angela Johnson, talent acquisitions manager; Valerie Loveless, marketing; Tyler Carpenter and Clint Hunter, digital content; Dru Huffaker, VP of sales; Shawnda Craig, designer; Kimiko Hammari, copy editor; and Heather Holm, editor-in-chief.

To my sister, Cindy Zedalis, who listened to my ideas, read very rough drafts, and picked up the phone when I needed to be calmed down from the ledge. It's what sisters do. She knows kids, too. To my brother, Gary. Your hacienda in New Mexico gives this writer a place to rejuvenate.

To my children, Eric and Kelly, who have taught me lessons that cannot be learned from a textbook. I love you beyond words. Kelly, without your keen eye and encouragement, *CS High* would still be a very rough draft. Eric, you have taught me that it's not about the cards we are dealt, but how we play the hand.

Finally, thanks to my two precious grandchildren, Isabella and Dylan, who keep me hopeful for the future. I hope they develop *some* interest in science, but they must follow their own journeys and their own hearts.

If I have forgotten anyone, you know who you are. Thank you.

ABOUT THE AUTHOR

JULIANNE M. ZEDALIS teaches AP/Honors Biology and forensic science in San Diego, California. She earned a graduate degree in biology from Occidental College. Over her thirty-year career, she has received numerous teaching awards, including the Presidential Award for Excellence in Science and Mathematics Teaching. She has worked with several academic agencies, including the College Board, as a subject matter expert and is a major contributor to several AP biology textbooks. In high school, Sherlock Holmes and Nancy Drew stoked her interest in science, and the original *CSI* television series ignited her passion for forensics. *Bugs, Bullets, and Blood* is one of her school's most popular classes.